BLUE

Book 3 in The MacLellan Sisters Trilogy

LUCINDA RACE

MC Two Press

This book is a work of fiction. Names, characters, places, and incidents are the product of the author's imagination or are used fictitiously. Any resemblance to actual events, locales, or persons, living or dead, is coincidental.

Published by MC Two Press

Edited by Mackenzie Walton
Cover Design by Jade Webb, Meet Cute Creative
Manufactured in the United States of America
First Edition 2019

ISBN Paperback 978-0-9986647-9-8
ISBN E-book 978-1-733161-0-2

I'm humbled by the love and support
I've received for the books I've published.
Thank you to all.

A special thank you to Joyce Young
www.joyceyoungcollections.co.uk
The wedding dress on the cover is from
Ms. Young's Tartan Collection.

CHAPTER 1

Grace smiled as she saw the *Welcome to Glasgow* sign on her way to the car rental counter. This trip was just what she needed after her sisters' weddings.

She was signing her name on the credit card receipt when she was struck from behind and shoved forcefully into the counter. Holding her midsection, she groaned just as a woman wrenched the garment bag from her hand and took off at a dead run.

"STOP! HELP! THIEF!" Grace grabbed her tote bag and ran after her. But high-heeled sandals and the slim skirt made it hard for her to stop the thief. The gap between Grace and her luggage was widening.

A man raced past her as Grace kept her eyes on the bouncing garment bag until the thief ducked behind a cement pillar in the parking garage. Her heart felt like a lead weight in her chest. How could she have let this happen? She slowed to a walk and stopped, her tote bag dragging on the ground as she turned to make her way back to the rental counter.

To her shock, the man who had run past was walking toward her with her garment bag slung over his shoulder.

With heaving breath, her eyes widened. Those eyes, that face, that man. She had seen him before. Mr. Green Eyes from the plane on her trip to Scotland last fall with her sisters. She hadn't realized how tall and heart-stoppingly handsome he was, with streaks of gold running through his dark brown hair, a chiseled jaw, a sensuous mouth and those beautiful green eyes. She would never forget those eyes.

"Miss?" His voice was deep and smooth, with a rich Scottish brogue. "Does this belong to you?"

Grace nodded, stunned. Her words came out in a rush. "Oh, yes. It's my wedding dress. I don't know what I would have done."

With a short bow, he handed her the dress. "He's a lucky man."

Before Grace could clarify her comment, he strode away. She called after him, "I didn't catch your name."

He flashed a smile that caused Grace's heart to race.

"Logan Campbell." And with that he turned.

Clutching the bag to her chest, Grace watched Logan walk out of the airport and out of her life.

The landscape changed from city and concrete to lush rolling hills. Clouds hung heavy in the sky with the threat of rain. Grace didn't care. She was right where she belonged. Replaying the scene in the airport, she realized she never said thank you to Mr. Logan Campbell. Her hand smacked the steering wheel. *He must think I'm a boorish American. Not bothering to offer him so much as a cup of coffee, let alone*

a heart-felt thank you. Nothing I can do about it now. I'll never see him again…well, except maybe on a plane.

She slowed as she entered the village of Stirling. Up ahead was her first destination: MacMeekin's Bakery. After easing into a parking space, she strolled over the cobblestones, swinging her handbag, and down the quiet street. It was midday, most of the locals were working, and tourists were likely off catching the sights.

The old bell above the bakery door jingled as she entered. "Well, hello, Grace, what a lovely surprise." Mrs. MacMeekin came through the swinging kitchen doors, wiping flour-covered hands on her apron. "Are your sisters behind you, dear?" She crossed to the door and looked down the street.

A stab of sadness hit Grace hard. She had never been in the bakery without her sisters or Gran.

"It's just me today." Grace's smile was half-hearted. "A vacation for one."

The older woman opened her arms. "Welcome home, Grace."

Mrs. M holding her tight almost felt like Gran had wrapped her arms around both of them. A lump lodged in Grace's throat.

With a kiss on her forehead, Mrs. M said, "So what brings you to Scotland?"

Grace cleared her throat and blinked away the tears that hovered on her lashes. "I wanted to get away for a couple of weeks. Enjoy some of your baked goods and wander the Highlands." She felt it best to not mention Gran's letter. At least not yet.

"Well, that certainly does sound lovely." Mrs. M chuckled. "I received a letter from your mother. She said Kenzie married a few weeks ago. Is he a good man?"

Grace grinned. "He's the perfect guy for Kenzie.

They've been best friends since they were babies. And let me tell you, Robbie Burns has the patience of a saint."

Mrs. M pulled out a chair from one of the round tables near the windows and sat down. "And Jamie and her husband Caleb, are they doing well?"

Grace settled in the opposite chair. "They moved into their new home, and I'm betting we'll be hearing the sound of little feet within the year."

Not one to sit still long, Mrs. M hopped up. "Tea and scones?"

Grace nodded. "Let me help you."

With a broad smile, Mrs. M said, "Nonsense. You sit and tell me why you really came back. Something tells me there is a bit more to the story than just needing to visit with your gran's old friend and eating cream buns." She bustled about making a pot of tea and plating teacakes and scones from the glass case. Grace got up and carried the cups and plates to the table while Mrs. M took a small tray and put the teapot, creamer and sugar bowl on it.

Grace waited until Mrs. M had sat down and poured them each a cup of tea. "Do you know how Gran met my grandfather?"

A gleam shone in the older woman's eye. "I do."

"So, you know about the wedding dress and the story that goes with it?"

"Aye." Mrs. M nodded and looked at Grace "Is this the reason for your trip?"

"Partly." Grace took a sip of tea and broke apart a scone. She nibbled on a small piece. Her eyes rolled back. "Just like always, Mrs. M, pure heaven."

Her gaze roamed the small but tidy bakery. She spied a picture of Gran and Mrs. M on the wall, and smiled. "Do you know the wedding dress is enchanted?"

"Yes, Arabel told me the story many years ago."

Solemnly, Mrs. M added, "We were friends for most of our lives."

"After Gran died, Dad sent the wedding dress, the MacLellan plaid and a brooch to us. There was a letter from our Great-grandmother. We didn't know about the family legend that if an unmarried MacLellan woman tried the dress on she would find her future. Heck, we didn't even know about the dress." Grace paused to sip her tea before continuing. "As you can guess from recent events, Jamie tried it on and married Caleb. Afterward Kenzie tried it on and realized she had been in love with Robbie forever, and they married. The dress was then handed down to me." She held up her hands. "And here I am."

"Did you try the dress on, dear?" Mrs. M leaned forward in her chair, her voice slightly breathless.

With a shake of her head, Grace said, "Each of us had one last letter from Gran tucked into our luggage. Jamie found hers right before our last trip here, Kenzie found hers before she went on the fateful hike, and I found mine the day after Kenzie's wedding. Gran told me to bring the dress back to Scotland without putting it on."

Mrs. M held up a finger, hopped up from the chair and hurried toward the kitchen. Her face was unreadable.

"Mrs. M?" Grace called after her. "Is everything all right?"

Over her shoulder, Mrs. M said, "Just one moment, dear."

Grace was confused. Maybe she had forgotten something in the oven? She strained to hear if there was a timer going off, but all was quiet. At a loss, she picked up the last bite of scone and popped it in her mouth, and then washed it down with tea.

Mrs. M walked into the room carrying a creamy white, medium-sized envelope. She handed it to Grace. "Your grandmother asked me to keep this for you. She said when you came in, without your sisters, I was to instruct you to read it after you try the dress on."

"But...I don't understand. Gran specifically said to not wear the dress."

Mrs. M sat down and patted her hand. "I remember her words exactly, as she had me repeat them back to her often. She said, 'Tell Grace she needs to go to the Blue Belle Woods within the week. But before she does, she's to put the dress on and look into the mirror. She will find the future she seeks.'"

Grace's hand flew to her mouth. "Did Gran know how everything would unfold for me and my sisters?"

The older woman's smile was all-knowing. "Your grandmother knew the sequence of events, nothing specific, but she felt it was imperative for you to come back to Scotland and put the dress on, here, where it all began."

Grace's shoulders slumped, stunned while she let this new information sink in. Wait until she called Jamie and Kenzie. They wouldn't believe it—well, no, they'd believe almost anything related to Gran.

The doorbell jingled and Mrs. M greeted her customer. "Grace, have another cup of tea and then I'll pack a box of goodies for you to take to the farm."

With a trembling hand Grace poured tea into her cup, to the point where it began to overflow into the saucer and on the table. Muttering to herself, she grabbed a stack of napkins to sop it up.

What does this all mean? Did Gran want the dress here so it could recharge or something? Maybe there isn't enough magic left for it to help me. Stop it, you're being foolish. Dress or not, if I'm going to fall in love, I will.

Pushing all rambling thoughts aside, Grace added cream to her tea. Mrs. M joined her after the customer left the shop carrying a huge box of pastries. She picked up her teacup. "I hope you'll come to dinner while you're here. Maybe you could bring some pictures of your sisters' weddings. I'd love to see them."

Grace smiled. "You could come out to the farm too. I'm a pretty good cook. After all I had one of the best teachers."

Mrs. M's eyes grew misty. "Aye, your gran was a wonderful cook, and I'd love to come to the farm. I haven't been there since she passed away."

Grace grinned. "Then it's a date." She held up her teacup and said, "Let's toast to Gran."

Mrs. M's look softened. "You are so like her, but"—she winked—"we can't toast to her with tea. I have something more appropriate."

Grace exclaimed, "Mrs. M!"

She batted her twinkling blue eyes. "'Tis only right." She hurried behind the counter and came back with a silver flask and two small glasses. "A gift from Arabel." She poured a splash of Scottish whiskey in each glass. Grace picked one up and held it aloft.

Mrs. M said in a clear voice, "To Arabel MacLellan, a dear friend and a special grandmother. We miss you."

Grace said, "To Gran." They clinked glasses and sipped the smooth, amber liquid. Each woman was lost in her own memories as they finished the smooth whiskey.

Mrs. M set her glass on the table and leaned forward. "What do you have planned while you're here? Other than Blue Belle Woods and having dinner with an old woman."

Grace toyed with her glass. "I'm not sure. Wander through the hills and I'll probably go fishing at least once. Being here alone is going to be an interesting adventure."

Mrs. M patted her hand. "If you get lonely, my door is always open."

Grace squeezed her hand. “Spending time with you is a little like being with Gran again.”

With a catch in her voice Mrs. M said, “Dear, that is the nicest compliment anyone has ever given me.” Giving Grace’s hand one last tug she said, “Now, let me pack up that box for you. I’m sure you’re anxious to get to the farm.”

Grace’s eyes swiveled to the street. “It has been a long trip and sitting on Gran’s patio is just what I need.”

CHAPTER 2

Grace dragged her heavy suitcases through the door into her grandmother's kitchen and kicked it closed with her foot. The silence was deafening. Maybe this wasn't such a great idea, coming to Scotland alone, surrounded by memories.

She opened the refrigerator and was happy to see a covered dish with a note on it and other staples waiting for her. They were from the caretaker's wife, Susan, with instructions for reheating the casserole.

She laid the note aside and took her suitcases upstairs, slowing as she walked past her grandmother's room. She pushed the door open wide and walked in. Taking a deep breath, she could almost smell lilacs, Gran's favorite fragrance.

She gave herself a hug and said, "I'm here, Gran," then left the room, closing the door behind her. For a moment she thought she heard her grandmother's voice answer her.

Her room was at the end of the hall. She remembered when Gran had it decorated with muted colors of purple and greens and the fluffiest pillows imaginable. It was hard to believe that was already fifteen years ago. Jamie and Kenzie had their own bedrooms at Gran's, decorated with their favorite colors too.

She pulled the soft floral drapes back and opened the window to let the cool, crisp air of late summer fill the room. She kicked off her sandals and wiggled her toes in the plush carpet before heading back to the kitchen. She could unpack later. It was almost eight o'clock at night in the States, so it was time for a glass of wine on the patio and a Skype call to her sisters.

Settling into a comfy chair, she set a glass of wine down and then fired up her laptop. *Boom bloop.* Jamie's face popped up on Grace's computer, and seconds later Kenzie appeared too.

"Hi there!" Her sisters smiled and started to talk at the same time. Grace laughed, "I can't understand if you're both talking."

Jamie raised her hand. "I'm the oldest, I go first."

Kenzie frowned at her. "Yeah, yeah, yeah. You know, that gets really old."

Jamie chuckled. "You're *punny*."

Grace giggled. "And that gets old too, Jamie." She sipped her wine. "Cheers!"

Jamie and Kenzie grinned and sipped their own wine. "It's just like we're all together," Jamie said.

Kenzie leaned forward. "So how is it there? Are you doing okay?"

Grace looked away from the screen and then back. "I'm not going to lie—it was tough walking into the house alone. It's really quiet here. But I'm fine."

"How was the flight?" Kenzie continued.

Grace's eyes widened. "Good, but you'll never guess what happened at the airport. At the rental car counter, someone tried to steal the dress. I chased after the thief." She paused. "Remember the guy with the amazing green eyes from the plane last year? He ran right past me and snagged the garment bag before it was gone for good."

"What?" Jamie asked. The look on her face was full of shock. "Did they arrest the person who tried to steal it?"

Shaking her head, Grace said, "No, she got away. I'm just happy I got the dress back and it's safely in this house."

Kenzie said, "I'm dying to know, did you try the dress on before you left?"

"Nope. I found my letter right after you got married and before you gave it to me. Gran asked that I bring it back here without wearing it." She shrugged. "So that's what I did."

Jamie's face fell. "So that means that Green Eyes isn't *your* guy, right?"

"Yeah, I guess so." Grace couldn't hide the disappointment in her voice. "But you'll never guess what else happened."

Kenzie arched a brow. "How could we, you're there and we're here."

She waved off her sister's impatience and told them how she stopped at Mrs. MacMeekin's bakery. "Gran left me another letter. She wrote I'm to try on the dress and then go to Blue Belle Woods.

Kenzie gave a big sigh. "Guess Gran still has her hands in things."

"I'm not sure why Gran wants me to go to Fairy Glen, but I can sit by the falls and look for a fairy or two. Heck, who knows what will happen?"

Finally rejoining the conversation, Jamie said, "Gracie, how would Gran know when you'd get the letter? It could have been winter for all she knew."

"I guess, but we've always loved going there and we haven't been back for a few years now, so it'll be nice."

Jamie looked concerned. "Be careful."

Grace smiled at her sister. "You're trying to mother me from across an ocean. Do us all a favor and try not to worry too much. But first things first, I have a dress to put on."

Kenzie let out a low whistle. "I'm looking forward to what you have to say after you do. It's going to fit you like a glove." She gave Jamie a playful nudge. "And you won't even have to tell us, we'll know."

Jamie nodded. "I knew when Kenzie put it on and we'll know when you do too."

"What happened, did you get an image of Kenzie in it or how did that work?"

Jamie waited half a second and smiled at Kenzie. "I saw her walking down an aisle wearing the dress. However,"—she winked at Grace—"she was wearing my veil."

Kenzie's mouth dropped open in mock shock. She protested, "It didn't work with my more understated look."

"You didn't wear the shoes either. You know, the pumps with the MacLellan tartan bows?"

"I have no idea how you ever walked in those. I wasn't about to break another ankle."

Grace chuckled as her sisters bantered about Kenzie's wedding ensemble. "I have to agree with Kenz. After breaking her ankle hiking, wearing three-inch heels wasn't a smart idea."

Kenzie pointed to the screen and grinned. "See, I was being smart to *not* wear them. Besides, high heels are a form of fashion torture."

Jamie attempted to keep a straight face and then laughed. "Out of the three of us, only Kenzie would equate heels with torture."

Grace took a sip of her wine. "It's amazing that Gran was able to guide you to such wonderful lives."

Jamie said, "How do you think she did it?"

Grace looked away from her computer to watch the sheep graze in the fields. "You mean did she have a touch of magic or is it in the dress from our Great-grandmother?"

Kenzie said, "It has to be all wrapped up with the dress. After all, Anne Mackenzie made it with the special thread."

"Maybe any time Gran thought about the dress, ideas just drifted to her. Our sweet Gran, she loved us and she's still pointing us in new directions from beyond."

Jamie agreed, "Kenzie is right. It has to be the dress. Which is why when I tried it on I could see a groom."

Kenzie nodded. "And I could see Robbie."

Grace concluded, "So who knows, maybe I will see a man when I try it on." She yawned. "I'm going to sign off for now. I'm exhausted. I need to go to bed."

Kenzie blew her a kiss. "Sleep well, squirt."

Jamie did the same. "Call if you get lonely."

Grace smiled. "I'm actually enjoying the quiet. Miss you guys."

She didn't want to tell them the truth. She felt lost at the family farm. For the first time in her life, she was completely alone.

CHAPTER 3

Grace nestled deeper in the cozy, soft bed. Through the window she watched the deep purple sky change right before her eyes, going from dark to lighter as the sun's rays spilled over the horizon. She wished Jamie and Kenzie were here. They loved a Scottish sunrise as much as she did.

The wedding dress was hanging over the outside of the closet door. The brightening sunrise cast a golden glow over the gown.

She sat up crossed legged on the bed. "Gran, do you think I should try the dress on this morning or wait until later?"

With the exception of the birds chirping outside the window as if saying good morning to the sun, there was only silence. Grace slid out of bed and held the dress in front of her. She looked in the mirror. Her chestnut curls tumbled over her shoulders as she moved from side to side, swishing the skirt and clutching the dress to her waist. She had a sensation of a flock of butterflies in her stomach. "I'm not ready to try it on."

What if there isn't anyone in the reflection?

She hung the dress back on the door and ran her hand down the length of the dress. "It's hard to believe four women wore this dress and it looked amazing on each one. Will I be the fifth?"

Feeling out of sorts, she grabbed comfy clothes. She had no definitive plans. But wasn't that what she was looking for, to do nothing unless the mood struck?

Grace was making breakfast when a knock on the kitchen door broke the silence. Wiping her hands on a towel, she recognized Simon standing on the back step. He was one of her Gran's closest friends and the retired farm manager.

She opened the door. A smile creased his face. "Good morning, Grace."

She held the door wide. "Simon, please come in. Would you join me for coffee or tea?"

"That's very kind of you. I don't mind if I do—coffee, please." With more pep than one might expect of a man in his eighties, he entered the tidy kitchen and pulled his cap from his head. "I still miss your gran. She was one in a million."

Grace laid a hand on his arm. "Yes, she was."

"Rumor has it you're here alone this visit." His pale blue eyes were mostly concealed by his bushy steel-gray eyebrows.

"Yes. It's just me." Grace took another mug from the cabinet and filled it with steaming coffee. "Please, sit," she said setting the cup on the table. "It's good to see you again."

The chair slid over the highly polished wooden floor, and the elderly man sat and watched as Grace took a plate from the cabinet and filled it with scones and cream biscuits. She joined Simon with a smile. "Dad says you're enjoying retirement, yes?"

"Aye, but it's strange. I've been coming here every day of my adult life to oversee the farm. Now my son Patrick has taken my place." His eyes dropped to his large, calloused hands. "Most days I stop by just in case I can help out."

Grace laid her hand on his. "Mom told me about Patrick. You did a wonderful job and I know Gran couldn't have kept it running all these years without your support after Granddad Rory passed away."

Simon blushed as Grace talked. "Ah, Grace, you are too kind."

"And all true." She held out the plate, and Simon selected a scone and took a bite.

"There's nothing like a scone from Mrs. M's kitchen." He wiped the crumbs from the corner of his mouth and grinned.

Holding her coffee mug with both hands, she leaned forward. "Tell me, how's the rest of your family?"

His eyes lit up. "Patrick's oldest son, Tait, is starting to help out around here. He's done with university, and has his degree in veterinary medicine. He wants to take over for the local vet when he retires, but until then Tait works in both places." He winked. "He's quite handsome and unattached."

With a playful laugh she said, "Simon. There'll be no matchmaking."

He shrugged. "Nothing wrong with getting reacquainted with an old childhood friend."

Taking a sip of her cooling coffee, she said, "I'm sure we'll cross paths at some point."

~

She was thrilled Mrs. M would be joining her for dinner. She discovered the farmers' market wasn't open until Saturday morning and she hoped this market would be the next best thing. Charmed as she entered the shop, it reminded her of a Whole Foods back in the States. Picking up a basket she wandered, selecting fresh produce, then salmon. Putting it in her basket, Grace turned, without looking and bumped into a customer.

"Excuse me." Grace looked into deep green eyes and stammered, "Oh, hello Mr. Campbell."

Dressed in jeans and a casual button-down shirt, he said, "We meet again." His voice was deep and smooth with the wonderful Scottish brogue adding to the thrill that raced through her. "Please call me Logan. And you are?"

Shocked into a momentary silence, she forgot to speak. Logan looked at her with an amused expression on his face. Recovering her poise, she extended her hand. "Grace. Grace MacLellan."

She couldn't help but notice their hands fit together like two puzzle pieces.

"It's a pleasure to meet you, Grace. I trust you're enjoying your stay in Scotland."

She drank in his face, committing the sharp angles and the cleft in the center of his chin to memory. His long, aristocratic nose was slightly off center, and those eyes, they seemed to hypnotize her.

With a shake of her head, she said, "Yes. But this isn't my first time here. My family owns a sheep farm about a half hour away. My sisters and I have been coming here every summer since we were born."

"You do look vaguely familiar. Would we have met before?"

She glanced at the floor and then back up, strangely disappointed he didn't remember her when she clearly hadn't forgotten him. "We saw each other last fall when my sisters and I were getting off the plane in Glasgow. You graciously let us off in front of you."

"Ah, I do remember three lovely American girls." His smile warmed his eyes. "Will your sisters be joining you?"

Grace shifted the basket from one hand to the other. "No, not this time. Both of my sisters recently got married. They're busy settling into married life."

"How nice for them." He stared intently as she talked.

Feeling a little flustered, she babbled on, "So it's just one MacLellan sister roaming the Highlands this trip."

"Well, I hope you enjoy your stay."

Disappointed she couldn't think of a way to continue the conversation, she said, "Goodbye, Logan."

"Goodbye, Grace." He nodded toward her basket. "Enjoy your dinner."

Grace watched Logan Campbell walk away, again.

Grace welcomed Mrs. MacMeekin into Gran's kitchen. She had set a table on the patio with wine glasses and candles.

"Dear, everything looks lovely." Mrs. M stepped through the side door and picked up a plate. "I recognize this china. It was your gran's favorite set."

Grinning, Grace said, "I thought we should enjoy some of the pretty things Gran tucked away for special occasions."

"And how is this a special occasion?"

Grace slipped her arm through Mrs. M's and they stepped into the garden, strolling in the cool evening air. The sun was slowly sinking towards the horizon. "After losing Gran, I realized every day is special. Why do we keep china and linens tucked away? We should seize every day and treasure it."

Mrs. M patted her hand and smiled. "Your gran would definitely approve of your outlook."

They stopped to look at the wild rose hedge growing along the wooden fence. Grace drank in the light fragrant scent. "I never told Gran how much I loved her garden."

"My dear, we don't need to tell the people we love how much every subtle nuance of life means to us, sometimes they just know."

Grace steered them back toward the house and asked, "Are you hungry?"

"I can't wait to see what you've fixed for dinner." Mrs. M's eyes twinkled. "I'm sure everything will be delicious."

"Did I tell you Simon stopped by today?" As the pair approached the house, Grace heard her cell phone ringing. "I'll be right back." She raced up the last of the path and flung open the door. Breathless she picked up the phone and said, "Hello?"

"Hi, Grace, this is Tait. Simon's grandson."

Grace pictured a short, sandy haired, freckle-face kid who hadn't quite filled out the last time she had seen him. "It's nice to hear from you, Tait. Your grandfather and I were just talking about you today."

"Gran-da said you were staying at the farm. I thought you might like to get out and about?"

Grace smiled into the phone. Simon, matchmaking already? "I don't have any plans at the moment, except maybe you'd like to go for a hike tomorrow?"

"Sure, I'll swing by. Say around ten?"

"That sounds perfect." The line was silent. Grace thought maybe they got disconnected. "Are you still there?"

She could hear him clear his throat. "Yes, well, all right then. See you tomorrow."

"Thanks for calling." Grace set the phone on the counter and took the cedar plank from the sink and the filet of salmon from the fridge. Time to grill. Mrs. MacMeekin was settled at the table, looking very relaxed.

"I'm sorry about the interruption. That was Tait Dennie. It seems Simon mentioned I was here, and now I have a hiking partner for tomorrow." She clicked the starter and the gas flame whooshed to life.

Mrs. M chuckled. "That Simon. It certainly didn't take him long to meddle in your love life, now did it?"

With a shake of her head, Grace said, "I'm not looking for a holiday romance. I just need to spend some time relaxing." An image of Logan popped into her head. She sighed.

"Well, dear, did you tell Simon that you were looking to rejuvenate your spirit without any complications?

Setting the fish on the side table next to the grill, Grace slid the plank and filet on the grate and closed the cover. "To be honest I didn't realize I had to say anything at all. I have a life in Vermont." She poured each of them a glass of wine. "Here you are, Mrs. M."

"Grace, would you please call me Flora? After all, you're an adult now."

"I'd be honored."

Flora said, "Maybe it's time for a new beginning."

Grace took a sip of her wine. "I get the feeling I am on the cusp of something, I'm just not sure what it is."

CHAPTER 4

Grace tucked an extra water bottle, a bag of oatcakes, cheese wedges and some sliced fruit in her backpack. Looking around for her hat, she heard a car door slam. She glanced out the window and saw a tall, slender, well-built guy crossing the driveway. *Is that Tait Dennie?* A sharp knock on the front door had Grace rushing to it.

Pulling the door open, she smiled. “Hello.”

“Hello, Grace, it’s nice to see you again.” The boy she knew had grown into a good-looking man. With his pale blue eyes and sandy brown hair curled at the collar of his jacket, and he still had freckles.

“Tait.” She held the door wider. “Please come in. I’m almost ready.”

He had to duck under the low doorway as he came inside. Glancing around the comfortable room, he said quietly, “It’s been a while but everything looks the same as the last time I was here.”

Grace cocked her head. “How long has it been?”

Tait followed her into the kitchen. Leaning against the

doorjamb, not looking directly at her he said, "You were still in braids and braces."

Surprised he remembered that little detail, she picked up her bag. "Wow, that's been years. Seems to me we have a lot of catching up to do."

I wonder if he's shy, the way he looks everywhere but at me. Fitting her hat on her head, she asked, "Any place special you want to go?"

"I thought perhaps Fairy Glenn at Rosemarkie?"

Tripping midstride, she righted herself. She thought fast. She couldn't go with Tait to the falls. That was a place she wanted—no, needed—to go by herself. "I was thinking we could just go out the back door and hike MacLellan land. It's been a long time since I've had the luxury of soaking up the scenery here." She looked up at Tait. "Would you mind terribly?"

"I'm happy to follow where you lead." He held open the back door and Grace stepped through it. Dark clouds lingered in the distance. "I checked the weather and we should stay dry."

Grace slipped her pack on her back. "Did you bring a backpack?"

He nodded and said, "I left it in the car. I'll be right back.

Minutes later, he came around the side of the house. "I locked the front door for you."

Grace touched her pack, confirming her house keys were securely attached. "Thanks. Are you ready?"

With a curt nod, the pair set off across the barnyard, hopping over the wooden fence that surrounded the farm and into the sheep shorn grass. Walking in companionable silence, Grace decided to break the ice. "Simon tells me you've become a veterinarian."

"After much studying I have become Dr. Dennie. It still

sounds weird to have *doctor* in front of my name, but I get to do something I've always wanted—help animals large and small." He looked at Grace out of the corner of his eye. "And you?"

"I'm a physician's assistant in general practice, and I love it. I have patients who I see regularly."

"Why didn't you become a doctor?"

Quick to answer, Grace said, "I have all the benefits of being in the medical field without much of the stress that comes from being a physician. And I work with a couple of doctors at the medical center where I have my practice." She grinned. "Kenzie calls me a junior doctor."

They climbed another fence and stepped into an upper pasture where the grass was longer. "How are Kenzie and Jamie?"

Grace beamed. "They're well. Kenzie recently got married. She and her husband Robbie, just returned from their honeymoon. Jamie and her husband, Caleb, moved into their new home."

Quietly, Tait asked, "And is there anyone special in your life, Grace?"

Surprised at the question—she heard an underlying hope—she said, "Not at the moment. I'm not looking for a relationship. I just bought Jamie's cottage and I'm happy."

Eyes downcast, he said, "Congratulations." But Grace didn't think he was thrilled with her answer.

"And you? Is there a special someone in your life?"

Tait climbed over a large rock and held out a hand as Grace followed him. "I dated a bit at university, but there wasn't a lot of spare time to get serious when classes were all-consuming."

Grace was going to give him a reassuring pat on the arm but thought better of it. She didn't want to encourage him. "Now that you're home, I'm sure you'll have more time to meet someone."

After a few more steps, Grace and Tait reached the highest peak. The valley stretched out before them like a deep green rolling carpet dotted with flowers. The sun played hide-and-seek between the dark clouds, and it was keeping the temperature cool.

"I miss this view." With arms open wide, Grace tilted her head back and turned in a circle. "Gran used to bring us up here at least once a summer, and it never fails to give me the awestruck feeling."

She could feel Tait watching her and not looking at the view. "I tagged along a few times with you and your sisters. Do you remember?"

She nodded and smiled. "You came around from time to time, but you were a short, skinny kid."

He laughed. "I grew up eventually. It took until I was almost nineteen to gain my height. I thought I'd be short forever."

"And now look at you." She waved a hand from the ground to the top of his head. "You have to be, what, six-four?"

"Close to that." He looked down at her. "Are you ready to have a bit of lunch?" He pointed to a couple of rocks with one that seemed to have a flatter surface. "How about over there?"

Grace adjusted her pack and sauntered over. She settled on a rock and began to unpack her food, laying out fruit, cheese and oatcakes. "Feel free to help yourself."

Tait hesitated before unpacking his lunch. He sheepishly pulled a measly-looking sandwich from his bag. "Your lunch looks like a small feast."

Grace squinted as the elusive sun popped out from behind a cloud. "Seriously, help yourself."

Conversation fell away as they ate. Grace looked at the darkening sky and frowned. "I think our trip back will be wet." She rummaged in her pack and looked up, annoyed with herself. "Did you bring a poncho?"

"I did." He pulled one from his pack and handed it to her. "Here you go."

With a shake of her head, she said, "I can't take it." As soon as the words left her lips fat drops of cool rain landed on Grace's upturned face.

"No worries, I packed two." He pulled another from the bag and slipped it over his head. Grace did the same and they packed up and set off at a quick and steady pace. Tait matched his stride to hers. They laughed and reminisced of summers past as the rain picked up.

Grace pointed to the family farm, which appeared in the distance. "I didn't realize how far we had hiked." She took a deep breath and laughed as the rain continued to fall. She said, "I haven't felt this at peace in ages."

A crease appeared across Tait's forehead. "Don't you relax back home?"

Grace dropped her arms and said, "Yes, of course I do." She chuckled. "But with two weddings in less than a year, life has been hectic."

"Is that why you came to the farm alone?"

She shrugged. Grace didn't want to share with Tait the real reason she was in Scotland. It would sound crazy. "It seemed like the right time to get away."

"How long are you staying?"

"A couple of weeks, more or less." Again, there were details hard to explain without revealing the contents of the letter.

The rain had slowed to a drizzle as Grace scrambled over the first of two fences ahead of them. Tait shifted his feet as she waited for him on the other side. “Do you have plans tomorrow?”

Grace could hear the hopeful tone in his voice. Not wanting to be less than truthful, she felt the direct approach was best. “Tait, that’s very kind of you but, well, I’m not looking for a vacation romance.” She watched as his face flushed scarlet and immediately regretted being presumptuous. “Tait…”

He held up his hand. “I’m sorry if you got the wrong impression. I just thought you might like to have some company while you’re here.”

Her voice softened. “Maybe we could grab dinner later in the week?”

Laying his hand atop the fence, he hopped over with ease. “Sure. I’ve been wanting to try a pub in the next village, it’s an old paper mill.”

Grace smiled. “That sounds nice. Can I let you know what night works best?”

Tait looked toward the farm and said, “Of course.”

In silence the pair crossed the open field, skirting grazing sheep as they grew closer to the barn. Someone was hovering in the driveway, a hand raised in greeting.

“Is that Simon?”

Tait chuckled. “Aye, I have a feeling he’s checking up on us.”

Grace’s head snapped in his direction. “He asked you to spend the day with me, didn’t he?”

Tait held up his hands in protest. “As I said yesterday, he mentioned you might like some company. Besides, I’ve had fun today. It’s been a while since I’ve wandered the trails with such a pretty companion.”

Immediately she regretted her tone. “Ah. That’s sweet.” Grace waved to Simon. “I’m going to ask him to stay for tea. Would you like to join us?”

Grinning Tait said, "Sure, I can help deflect Gran-da's gentle interrogation about our non-date."

"Hi, Simon," she called. "Tea?"

A wide grin split his sun-wrinkled face. "I thought you'd never ask." He held a box aloft. "I have cakes."

Grace chuckled. "I get the feeling we've been set up."

Tait softly said, "He's just a kind old man looking out for us both."

Grace threw her arms around Simon and hugged him tight. "Come inside and out of this drizzle. I'll get the kettle on, and maybe you and Tait could start a fire in the living room?"

With his pale blue eyes twinkling, Simon said, "If you two would like to be alone I can make myself scarce."

Grace linked her arm through his, her voice playful but stern. "You'll do no such thing, Simon Dennie. It's tea for three."

"Well, you've convinced me, Grace." He looked back at Tait. "Are you coming?"

"I'm right behind you, Gran-da, just let me pop in and say hi to Dad." Tait veered off toward the barn. "I'll be in shortly and I'll get the fire crackling in two shakes of a lamb's tail."

While Tait disappeared out of sight, Simon said with a mischievous gleam, "Did you and Tait have fun today?"

Like her sisters, Grace could speak with a good Scottish brogue to sound more like her gran. She admonished him, "Simon, now you'll not be doing any of your matchmaking. Your grandson and I are friends, nothing more will come of it."

They stepped into the kitchen as Simon said, "You can't blame an old man for wanting the very best for his dear grandson."

"What makes you think I'm the best for Tait?" Grace moved about the kitchen with ease.

Simon settled into a chair and held out the box. "You're Arabel's granddaughter. You're very much like her, you know. A kind woman to your very center."

Grace's eyes met his before taking the outstretched pastry box. She set out cream buns and teacakes on a serving plate and turned to take three mugs from the shelf. Simon fell strangely silent.

Grace dropped into the chair next to him. "Did you care for Gran?"

His eyes grew misty. Softly, he said, "After I lost my dear wife and Rory passed away, your gran and I spent a great deal of time together. Losing a part of my heart was easier to bear with her."

"Did you and Gran talk about me?"

Simon said, "No. When I saw you the other day I thought it would be nice if you and Tait had an opportunity." With a catch in his voice he added, "He's a good man, Grace."

"I can see that, but I don't know what my future holds." She slowly looked into his eyes. "Do you know about the dress?"

His eyes grew bright. "Arabel had no secrets from me."

Grace dropped her voice low. "So…" The word came out very slowly.

Simon stated with simplicity, "Aye. I know about the dress and that's why you're here."

Grace's mouth fell open and she stammered, "Did Gran tell you Tait was my future?"

CHAPTER 5

The back door opened and Tait came in. Seeing Grace clutching Simon's hand, he dropped to one knee. "Grand-da are you feeling all right?"

Simon chuckled. "I'm fine. I was just telling Grace that Arabel and I used to spend quite a bit of time together in recent years and I was fond of her."

Grace heard the kettle starting to gently whistle. "I'll get the tea." She said to Tait, "Would you mind lighting the fire? It'll take the chill off."

Tait glanced at his grandfather. "Are you coming?"

Simon slowly stood up and gave Grace one final look before following Tait into the other room, leaving Grace to digest this new bit of information.

Did Gran want her to marry Tait? Was Gran hoping for a good old-fashioned matchmaker like Simon to guide her? With a shake of her head, Grace thought, *I need to go to Rosemarkie. I just know that is significant for me.*

She poured the steaming water over the tea leaves and set everything on a tray when Tait appeared in the doorway. "I'll get that for you."

Grace looked up and smiled. "Thank you, Tait." She felt no sparks when she was with him. It was different when she looked at Logan. *But you know almost nothing about the man, other than he lives somewhere in Scotland and, most likely, you'll never see him again.*

"Are you feeling okay?" Tait's voice penetrated her thoughts.

"Huh? Oh, sorry. My mind wandered. Guess it must still be jetlag." He set the tray on the coffee table and Grace poured three cups, automatically adding milk to Simon's. She looked at Tait. "Sugar?"

"No thanks."

She handed him the cup as her mind drifted to the wedding dress. The cup tilted and hot tea spilled on the table, just missing Tait's hand. Her eyes widened. "I'm so sorry."

He took a napkin and sopped up the tea. Dropping it on the tray, he said, "Our hike must have taken more out of you than you realized. We should go."

Simon looked at her. "Grace?"

"Don't be silly. I'm fine." She held out the cake plate. "Please, let's enjoy our tea."

After they left she hurried upstairs in search of Gran's letter. Maybe there was a clue she missed when she read it the first time. Taking the large creamy white envelope, Grace went back into the living room and sat by the fire. Smoothing the pages flat, she read:

My dear Grace,

By now your sisters are married and you're wondering, am I next? I'm sure you were anxious to find your letter as you've always been the lass who loved a surprise. You were sound asleep when I tiptoed into your room and slipped a wee little note into your pretty pink bag.

With two weddings come and gone, I'm sure your sisters were stunning brides. Each one of you reminds me of myself when I was a young woman. You're a tenderhearted woman with a great capacity to love. However, you tend to follow your sisters' paths and not where your heart lies. It's time to branch out on your own and live your best life. It's scary, but if you would indulge my last request, go to Scotland. Bring the wedding dress back to the farm—you must try it on in there. I know what you're thinking, how will it look on you as your figure is much different than Jamie or Kenzie's? Trust me, it will be a perfect fit.

There are so many stories I remember about my sweet lass. The most precious was the night you ate the shortbread and Jamie tried to cover it up for you. Ah, so much like your Great-gran. She too loved her shortbread.

Pack your bags, child. Take a few weeks to wander the Highlands and discover for yourself where you belong. You are a MacLellan and you'll find your future on Scottish soil. Grace, open your heart to love and you will discover a life filled with joy. Take the first step, book a flight, pack the dress and find your way back to where our legacy began.

My darling granddaughter, the morning light is chasing away the darkness of night. Today is our last day together. It will be memorable, just as you are. Stay connected to your sisters but don't be afraid. Your life is about to change, and I promise good things are waiting for you.

Keep your heart open to all possibilities and love will flourish.

Until we meet again—

All my love, Gran

. . .

Grace clutched the pages to her heart and tears slid down her cheeks. "I miss you, Gran, so much."

She jumped up and laid the pages on the hallway table. After grabbing a rain slicker from the coat rack, she slipped it on and pulled the door closed. She needed to talk to Gran.

On the walk to the cemetery, thoughts swirled. How was she to know what she was really supposed to do? Was she to date Tait, or try the dress on, go to Blue Belle Woods and just soak in the ambience? Too many questions with no idea what to do next.

Trudging down the long gravel drive, she turned onto the path that would lead to the church. Walking usually cleared away the cobwebs, but not today.

Grace started to jog and then broke into a run. She could see the steeple ahead as the clouds parted and a sunbeam caught the stained-glass windows. The light refracting looked like jewels. Hesitating at the gate, she took a deep breath. Grace pushed it open and stepped through it.

Picking her way around the headstones, a small smile played over her face. Dad had the bench installed at the family plot. Grace bent over and traced Gran's name on her headstone.

"Hi, Gran. It's been a while since I've been here. But you know a lot has happened." She dropped to the hard, stone bench and fell silent. The birds chirped as the sun warmed her face. "I talked to Simon, and I have a strong suspicion you two were in cahoots."

She slipped off the raincoat. "I'm going to try the dress on tonight before bed and I'll go to the falls tomorrow." She stared at the headstone. "Does that sound like a good plan?" A sob filled her throat. "Oh, Gran, I shouldn't have come alone. I'm lost and don't have any idea what path I'm supposed to take. But is that what you want? For me to really have to look inside myself?"

For one long minute Grace sat on the bench. Waiting. With a strangled laugh she said, "I was hoping somehow you would reach beyond the grave and hand me another letter telling me exactly what I need to do."

There were still many hours before sunset as Grace rose from the bench. She laid a kiss on her fingertips and touched Great-grandmother Ann's headstone, which sat next to Gran's. When she looked up, Flora was standing next to the gate waiting for her.

Grace hurried over. "Flora, how did you know I was here?"

"Just a hunch." Flora grasped her hand. "Will you take a walk with me and we can talk?"

Grace fell into step next to her. "Tait and I went on a hike today."

"You did? And did you enjoy yourself?"

Grace asked, "Did Gran think that Tait is meant to be my life partner?"

"Oh, my dear, your grandmother wanted you to marry the man who you would love with all your heart. She would have been thrilled if you fell in love with a Scot, but the most important thing for her was that you open your heart and find lasting love. She never wanted you or your sisters to live a solitary life."

Grace looked at Flora. "To answer your question, we had a nice time but there wasn't a single spark."

Flora slipped her arm through Grace's. "Well then, that is something to consider, isn't it?"

Grace said, "Simon stopped by and told me about him and Gran; he said they became very good friends. Why didn't they ever marry?"

"I'm not sure. I always thought they would."

The women walked side by side. Grace was quiet for a few moments and asked, "Do you think she journaled about it?"

A small smile played over Flora's face. "I wouldn't be surprised at all. She loved to write in her journals. Often she'd encourage me to do the same, but I told her my life was far less interesting than hers and that after I was gone all that I'd need to leave behind were my recipe books."

"Well, let's not talk about you going anywhere for many, many years."

Flora's car was parked up ahead and they strolled arm in arm. "Can I drop you at the farm, Grace?"

Flora's sweet smile reminded her of Gran. "No, I'd like to walk. But I'll see you very soon." Grace kissed her soft cheek. "Thank you, Flora. I'm sure Gran sent you to me."

Flora brushed a stray curl of Grace's hair off her face. "Her spirit lives in us both."

Fresh from a soothing shower, tendrils escaped from Grace's loosely formed bun. She gazed at the wedding dress hanging on the closet door. She was sure it would never look as good on her as it had on Jamie and Kenzie.

Taking a deep breath to settle her nerves, she announced to the girl standing in front of the mirror, "It's time."

Butterflies took flight in her stomach, and her heart quickened. Grace held the dress in front of herself. *Stop stalling.*

Slipping the dress from the padded hanger, she then loosened the soft laces in the back. Taking a deep breath to steady her nerves, she stepped into the full sweeping skirt, and put her arms through the sleeveless bodice. *Good thing Gran was well endowed or I'm sure this would never fit.*

Reaching behind herself, Grace did her best to pull the laces taut. The dress molded to her curves. *Oh my, the girls were right, it's like the dress was made for me.*

Moving away from the mirror so she could get a look at the gown, she sucked in a breath. "If I had tried on a thousand dresses, this would be the only one I could ever marry in."

She moved her hips left and right, the skirt caressing her legs with a *whoosh, whoosh*. The only thing that would make the gown over-the-top beautiful was the MacLellan plaid secured over one shoulder with Gran's brooch. The finishing touch would be Jamie's heels with the cute tartan bows on the backs. And she would carry...heather, white and lavender, and of course bluebells, all tied with a plaid ribbon. Grace could picture it all so clearly.

And as she stood there daydreaming, she saw a shadow in the mirror. Over her shoulder stood a tall man with his back to her.

She peered closer. "Who are you?"

Hoping for some kind of sign or answer of sorts, she stared at the mirror, afraid to look away. Compelled to turn around to see if there was some sort of answer in the room, she picked up the skirt and took a step. It was then that the image faded.

An anguished cry escaped her lips. "NO!"

CHAPTER 6

Grace slumped to the floor, the dress puffed up around her. She had no idea why she felt as if she had just lost her last friend. After all, she reminded herself, it was just a vision.

Her cell phone rang and she looked at it: Jamie.

"Hi, Mac." Grace lapsed back into using Jamie's childhood nickname. "What's going on?"

"I got the feeling you needed to talk."

Grace smiled into the phone and didn't say anything.

"You're wearing the dress, aren't you?" Jamie's voice was gentle.

"How did you...oh wait, you told me you'd know. Do you think Kenzie knows too?" Grace could hear Jamie's office phone ringing. "Hold on a sec."

Grace could hear Jamie talking, but she wasn't sure to whom.

"Hi again. That was Kenzie asking if I was talking to you. She got the feeling you were very sad."

"I don't get it." Grace's face formed an unseen pout. "How come I had no idea when you or Kenzie tried on

Gran's wedding dress, but I put it on and you both know?"

"I don't have all the answers, but Kenzie and I have talked about it. We believe because we have worn the dress on the happiest days of our lives it has given us a special connection to it and each other."

Grace said, "Jamie, I saw a man in the mirror, but only from behind. I had the feeling he was in the room with me, and when I turned he faded away. I thought I would see something more definitive."

"Oh, Gracie, when the time is right you'll figure out who he is."

Grace straightened her shoulders and got up from the floor. "You're right. I need to go with the flow and follow the rest of Gran's request. Tomorrow I'm going to the falls and just let whatever happens happen."

"Before you hang up, I'm dying to know—how does it look?"

Grace looked in the mirror. She chewed on her lower lip.

"Grace, are you still there?"

She smiled and tossed back her head. "Let's just say you and Kenzie were right, it's like the dress was made for me."

She heard Jamie let out a whoop. "We knew it!"

Grace chuckled. "Good night, Jamie."

"Send me a picture of the falls tomorrow and," Jamie teased, "remember to be on the lookout for a fairy or two."

"I won't forget." Grace swallowed a lump in her throat. "Mac, thanks for calling."

"Not a problem, squirt."

The line went dead and Grace tossed her phone on the bed. "Gran, well, what do you think? Do I do the dress justice?"

A soft breeze ruffled the curtains, causing them to connect with her arm in an almost feather-like touch. Grace smiled.

With the windows down, Grace cruised down the two-lane country road. She had tossed and turned for most of the night wondering what might happen at the falls. Close to dawn she fell into a deep, dreamless sleep.

Waking somewhat refreshed Grace tucked a light lunch in her pack, she was excited to get going. This was the first time Grace was driving to Rosemarkie by herself. The GPS announced she needed to take the next turn. Her heart lightened as she drew closer. This was one of her favorite places in Scotland—not only were the falls stunning, but when the bluebells were in bloom it was beyond spectacular.

Up ahead she saw a sign on the side of the road. She had arrived. There weren't many cars in the parking area. Grace parked, and after grabbing her pack, she locked the door and pocketed the keys in her side zipper pants pocket. Anxious to get on the path to the falls, she wasn't paying attention and stepped in front of an oncoming SUV. The blaring horn caught her attention and she jumped back.

With a wave of her hand to the unseen driver, she called, "Sorry…" The vehicle slowly drove around her and made its way out of sight. "Well, someone was sure in a hurry."

With a spring in her step, she began the easy but muddy trek through the woodlands. Grace stopped on the first bridge and watched the stream flow underneath it. Listening to the variety of birds was like putting a song in her heart. She continued down the path, strolling past the millpond. The wildflowers danced in the light breeze, and she wandered a little farther, letting the magic of her surroundings restore her spirit.

Her ears caught the sound of rushing water, and around the last bend the first set of falls came into view. She halted in her tracks, awestruck by the beauty that surrounded her. The falls were just as she remembered.

Standing amongst the ferns, she drank in the familiar sight. The deep emerald-green moss dotted sections of the craggy outcropping as a cascade of water slid over and around on its journey to the pool at the base. She felt a peace that only this spot had ever given her. She took a deep, cleansing breath of cool, fresh air into her lungs, unsure how long she stood rooted in one spot. She enjoyed her solitude.

"All I need is to find a good spot for fairy gazing." Grace found a place to perch, drink some water and eat part of her sandwich. She wasn't in any rush for lunch. Instead she pulled out her cell to snap some pictures, wishing she had remembered to bring her good camera. It was a perfect day to take photos.

Wanting to reach the next falls, she walked up the wooden steps, looking around she saw a Britain's dipper, the only aquatic songbird in Scotland, perched on a rock at the water's edge. Impatient to feel the water on her skin, she slipped out of her hiking shoes and socks. After rolling up her pant legs she looked around and saw an old moss-covered log, jutting from the water. It was filled with coins. How many years had they been there and why? She seemed to recall Gran telling her that people pounded the coins in for good luck.

"I hope everyone got what they were wishing for." Grace wiggled her toes in the cool, refreshing stream. "Ah."

She found herself blinking. Were her eyes playing tricks on her? Was that man walking toward her Logan Campbell?

~

His thoughts drifted back to bumping into Grace MacLellan at the market. What was it about that blue-eyed woman that had him longing to run into her again? She was engaged to another. Maybe it was a good thing he had followed his heart and driven to the glen in Rosemarkie—it was just what he needed to push her from his thoughts.

He began to cross the bridge and looked up. There she was, wading in the stream. The look of pure delight splashed across her breathtakingly beautiful face with the sun highlighting the copper highlights in her dark brown hair. *There I go again, using flowery words about this woman.*

He'd never admit it to anyone but he knew from the first moment he laid eyes on her on the plane last fall, he'd been captivated. Not that he ever dreamed he'd see her again, much less three times in the span of a few days.

As he watched her frolic, totally comfortable in her skin, he wondered how it would feel to join her. Though tempted to let go of all his straight-laced and uptight ways, he held himself back. He had no right. Looking around, he wondered, where was her fiancé?

Her eyes captured his. "Logan?"

He leaned over the railing. "Hello, Grace." She didn't look pleased to see him.

She glanced around. "Are you following me?" A flash of apprehension appeared in her eyes.

"I had no idea you'd be here."

She watched him warily.

He kept his gaze steady, not blinking. "I was getting

ready to go into the office this morning when I had the sudden urge to play hooky. If you knew me you'd know that is completely out of character. I jumped in my car and here I am, wandering among the greenery." Lifting his head, he slowly looked around. "It's one of my favorite places; I come here when I need to think about things." He closed his eyes and listened to the sounds of the water and birds. "It provides me with perspective."

"Well, then I won't disturb your personal reflection time." Grace took a step and lost her footing, going down in a deeper pool of water and ending up on her butt. She blinked water droplets from her eye lashes. Laughing, she looked up at Logan. "Guess I should have watched my step."

He rushed around to where he could make his way into the stream, heedless of the fact he was wearing hiking boots, and helped Grace to her feet. "Just look at you. Soaking wet." Not letting go of each other's hands, the couple carefully made their way up the small embankment to the path. "Are you hurt?"

Grace shook her head and beads of water sprayed her rescuer. "No, just my ego is a little battered. It never looks good to trip and fall in front of a stranger."

He pulled out a crisp white linen handkerchief from inside his jacket and handed it to her. "You can dry off your face."

She stared at the piece of cloth. "This is much too nice to get water-logged." She handed it back to him.

"I must insist." Logan gently pressed it back in her hand. "It's why I carry one at all—to help a lady in distress, especially those who happen to fall into a stream."

Grace giggled like a schoolgirl in an attempt to squash her nerves. "How wonderfully chivalrous of you." She took the handkerchief and used it to pat her face dry. She gave an involuntary shiver. "Would you mind if we moved into the sun? I may have a hope of drying off just a little before I make the drive home."

Logan guided her to a bench and sat down next to her. "Is this better?" Grace smiled at him. Once again, he was inexplicably drawn to her. She was even lovelier than he remembered.

"How was your dinner the other night?"

"Dinner?" She furrowed her brow. "What did...?"

"When I bumped into you at the market you were purchasing items for a special dinner."

Her sunny smile soothed the complex feelings he had about her making dinner for another guy. *Are you insane, man? It is perfectly normal for Grace to prepare a meal for her fiancé.*

"Oh, yes. Actually, I made dinner for my late grandmother's best friend. She's a wonderful lady. I've known her my entire life, and she happens to own the best bakery in the world."

His eyebrow arched. "That is quite an endorsement."

"And one-hundred percent true. Have you heard of the MacMeekin's Bakery in Stirling?"

His eyes grew wide. "Flora MacMeekin?"

"Yes, do you know her?" Grace asked.

Aunt Flora? "As a child my father took me there often. She is a wonderful lady and just happens to be my aunt. Have you ever had one of her shortbread cookies?"

"Are you kidding? She's wonderful." Grace chuckled. "And when we come to Scotland the bakery is the first stop before we get to the farm." She leaned back on the bench. "I love everything she bakes. Heck, I think just walking in there I gain five pounds, and it's worth every buttery bite."

"How often do you visit?" Logan leaned over and plucked a leaf from her hair.

She sighed. "Not as often as I'd like. Once, maybe twice a year."

"Do you still have family in the area?" He wanted to know everything about her and shut out the little voice that kept reminding him a deeper relationship was pointless.

Grace folded the now damp handkerchief and handed it back to him. Smiling her thanks, she said, "My parents recently retired, so they're living between the family farm and our home in Vermont. Dad is originally from here."

"And you spent time here as a girl?"

"Every summer my sisters and I would stay with Gran and become wee Scottish lasses." Grace's attempt at a brogue made Logan smile. "It's a great way for a child to grow up surrounded by the hills and valleys. Wading in streams, casting a line and even looking for fairies in the waterfalls."

"You fish?"

She flashed him a surprised look. "With the best of them. Gran taught us the fine art of casting as soon as we could hold a pole. Even Mom has gotten into the act, as long as she doesn't have to take a fish off her hook." She grinned. "Heck, I can even clean them."

With a bemused look, he said, "I'm impressed."

She stretched out her legs in front of her and wiggled sock-covered toes. "This is nice." She gave a slight shiver and stretched her arms over her head.

"You're cold." It wasn't a question but a statement. Logan started to pull off his lightweight jacket to hand it to her. Grace held up her hand.

"I'm drying off. I'll put my boots on and finish my hike to the top." She cocked her head and gave him a warm, friendly look. "I'm happy to share my lunch with you."

Logan was taken aback. Quickly covering his surprise,

he said, "I'd enjoy having lunch with you, but there's a small outdoor café on the grounds. We could walk over—it's not far."

Grace glanced down at her soggy clothes. "I don't think I should be eating at a restaurant, but my offer stands. It's not fancy, but I have plenty."

He considered pushing the café again but threw up his hands. A slow smile spread across his face. "Why not? It's been a long time since I've eaten next to a bubbling body of water." He winked. "Who knows, we might even spot a fairy peeking out of the trees."

Her blue eyes grew wide and she dropped her voice. "So, do you believe in a bit of wee fairy magic?"

His voice held a hint of amusement. "Would you think less of me if I said yes?"

Grace gave one shake of her head and hid a smile behind her hand. "Not at all. In fact, I'd be concerned if you didn't. After all, you live in Scotland and you're surrounded by it." She bent over to pull her socks up and her boots on, then jumped up from the bench and slung her backpack over her shoulder. "Ready?"

With a sweep of his hand, Logan said, "Ladies first."

Grace started down the path with a spring in her step. Logan fell in behind her. *What the heck am I doing following an engaged woman down a path in one of the most romantic settings in all of Scotland?*

She turned around and flashed him a smile that quickened his step.

"I'm right behind you, Grace."

CHAPTER 7

Grace wondered what she was thinking, inviting Logan Campbell to share her measly lunch. She had some fruit, crackers and cheese along with the last of the scones from Flora's place. She glanced over her shoulder; Logan was on her heels.

With the final last few steps ahead of them, Logan slowed. "What do you think about this spot?"

Grace pivoted and looked around. "It looks perfect." Dropping the pack on a moss-covered log, she said, "I hope you're not disappointed with lunch." She opened the bag and pulled out two bottles of water, along with the other items. The last were the scones. "These might be a tad dry—they're leftover from a couple of days ago from MacMeekin's."

"I'm sure they'll be delicious."

Grace sat on the ground and patted the spot next to her. "Have a seat."

Logan dropped down, his back against the log. The sun peeked through the tree limbs overhead causing a soft filtered glow in the clearing. Grace handed him a bottle, then with a flick of her wrist laid out a small checked tablecloth and then placed the food on top. "Help yourself."

"Everything looks delicious." He winked, "I'd love a scone."

After pulling a napkin from the bag, she handed it to him. "It doesn't matter to me how old the scone is, Flora's are the best."

Accepting the napkin with a smile he asked, "So, tell me, what do you do for work?"

"I'm a physician's assistant at a medical center. It's a general practice. I treat everyone from toddlers to the elderly, and I love the variety." Nibbling on a cracker, she asked, "What about you?"

He hesitated looking into the distance.

"I'm sorry, you don't have to tell me if it's personal."

He met her gaze. "I've inherited a family business, among other things."

Grace wondered why he was vague. "Don't you enjoy what you do?"

"Very much, but I've been working in the business since I was in school and there isn't much of a challenge. Recently I've been thinking of expanding, maybe opening a small boutique hotel or something of the sort."

"That sounds interesting. I wouldn't have any idea how to run one, but I love staying in them."

He studied her and continued, "I would hire someone to run it for me, but it might be a nice change of pace."

She held out the bag of sliced cheese to him. "That's what I love about being a PA, it's never the same from patient to patient. Even during cold and flu season, each patient deals with illness very differently."

Logan selected a piece of cheese. "Do you live near your sisters?"

"I do. In fact, I just bought my sister Jamie's cottage.

She and her husband Caleb recently moved into their new old farmhouse."

Giving her a quizzical look, he said, "I'm not sure I understand what you mean."

With a laugh she said, "Jamie and Caleb bought a really rundown farm, and the house was in bad shape. Once they started renovating they discovered all sorts of issues with the electric and plumbing. It turned into a major rehab and Jamie doesn't do anything halfway, so before they finished the entire place was demo'd to the studs. After installing all new electrical and plumbing they hung sheet rock and new windows and doors. It looks like it's old, but it is brand-spanking-new."

He picked up a scone and took a bite. "That sounds ambitious, but I have a great deal of respect for people who lovingly restore an old building. There is usually so much history lost in the name of progress."

Grace nodded. "I couldn't agree more, which is why I love the cottage. Jamie did the same thing with that a few years ago, but it's too small for them to raise a family." Her voice drifted off, a stab of homesickness caught her off guard. "It really is a nice place."

"And your other sister?" he prodded.

"Kenzie?" She chuckled. "She loves condo living, but I have a sneaking suspicion that might change. Her husband Robbie and his family own a horse farm and stable. It's been in their family for generations, and as a wedding gift his dad gave them a parcel of land where they can build a home."

"That is a wonderful gift." He wiped the crumbs from the corner of his mouth. "It sounds like you're close with your sisters and their husbands."

"And with our parents too. We have Sunday brunch when we're all in town, and if my parents are here, in Scotland, my sisters and I get together, have a meal and Skype with them."

Grace looked down and discovered they had managed to eat everything she brought. "Well, I've rambled on enough. I must have bored you to tears."

"Not at all, it's been fun, and a nice way to spend the afternoon." Logan stood up and held out his hand to help Grace to her feet. "But I need to be going."

Grace glanced at her watch and exclaimed, "I had no idea it was so late! The day has gotten away from me. I'm supposed to be somewhere." The last thing she wanted to do was appear to be a lonely, needy tourist to Logan.

"Grace, before we go, how would you like to hammer a coin in the money log for luck?"

"That's something I haven't done since I was a child." She dug in her pockets but came up empty. "Sadly, I can't today."

Logan held up two coins. "One for you and one for me."

"Were you a Boy Scout as a kid?"

With a smile he said, "They do have Scouts of Scotland, but sadly I wasn't able to join. However, I do believe in always being prepared." He gave her a sideways grin. "That is their motto and one I strive to live by."

Grace accepted a coin and hastily stored the remnants of lunch in her bag. "Let's go pound some coins into a log and ask the fairies to spread a little magic."

Grace didn't remember when she had so much fun without her sisters. This was the kind of silly stuff she'd do with them, but never a guy, especially someone she just met. But what did it matter, really? It wasn't like they would see each other again.

After a short stroll, they came upon the spot and picked up a small hammer leaning against the log. Grace positioned her coin horizontally and gave it a *whack, whack, whack*. Logan gave an appreciative nod and followed suit.

They stood back and admired their handy work. He said, "I think that will make the fairies very happy and the waters of Rosemarkie Glen will run clean and pure."

"Let's hope so." She turned and stopped short. "Logan."

He turned and followed her arm to see where she was pointing. Grace stepped closer. "Look." With an outstretched hand, she traced the outline with her finger. "Someone carved a beautiful heart in the tree, but it doesn't have any initials. I wonder who it was."

He took a step closer, a hairsbreadth from her, and said very softly, "Maybe it was meant for all lovers. If they are here with the one they love, they will believe it was carved especially for them."

With a sigh filled with longing, Grace breathed, "How romantic."

"Maybe the next time you come to Rosemarkie it will be with your sweetheart."

Grace wondered if she would. Quietly she said, "Maybe."

Logan and Grace made their way back to the parking lot. An internal battle waged. He shouldn't have spent the afternoon with her, but he was inexplicably drawn to her. And he definitely should have asked her about the fiancé.

He was going to be selfish and enjoy these last few moments with Grace. He kept one eye on her and the other on the path. She radiated contentment.

Standing at the edge of the parking lot, he said, "Well, I

must be going. I've played the wayward company man for long enough today."

Grace laughed, which made his heart quicken. It was a sweet, pure sound. "I'll be headed home and to a hot shower."

He watched her blush, a most charming shade of pink. "Perhaps we'll run into each other again during your visit." He'd leave it up to fate.

"Life is certainly unpredictable. After all, who would have expected us to bump into each other so often during this trip?" She took off her sunglasses and looked into his eyes. "Thank you for an enjoyable day. It was certainly unexpected."

Downplaying his delight in meeting up with her, he met her eyes. "I appreciate the company in a picture-perfect setting. It was just what I needed before I slog through a mountain of paperwork." Who was he kidding, paperwork was the last thing on his mind. He knew once Grace went her way, the loneliness that enveloped him would come back with a vengeance.

She held out her hand, and he hesitated. Should he shake it?

"My bag?" she asked.

"Oh, right." Logan passed it to her.

Grace said, "All right then."

Was she waiting for something else? He frowned and said, "Well, goodbye, Grace, and drive carefully."

He hesitated as she turned and then said, "See you!" over her shoulder.

He waited until she was driving down the road before he made his way to his SUV. Climbing into the luxurious interior, he looked at the passenger seat. Grace would enhance the view if she were sitting next to him.

He could feel his shoulders sag. "Logan, old man, pull

yourself together and get to the office before the entire world wonders what happened to you." The engine roared to life and he eased out of the parking lot.

Grace's thoughts tumbled as she tried to make sense of what just happened. She wasn't interested in a vacation romance but meeting Logan Campbell had somehow changed that. She was surprised he didn't ask for her phone number and even more so that she really wanted him to.

Why didn't he ask me on a date? Inwardly she groaned. *Oh no. I'll bet he thinks I'm getting married because of the wedding dress.* The drive home would give her time to think about what it may or may not mean in the overall plan for her life.

After spending the afternoon in search of the journal Simon said Gran left for her, a sharp rap on the back door interrupted Grace. Running a hand over her curls, she hurried to the door.

"Tait? This is a surprise." She opened the door wider. "Come in."

As he ducked under the archway, he stopped in the front hall. "I'm sorry to drop by without calling, but I was thinking, if you're free, would you like to run into town and have tea at MacMeekin's?" His face flushed a deep shade of red.

Looking down at her outfit, she said, "That sounds like fun. I could use a break. Can I have a couple of minutes to change?"

"You look great, but of course I'll wait."

Grace shut the door and ushered him into the living room. "I won't be long. Make yourself comfortable."

Tait looked around the room and chose a rather uncomfortable hardback side chair, but it did have the best view of the farm.

Grace raced up the stairs into her room. Pulling open her closet, she pulled out a jean skirt and a pullover sweater. With a dash of mascara and a clip to tame her unruly hair, she was satisfied. After walking down the back stairs, she slipped into her sandals and picked up her handbag, making sure the kitchen door was locked.

She called, "I'm ready."

Tait was standing in the front hall waiting for her. She flashed him a sunny smile. "See, changed in under ten minutes."

He opened the door and Grace walked out first. "Do you have your keys?"

She nodded. "I do."

He flipped the lock on the door and pulled it tight, checking to make sure it was secured. "We'll take my truck if that's okay with you." He glanced at her bare legs. "It's kind of high."

She breezed down the front walk. "Don't worry, I can climb into your old truck." She pulled open the door and hopped in, proving her point.

Tait slid in and drove cautiously down the driveway. "I'm glad you're able to come with me today."

Grace glanced over to him. "I've had a busy day. I've been looking for my gran's journal, and maybe some time away from the house will provide me with a much-needed epiphany." She laughed. "Or who knows, maybe by magic they'll be on the table waiting for me when we get back."

Tait drove for several miles without responding before

he gave her a sidelong look. "Do you believe in all that nonsense?"

Grace was taken aback. "Don't you? After all, you've grown up around the legends."

She stared at him as he said, "Other than going to church, I don't put much stock into anything I can't see or touch."

In a small voice she said, "Oh." Grace looked out the window as pastureland gave way to more frequent houses. She was hurt that Tait would be so cavalier about his heritage; did that mean he thought she was silly? What did it matter if he did? The silence in the truck was irritating Grace, making her wish she hadn't agreed to tea.

The truck slowed and Tait said, "I'm sorry. I'm more of a practical man and I thought, given your profession, you would be too."

With a wave of her hand she said, "It's not a big deal." She pointed to an open parking space on the street. "Here we are."

Grace waited until they were stopped before unbuckling her seatbelt and hopping down. Straightening her skirt, she waited for Tait to come around the truck. They walked to the bakery, and Tait held the door for Grace. It took a moment for her eyes to adjust from the bright sun to the interior lighting. Expecting Flora to greet her, she stopped mid-step.

"Logan!" Her heart skipped a beat. "I didn't expect to see you today."

He looked up and his eyes twinkled as they met hers. "Hello, Grace. This *is* a surprise."

CHAPTER 8

Grace watched Tait's eyes move from her to Logan. She took a step toward Logan. "Logan, this is Dr. Tait Dennie. Tait, this is Logan Campbell."

The men shook hands and Flora came through the swinging kitchen door. "Grace, I thought I heard your voice." She beamed. "I didn't realize you and Logan knew each other."

She embraced the older woman. "We've bumped into each other a couple of times. However, I had no idea he'd be here today." Grace saw the look of confusion on Flora's face. "He's the man who saved my dress at the airport. Then when I was shopping for our dinner, I ran into him, and yesterday he pulled me out of the stream at Rosemarkie."

Flora's eyebrow arched. "Really now. That is very interesting."

Grace's smile bounced between the people surrounding her. "He was most gracious on each occasion." She turned to Logan. "What brings you to MacMeekin's?"

"After talking with you about the delicious baked goods, I wanted to stop in and pick something up for the office and of course to see my aunt." His voice was rich and smooth. She could listen to him talk for hours and never get tired of the melodic sound of his voice.

"What a coincidence. Tait stopped over and asked me to tea. Would you care to join us?"

Tait frowned and Logan said, "Another time, perhaps. I do need to get back to the office. Aunt Flora, would you fill up a couple of boxes with a nice assortment?" He reached into his suit jacket and withdrew his wallet.

"Certainly." Flora bustled around the case and selected two large boxes. "Will these be big enough?"

Logan nodded and smiled. He turned to Grace. "Please enjoy yourselves."

Tait escorted her to a vacant table as far from Logan as seemed possible. He held the chair for Grace, and then he sat down, effectively blocking her view of the shop and the tall, handsome man at the counter.

She strained to eavesdrop on Logan and Flora's conversation, hoping to glean a bit more information about the mysterious man. Avoiding Tait's gaze, she pretended to study the menu. She casually watched Logan leave. He gave her a quick smile before the door swung closed behind him.

Flora picked up a teapot and two cups. She carried them to Grace's table and set them down. "Tait, I'm sorry we didn't get a chance to say hello with Grace and Logan chatting. It's good to see you again."

"Thanks, Mrs. M. It's good to be back." He smiled at Grace. "And it is a nice surprise that Grace is here on holiday."

"Aye, it is good to see her again." Flora patted Grace's shoulder. "I'm going to bring you an assortment.' She smiled at Tait. "Grace always has a difficult time choosing. Whatever is left you can take home with you."

The door opened and a customer came in, cutting Grace off from asking the question uppermost in her mind. She had to be patient.

Flora returned with a large plate brimming with sweet cakes and assorted pastries. Fishing for details, Grace casually said, "So you're Logan's aunt?"

Flora didn't meet Grace's gaze. "His mother and I were sisters."

Grace took a sip of her tea. "It really is a very small world."

Flora gave a wry laugh. "And it gets smaller every day, my dear lass." She left to go back into the kitchen.

Tait held out the plate to Grace, and she selected a small fruit tart. "Thank you."

"So, you say that Campbell fellow helped you at the airport?"

Grace really didn't want to relive the story, so she kept it simple. "He was a true gentleman."

Tait was silent for a few uncomfortable moments. "Well, I'm glad he was there to be of assistance."

Grace gave him a sharp look. Could Tait be jealous? "Me too. I would have been devastated if I'd lost Gran's dress." She wiped her mouth with the corner of the cloth napkin. She feared Tait had the wrong idea about having tea together. It seemed clear to Grace that he was getting territorial about her.

Not wanting to hurt his feelings, she said, "This is nice, but I should be getting back to the farm." She remembered where Gran had always kept the journals.

"We just sat down." Tait scraped back his chair and picked up the plate. He didn't attempt to disguise the hurt in his eyes. "I'll have Mrs. M wrap these up for you."

"You should take some too." Grace knew this had been a bad idea. It had given Tait the wrong impression.

He shook his head. "I can have them anytime."

Grace pulled out her wallet.

With a shake of his head Tait said, "Grace, let me take care of the check."

She knew he was raised to be a gentleman, and to push the issue of paying for the pastries would be rude. "Thank you, Tait. I will enjoy them for sure."

They approached the counter and Flora smiled. "Did you enjoy your tea?"

Grace leaned over and pecked her cheek. "Best in the world."

Tait reached into his pocket and Flora waved a dismissive hand. "It's all taken care of, Tait."

"Mrs. M, I insist."

"No, the bill has been paid for. Logan took care of it before he left."

Her words made Grace's heart flutter. Logan had paid? "I wonder why he didn't join us."

Flora laid a hand over her heart. "Logan Campbell is a very nice man who does kind things on the spur of the moment and I, for one, have never been able to figure him out."

Grace sputtered, "I'd like to thank him."

"The next time I see him, dear, I'll pass it along." Flora's eyes twinkled. "I'll see you soon?"

Grace smiled. "I'm sure you will. Thank you again, Flora, everything was delicious as always."

Tait was strangely silent during the exchange and dropped some money in the tip jar before he turned toward the door. He waited until Grace was next to him before pushing it open. In silence the pair walked back to his truck.

"Tait?"

He grumbled, "When I take a girl someplace, I expect to pay."

She gave him a searching look and overlooked that it sounded like he thought they were on a date. "It was just a kind gesture, nothing more."

He softened. "I'll take you home."

Somehow Grace knew it was going to be a very quiet ride.

Logan drove quickly away from his aunt's bakery. He was thrilled to have bumped into Grace again but not happy to know she was engaged to a doctor. He needed to talk to Aunt Flora and see if she knew anything more about Dr. Dennie and when they were to be married.

Logan could see the glow of the city limits of Glasgow ahead of him. He slowed and pulled over to the side of the road. He hit a button on his phone and he could hear ringing on the other end.

Aunt Flora's voice came through loud and clear. "MacMeekin's Bakery."

"Hello, Aunt Flora."

With a soft chuckle she said, "I wondered how long it would take for you to call."

He grinned into the phone. "I'm not sure what you mean."

"I haven't seen that look in your eye in a very long time. You couldn't keep your eyes off Ms. Grace MacLellan."

"She is something special."

"Yes, she is and I'm glad you can see that."

"Thanks for not mentioning the connection between your bakery and the company."

"Why?"

"I'm not ready for her to know, at least not yet."

A car whizzed by his SUV.

Aunt Flora's voice held a warning tone. "Don't wait too long before you tell Grace everything."

Without responding to her statement Logan said, "I was wondering if I could come out tomorrow and take you to dinner. I need your advice."

"I have a feeling I know what the topic will be, but of course. Come by my house and I'll cook. It has been a long time since the two of us have shared a meal."

Logan realized his aunt must be lonely, as they were all each other had. "I'm happy to take you out."

"Nonsense," Aunt Flora admonished. "We'll have dinner at home. I'll see you promptly at six."

Logan laughed. "I promise I won't be late." He disconnected and leaned his head back against the seat. He had spent years living with her after his father died. Flora must have felt that her only living relative had abandoned her, and for that he felt like a failure. If only his mother and sister hadn't died in the ferryboat accident. Life would have been very different.

He glanced in the rear and side view mirrors and pulled back onto the road. He'd burn the midnight oil to make sure he got out of work on time tomorrow. "I won't disappoint Aunt Flora again."

Grace hopped down from Tait's truck with the goodie box. He gave her a curt goodbye. She watched as the tires kicked up dust as he drove down the drive. Better to have him disappointed now than later.

Straightening her shoulders, she walked with a new

sense of purpose, to read the journal. She knew exactly where to look—in the hutch drawer. Fumbling with the keys Grace practically fell through the door in her haste. She threw down her bag and kicked off her sandals.

Hurrying into the formal dining room, Grace put the bakery box on the table and pulled open the first of the top three drawers. Linens. The next contained a box for silverware, and then she pulled open the middle drawer. She reached inside and her fingers skimmed the cover of a thick, leather-bound book. "Gran's journal."

Grace clutched it to her chest. Pushing the drawer closed, she carried it into the living room. Taking a deep breath, she laid it on the coffee table.

Do I call Jamie and Kenzie, or do I go ahead, read it and fill them in later? The clock ticked, and Grace made a decision. *This is my journey. I'll read it first and then call my sisters.*

Shadows were creeping into the corners of the room. Grace poured herself a glass of wine and snapped on a couple of lights. Once she started, she didn't want to stop.

Making herself comfortable on the sofa, she picked up the thick book and flipped open the cover. Grace traced Gran's name.

Arabel Mackenzie MacLellan
For my granddaughters

Grace skipped the first few pages, as it was about the weather. She turned the page and stopped to read the next entry.

My dear granddaughters Jamie, Kenzie and Grace have just left to return home to Vermont. The house is quiet, as it typically is when the little bundles of energy leave. My darling Rory is watching down on me, keeping me company from afar. It will be many years before we see each other again.

During the visit I paid special attention to my little one, Grace. I worry for her. The future that surrounds her is not clear to me. After holding the wedding dress, my dear mother sewed with her hands, I can see their future. Jamie, our firstborn, will marry a good Irish man and her future is bright and filled with love and much happiness. My dear Kenzie, our strong-willed and fiercely independent lass, will take her time finding love. When she does, it will be as deep as the loch and strong as a mighty waterfall with a man she has known her entire life. But little Grace, whose heart is loving and pure, will need to find her way back to where it all began to discover where she truly belongs.

Grace looked out the window as she rubbed her eyes. She could almost hear Gran speaking the words she had written. *But why was my future unclear?*

She turned the page. Gran talked of the weather, the upcoming harvest and fishing with Simon. Grace paused on the next entry.

I have packed the wedding dress, brooch and our plaid for the girls with instructions for James to give it to them once I'm gone. When the time comes to give each lass her letter, I will instruct Grace to bring the dress home, to Scotland. It is here she will find the path to her future.

But, Grace thought, it didn't. "I saw the back of some man's head. How do I know who it is? Just like Gran had said, it wasn't clear."

Her hand flew to her mouth. *What if I tried it on too soon, before it had a chance to recharge the enchantment and I've ruined my chance at finding long, lasting love?*

Goose bumps danced up Grace's arm and, setting the journal aside, she went to get a sweater. Her stomach grumbled, but she ignored it—she needed more answers, and hopefully they were within the pages of the journal. Putting her arms through an oversized fleece, she sat back down.

Gran wrote:

I've decided not to tell the girls about the wedding dress, just as my mother withheld the information from me. But over the last few years there have been times when I've wanted to reassure Grace the magic of the dress will guide her. But how could I do that? They should only discover the existence of the dress when they are ready to open their hearts to love. The only comfort I have is when I've gone to be with Rory the girls will be confident young women, and ready to understand all...

New entry:

Grace, I believe you will read this journal after you've returned to Scotland alone. I've enlisted Simon's help to encourage you to find this book. Oh, I wish I were sitting next to you on the sofa. There is so much I would want to explain, but this is the way it must be. I'm confident you will find your path. Last night I had a dream of you wearing the dress, and I must say you were a stunning bride. Your curls tumbling down your back, our plaid as your train and your flower choice was absolute perfection.

Grace's hand flew to her throat. That was exactly how she saw herself in the mirror. How did Gran know?

I know you're wishing you could ask me who he is. As I packed the dress, I saw him. He's a fine man. One I'd be proud to call my family. Be patient, dear child. He is coming as fast as he can and will be standing beside you for all time. I love you with all my heart.

Grace leafed through the remaining pages in the journal. They were blank. She gently closed the book and sat in silence. Darkness had long since fallen, and she was at a loss. The emptiness in her stomach matched her heart.

"Gran," she cried, "what am I supposed to do?"

Silence answered her.

CHAPTER 9

Logan looked at his watch again. He was the boss, and he was calling it a day. He closed his laptop and slid it into his briefcase. He yelled to his assistant, "Tracey, I'm leaving," unconcerned if she heard him or not.

He noticed traffic crawled on the city street outside his office. Making his way to the parking lot, he jumped into his SUV and eased into traffic. The snail's pace suited him just fine so he could replay the wonderful dream he had last night. Grace was in his arms as they stood in a field of bluebells. Her long curls were teased by the breeze. He had reached out, cupped her cheek and, mesmerized, he fell into the depths of her crystal-blue eyes.

A blaring horn drew him back to the present. Logan pressed down the gas pedal and cleared the slower traffic before merging onto the highway. Cruising along, he wondered what his aunt would cook for dinner, not that it mattered since everything she made was amazing.

His cell rang. Pushing the hands-free button on the steering wheel, he said, "Hello, Aunt Flora."

"Logan." Her voice held a musical quality he loved. "I wanted to make sure you were on your way. I know how you can get distracted at the office."

"I should be home in less than thirty minutes. I left early and traffic has finally lightened up."

She chuckled. "Are you anxious for some home cooking, or to discuss the lovely Grace?"

Logan grinned into the phone. "Is both an appropriate answer?"

"Of course it is. Be a dear and pick up a bottle of wine. I'm in the mood for a glass of pinot noir."

He snorted. "I know what that means—we're having fresh trout for dinner. I presume Simon Dennie dropped by."

A light bulb went off in Logan's head. Tait Dennie was Simon's grandson. He smacked the steering wheel with his hand. That's how they'd met.

"Logan?" Aunt Flora's voice broke his train of thought.

"Yes, I'll pick up a bottle. I'm going to let you go, but I'll be there very soon."

"Drive carefully."

"Of course. Bye."

Logan disconnected the call and stared ahead. *They've probably known each other their entire lives. No wonder Grace looked comfortable with him. It's natural they would keep in touch, and they share the love of medicine, even though Tait takes care of animals. If Aunt Flora tells me to back off, I will.*

Grace relaxed on the patio in the early morning sun until the lure of fishing propelled her to take action. As she loaded her gear in the car, she saw Simon strolling across the barnyard. She waved. His face lit up and he hurried in her direction.

When he grew close, he called, "Morning, Grace."

"Good morning, Simon." She glanced at the blue sky and puffy clouds. "Lovely day, isn't it?"

"Aye." He glanced at her car. "Are you headed out to cast a line or two?"

"I haven't fished since I got here. I want to see if I can reel 'em in. Would you care to join me?"

He pushed back his cap and studied her. "Are you sure you'd like an old man as a fishing buddy? It might suit to take someone else with you."

She wagged a finger at him. "I asked if you'd like to go, not anyone else. Are you interested?"

With a snort he said, "Am I a Scot?"

She threw back her head and laughed. "Oh, Simon. You most certainly are. Do you have your gear in the truck or do we need to swing by your house?"

"Now, Grace, I think you've forgotten my cardinal rule, always be ready to go fishing."

She jerked a thumb toward his truck. "Grab your gear and I'll grab a couple extra bottles of water and some snacks. We'll meet back here in a couple of minutes."

With a half turn Simon said, "I'm going to let Patrick know where I'm going just in case he comes looking for me."

"Good idea." Grace watched as the older man quickened his steps. She was glad she asked him; it would be sort of like fishing with Gran again. Simon had occasionally accompanied them on their jaunts to different streams. She hurried into the house and finished gathering what was needed before heading back to her car.

Simon was wearing his vest and had his hip waders, a tackle box and a pole sitting next to her car. His smile was broad as he walked to Grace. "I told Patrick I'd bring home supper."

Grace took his pole and box and stowed them in the back. She said, "We'd better hope they're biting since we're both counting on dinner." She winked. "We might be swinging by the market if we come up empty."

Simon chuckled and stowed his waders in the back of the car. "You have so little faith in our skill, Grace."

Smiling, she shut the back. "We do have skill, but those fish have a goal to keep swimming." She hopped behind the wheel. "Any place special we should go?"

"For old time's sake, let's go to Arabel's favorite spot." He looked at her. "Is that okay?"

Grace patted his hand. She noticed the skin was thin and wrinkly, his fingers gnarled from years of hard farm work. With a gentle smile and a tilt of her head, she said. "I think that is a perfect spot."

Without rushing, Grace pulled out on the two-lane country road with the windows down and the wind caressing her face. This was exactly the right thing to do today.

"I understand you and Tait have spent some time together."

Grace gave him a wary look. "We did."

He gazed out the window. "Do you think you could have feelings for him? He's a good man and thinks the world of you."

"Oh, Simon. You're right, he *is* a good man, and he deserves a wonderful woman, but that's not me."

He held up his hands in defeat. "I won't ask you again. But thank you for indulging an old man's foolish hopes."

Grace slowed and put on her blinker. She stopped in the small parking area and turned off the car. Turning in her seat, she faced Simon. "It is very sweet that you think of me so highly, and I do value Tait's friendship. But that's all we will be, friends." She leaned in and kissed his weathered cheek. "Now, I don't know about you, but I'm itching to cast a line into that fine-looking stream." She pointed out the window. "Did you see that?" She laughed. "The trout are just leaping out of the water, taunting us."

Simon laid his hand on the door handle. "You really are a rare woman and so much like Arabel. It makes me miss her even more."

She swallowed a lump in her throat. "That is quite a compliment, Simon."

Wearing hip waders, fishing vests and oversized hats, Grace and Simon stood quietly, thigh-deep in the cold current in the riverbed. Her first cast of the day sailed over the water before slipping underneath the surface. Grace jerked the line heavenward. The cadence of the cast, back and forth, as the line glided on the air, presenting the fly to the fish, was restorative. The rhythm of casting was second nature to Grace. She and her sisters had been fly-fishing since the moment they could hold a rod. She missed sharing this with her sisters, but standing next to Simon seemed right.

The fly went plop, plop, plop on the surface with each cast. Simon quickly landed a large trout and stored it in his bag. Grace was next, bringing up a fourteen-inch rainbow, which she promptly added to Simon's bag. Within a short while, they had their limit, and after spending some time fishing and then releasing them, the pair was ready to go home.

Grace looked in the bag and pulled out her two.

"These are bigger than I need. Maybe I'll stop by Flora's and see if she'd like one." She quickly set about to clean them.

Simon worked next to her doing the same. "Arabel did a fine job teaching you about the sport and how to be a good steward to nature."

Grace pushed the brim of her hat out of her eyes with her forearm. "If it's not worth learning how to do it right, it's not worth doing."

"She said that often too." Simon smiled and paused as he opened a cooler in the back of the car. "Are you going to drop the fish off to Flora on the way home?"

Grace grinned over her shoulder as she walked to the edge of the stream, bending low to rinse her hands. "I'll call her before we leave so she can meet me outside. I wouldn't want to *perfume* her shop with a fishy odor." She wrinkled her nose. "That wouldn't be good for tourist business."

Simon snapped the lid of the cooler tight. "Knowing Flora, it wouldn't bother her in the least. She loves a fresh trout dinner."

Grace dried her hands on a towel and tossed it in the back of the car. "Ready?"

"When you speak with Flora, ask her if she'd bag up a few scones for her old friend." He flashed her a toothy grin.

Grace pulled out her phone and said, "That's a good idea. Maybe she'll pack up two."

Flora was waiting on the sidewalk holding two white boxes, grinning from ear to ear as Grace got out of the car. "Grace, dear, it was lovely of you to call. I must say it couldn't come at a better time. I'm having company for dinner and it saved me a trip to the market on the way home."

Pulling open the hatch, Grace frowned. "Flora, do you have something I can put it in? I have fish for both of us and nothing for you to carry it in."

Simon called from the front seat, "I have a heavy-duty plastic bag in my box. It's tucked under the lid. You can use that."

Flora took a few steps and handed Simon a box through the open window. "This is for you."

With a chuckle, he said, "I'm glad I had the bag then. We'll be even?"

She gave a hearty laugh. "A plastic bag for a box of sweet treats. Somehow I think we both made out tonight."

Grace walked over to where Flora and Simon were chatting. She extended the bag and Flora handed her a box. "I tucked in a few items for tea and something to go with your dinner tonight."

"Thank you, but that wasn't necessary." Grace peeked inside. "Biscuits—oh, they look delicious." She pulled the top up higher. "Scones, shortbread and teacakes." She closed the lid and smacked her lips. "I haven't had those yet. I love the marshmallow in them."

"I hope you enjoy every morsel." Flora examined the filets Grace handed to her. "That was a mighty big fish you landed, Grace."

She jokingly bowed and said, "Thank you. I haven't lost my touch after all."

Flora said, "You've got good Scottish blood running through your veins and the fish know it. I'll bet they leap from the water into your net."

Grace laughed. "If only it was that easy." She dropped a kiss on Flora's cheek and announced, "We need to be off. Patrick is going to wonder where we are." With a jaunty wave, she hurried around to the driver's seat and called out, "I'll see you very soon."

Grace could see in her rearview mirror Flora watch and wave as they drove away. She mused, "I hope she and her dinner guest enjoy the trout," then said to Simon, "we should try to get out one more time before I go home."

"And when might that be, Grace?"

She did a quick calculation. "Two weeks and two days."

Simon chuckled. "Glad to know you're not counting the days until you leave."

"Heck no. I'm counting the days I get to keep having fun." She glanced at him. "And I do mean lots of fun."

Aunt Flora was waiting by the door when Logan pulled into her driveway. He looked around the tidy fenced-in yard and couldn't help but feel his worries slip away. He dashed up the steps, taking them two at a time, and swept her off her feet.

Laughing, she said, "Put me down before you drop me."

"Hello, Aunt Flora, and for the record, I'd never drop you." He planted a kiss on her cheek and carefully set her back on her feet. "Oh, wait." He hurried back to the car, grabbed a bag off the passenger seat. As he walked toward the door he said, "I didn't forget the wine."

She stepped over the threshold. "Come in and you can pour. I have a sneaking suspicion you have something important on your mind."

He closed the door after them and followed her into the kitchen. He pulled open a drawer to retrieve the corkscrew. Making short work of the cork, he poured two glasses of aromatic wine. Logan handed her a glass. "Here you go. Have a taste," he encouraged.

She took a sip. "This is exceptional. Just right for our dinner. We're having your favorites—trout, baby peas and biscuits."

He trailed behind her as she went into the front room and waited until she got settled. Then he sat, his long legs stretched out in front of him. "I'm not sure where to begin, and I hope you don't think I'm foolish, but I need your advice."

"That's why I'm here, Logan. So, tell me." Aunt Flora set her glass aside and leaned forward.

"Last year, when I was flying home from signing that deal to expand the business to the United States, there were three American girls in the seats in front of me."

Aunt Flora's eyes widened. "The MacLellan sisters?"

He nodded. "The same." He took a drink of wine and continued, "And when I saw Grace, even though I didn't know who she was at the time, I felt an instant connection?" He shrugged. "They went their way and I mine. But she began to appear in my dreams."

"Really?" Aunt Flora scooched to the edge of her chair.

"I didn't think I'd ever see her again until last week when she was at the car rental counter at Glasgow International and a thief took off with her wedding dress. I chased it down and brought it back to her. Then I bumped into her at the gourmet market and again at Rosemarkie."

Confusion flashed across her face. "I don't understand, Logan, what is the problem?"

He hopped up and, with palms flung wide, began to pace. "Aunt Flora, she's engaged to be married to Dr. Tait Dennie."

Aunt Flora's mouth dropped open and she laughed. "What did you say, engaged to be married? Wherever did you get that idea? And to Tait?"

CHAPTER 10

Logan sputtered and sank back in the overstuffed chair. "Stop. This is not a laughing matter. The woman I've been dreaming about for months is going to marry another man."

"Logan Campbell!" Aunt Flora's tone was sharp. It was the same one she had used on him when he was a teenager.

His eyes met hers. "What?"

"Did you hear what I said? Grace is not engaged to Tait or anyone else, for that matter."

Stunned, he sat up straight. "Are you sure? How do you know?"

Aunt Flora casually picked up her glass and sat back in the chair. "I've known her all her life, and she and Tait have been friends since childhood. But there is nothing romantic between them."

"Really?" he questioned. "But when I brought back the garment bag I'm positive she said it was her wedding dress."

"I'm sure she did. What you don't know is her grandmother sent an heirloom wedding dress to the girls in Vermont. Her sisters, Jamie and Kenzie, recently married, wore that very dress and Grace was bringing it back to Scotland. Yes, someday it will be her dress. So, you can understand how devastated she would have been if anything had happened to it."

Slowly he nodded and a smile spread across his face. "So this means I can ask her out on an official date."

Aunt Flora grinned. "Nothing would make this old woman happier."

Logan did a fist pump. "Yes!"

"Now that we've resolved the issue of whether or not you can ask Grace out on a date, there is the matter that she is here on holiday and not planning on relocating."

He grinned. "My dear aunt, first I have to get her to fall head over heels in love with me and the rest will take care of itself. After all, I'm a great catch."

"Logan." Her voice held a cautionary tone. "She's not like those girls you've dated in the past, dazzled by your money, good looks and charm. She's a beautiful, intelligent girl with strong ties to her family. You won't be able to bowl her over with your 'stuff.'"

He leaned back and grew thoughtful. "Do you think I should keep the fact that I'm very financially secure to myself?"

"Money won't matter to Grace. She'll be attracted to the caliber of you as a person." Setting her glass aside, Aunt Flora rose. "As a matter of fact, the fish we're going to enjoy tonight was freshly caught today, by none other than the lovely Grace."

"Interesting. I knew she liked to fish but didn't realize she was going while she was here." Logan stood. "Let me finish dinner for us. You can sit and tell me more about Grace MacLellan, her likes and dislikes."

Aunt Flora raised one eyebrow. "Won't that give you an unfair advantage in your pursuit of her? As she basically will know nothing about you?"

"I intend to sweep her off her feet." He patted the middle of his chest. His voice and eyes softened. "She makes me feel again." He grasped his aunt's hand. "For the first time in a very long time it matters that someone likes me for me."

"She's a good person, but mark my words, if you hurt her, you'll have me to answer to. She is my best friend's granddaughter and I have an obligation to Arabel."

Logan said with sincerity, "From the bottom of my heart I promise, Aunt Flora. This is one time I'm committed to being the best man I can be. I'll make you proud of me."

Aunt Flora patted his cheek. "Now, when are you going to tell her that you are owner and CEO of Tartan Bakery, along with a string of hotels and businesses?"

"You're right. She's not like the other women I have dated where money was my most charming attribute. If it won't impress her, there's no reason to bring it up."

Grace perched on the edge of her chair, waiting while Jamie and Kenzie logged into Skype. *Bloop.* Their smiling faces appeared on the screen.

"Hey, Grace," they said in unison.

"Hi, Mac, Kenz." She smiled. "How's everything back home?"

"All's good here. Nothing new to report," Jamie said. "How's things on the farm?"

Grace was nodding. "All's fine here too. The weather has been almost perfect, and yesterday I went fishing with

Simon. I had fresh trout for dinner and I even dropped one off to Flora."

Kenzie leaned in toward the screen. "How come you didn't ask her to join you?"

"She was having company, but I'm sure before I leave we'll do dinner at least one more time."

Jamie's head bobbed. "Anything else going on?"

"Like what?" Grace attempted to avoid the implied questions about what was really happening.

"Grace..." Jamie's tone was firm and gentle at the same time.

"I found another journal." Grace let the mini bombshell land where it may.

Kenzie said, "And? Don't keep us in suspense. Have you read it yet?"

Grace admitted, "I've been scanning it. Gran meant for the three of us to see it. I'll bring it home when I come. It's got a lot of neat stuff about when we were young, but also a few tidbits about our futures."

"Like what?" Jamie demanded.

Grace said in a rush, "Gran knew you'd marry a man who was Irish and she knew Kenzie would find love with someone she had known her whole life."

"Gracie, what did Gran say about you?" Kenzie asked her softly.

"She explained that my future would be found here, in Scotland." She choked back a sob. "Gran said she could see me on my wedding day and the man I would marry, but she didn't tell me who it was."

Jamie laughed quietly. "Gracie, would you really want Gran to tell you? Wouldn't it take all the thrill and adventure out of falling in love if she had? And finding true love is amazing and breath-taking all at the same time."

"I guess." She frowned.

Kenzie said, "If I had known Robbie was my future, I don't think I would appreciate how deep my love is for him. Or worse, I might have run in the opposite direction, saying there was no way Gran could know what my future held."

Anxious to talk about something else, Grace said, "Are Mom and Dad excited to get back to the farm?"

Jamie looked at Kenzie before answering. "They're planning on the fall, and then they'll spend Christmas in Scotland."

"What?" Grace's mouth dropped open. "Spend the holidays without us?"

"No, Gracie," Kenzie said, "they want us all to be in Scotland. Together."

Grace didn't attempt to keep the frustration from her voice. "I don't know if I'll be able to get time off from work. You and Jamie are both self-employed, so it's a little easier. I usually have to take call, at least one of the holidays the office is closed."

"Grace, relax. We can sit down with Mom and Dad and it'll work out." Jamie smiled. "I promise, we'll be together for the holidays."

"I'm not holding out a lot of hope, but I'll worry about that in a few weeks. I think I might saddle up a horse and head up the hills for a short ride before dinner."

"Sounds good, kiddo." Kenzie said. "We'll talk on Sunday?"

Faking a smile, Grace gave thumbs-up. "Bye, girls."

She disconnected and closed her laptop. She didn't want to go for a ride. Maybe she'd walk down and visit Gran. After slipping her cell in her windbreaker, she tied her sneakers and off she went. But before she reached the end of the driveway, her phone rang.

"Hello?"

"Hello, Grace." She'd recognize that smooth brogue anywhere.

"Logan, hi. How did you get my number?"

"I hope you don't mind, but I asked Aunt Flora for it, and after I promised to be nothing but a gentleman, she agreed to give it to me."

Her heart fluttered and she sighed. "All right then." She was flattered he had gone to the trouble of getting her number.

"I was wondering if you'd care to have dinner with me tomorrow night. There's this great restaurant where all the furniture is from secondhand shops but the food is absolutely amazing. If you'd like, there's a pub with live jazz music within just a short walk."

She hesitated and did a mental check of the clothes she brought with her. She had a nice dress for dinner. "That sounds great. If you text me the address, I can meet you there."

With a low, sexy chuckle he said, "Now, you just heard me say I promised Aunt Flora I'd be a gentleman, so what kind of man would I be if I didn't pick you up?"

The sound of his laughter caused Grace's pulse to quicken. "I don't want you to go out of your way. It's no trouble, really."

"Grace, I insist. I'll pick you up around five?"

"Do you know where I'm staying?" she asked.

"It's a small village," he said with a chuckle, "and everyone knows about the MacLellan farm, they raise the best sheep in the county."

"Okay. Well, then I'll be ready." She kept her voice steady and did a jig in the middle of the road.

"I'm looking forward to it. See you tomorrow, Grace."

"Goodbye, Logan."

With a new pep in her step, she headed down the road.

CHAPTER 11

Grace had soaked in a long, hot bubble bath in anticipation of the evening ahead. She dressed in a simple, knee-length, aubergine-colored shift, with long chiffon sleeves and a dramatic deep V exposing her back. She carefully pinned her curls on top of her head, highlighting chandelier earrings which swayed as she moved her head from side to side. The finishing touch: strappy, high-heeled silver sandals.

Turning as she looked in the three-way mirror to view herself from all angles, she was satisfied with the effect. Hopefully she'd make a better impression on Logan since the first time he saw her on the plane, travel weary and her hair a mess.

Grace heard a loud knock on the door. With one final check of her makeup, she took a deep breath and exhaled. It did nothing to quiet the butterflies inside her. She descended the stairs, taking deep breaths, and walked into the front hall. Grace pulled open the door; her eyes sought his. In an instant she knew she had chosen the perfect dress.

~

Logan's mouth went dry and he felt his eyes pop. "Grace, you are beautiful."

He picked up her hand and kissed it. His gaze lingered on her full, deep-red lips. He wondered what it would feel like to crush her to his chest and to kiss them. But for tonight he was going to be the gentleman she deserved. He didn't want Grace to think he was attracted to her primarily for her physical attributes. It was so much more than that, and he had no way to describe it at the moment.

He was enchanted as the rush of pink filled her cheeks and her deep blue eyes sparkled.

She asked, "Am I overdressed?"

He was still holding her hand and let his eyes drink in the sight of her, from chestnut curls down her long graceful neck, her earrings hovering where he'd like his lips to be. "You are perfection." For a second or two, his eyes slid over her legs, to the graceful turn of her ankle and the barely-there shoes.

Her cheeks went to a new delightful shade of magenta. "Thank you," she stammered.

"Shall we go?"

"Let me grab my bag."

As Grace turned to pick it up, Logan saw the back of her dress, desire flared deep within him. Reminding himself to focus he held the screen door while she locked the main door, and then he held out the crook of his arm for her to take. He didn't want her taking a tumble on the stone path.

"It's a beautiful evening," Grace breathed.

His eyes were on Grace. "It certainly is."

Opening the car door, he helped her into his SUV. He had wanted to bring his vintage Jag, but that was the usual move to impress a lady. He was determined this was going to be different. In a few quick strides he was behind the wheel and they were off down the road.

She gave him a killer smile, which made his heart flip. *Who is this woman and what spell has she cast over me?*

Grace's head swiveled. *Oh, shoot, was that Tait's truck we just passed?* She didn't want him to see her on a date with Logan since she had proclaimed she was here to relax. But wait, she spent time with Tait. This was exactly the same thing, she reassured herself. *Yeah, right, who are you trying to kid?* This was not the same as when she had tea with Tait.

She glanced at Logan. He looked so handsome. His light brown hair was cut short and simply styled. He must be at the barber all the time to keep it looking sharp. She longed to reach out and trace her finger over his strong, sturdy jaw line, and touch the deep dimples that appeared in his cheeks when he smiled. She liked that he wore a classic button-down shirt, sleeves turned back to expose his muscled forearms, and dark pressed jeans outlined his long legs. Logan Campbell was hot. She laughed to herself and wondered, what would the reserved Mr. Campbell think of being ogled, even if it wasn't apparent to anyone but her?

Interrupting her inner monologue, Logan said, "A penny for your thoughts?"

She flashed him a smile. "I'm looking forward to tonight. You didn't tell me where we were going so I couldn't check out the menu, but the decor sounded intriguing."

"My assistant says it is one of the best in the city and recommends anything with seafood, venison, duck or beef." He chuckled and continued, "And she reminded me twice about the seafood."

"It sounds like the seafood dishes are among the best." She nodded. "Good to know." She liked the talk of food, it diffused the electricity in the air.

He grinned. "And for dessert she said the hot lemon meringue pie is not to be missed."

Her eyes grew wide. "I love dessert and that sounds amazing. It's making my mouth water just thinking about it."

Teasing he said, "Maybe we should have dessert first."

She sighed. "A man after my own heart."

The car slowed as they merged onto the highway. "We'll be in the city in no time at all." Logan expertly maneuvered the SUV through the heavy traffic. Conversation was about activities Grace shared with her family, and Logan talked about his ideas for expansion into new markets for his business.

"It sounds like you're out to conquer the world." Grace looked at him. "How did you get started in the company—were you fresh out of university?"

He wondered how he should answer this question without giving away too much information. "I went to business school and jumped in with both feet. With my aunt's guidance, I became the moderate success I am today."

Grace sensed there was more to the story but asked, "Do you have brothers or sisters?"

He felt his heart constrict with the familiar vise. "My mother and sister died in a ferry accident when I was about fourteen and my dad died shortly thereafter. Aunt Flora raised me." He glanced at Grace. "I was one angry adolescent, and thankfully she has the patience of a saint."

"I'm sorry." Her heart broke for Logan. To have suffered

so much loss no wonder he seemed so closed off. Reaching over, she laid a hand on his arm. "She's a wonderful person."

"That she is." Logan slowed the car and took the next exit. "Enough of my past. Let's focus on the evening." He looked out the windshield. "Hopefully it won't rain tonight."

She glanced at her tiny handbag, "I don't have an umbrella tucked away in here; it's not exactly roomy."

"Not to worry. It wouldn't dare rain until I have you safely delivered home." He pulled to a stop in front of the restaurant. The sidewalk was crowded with people bustling around, probably headed home for the evening. Logan pointed across the street. "There's Number Ten."

She noticed people were standing in line waiting to get inside. "It looks crowded."

With hand poised on the door handle, Logan grinned. "Never fear, there is a table waiting for us." He pushed open the door and hurried around the front. Grace's door was open and he extended his hand for her. Taking it, she stepped onto a crack in the brick sidewalk, promptly losing her footing and tumbling into his arms.

"Steady there." His voice was husky.

"Um, thank you." Grace smoothed down the front of her dress and brushed a curl from her face. She closed the door and Logan hit the lock on the key fob.

Hand in hand, the couple crossed the street. Logan steered her past the line, walking into the restaurant. The spicy aromas of food tantalized Grace's senses. Her mouth watered with anticipation. Logan escorted her toward the host station.

"Good evening, Logan." A young man welcomed them with a warm smile. "Your table is ready. Follow me, please."

"Hello, John."

Logan and Grace wound around a few tables until they came to a corner booth. The host left the menus on the table and said, "Your waiter will be over shortly. In the meantime, can I get you something from the bar?"

"Grace, what would you like, wine?"

"Pinot noir?"

Logan smiled. "As the lady requested."

The host moved away and Grace leaned forward. "You haven't eaten here before?"

With a shake of his head, Logan said, "This is my first time."

Grace glanced around the busy restaurant. "But he knew your name."

"I think I mentioned about opening a hotel—I interviewed John as the dining room manager."

"Oh, how many businesses are you involved with?" she asked.

"Just the two." At least that was a half-truth; the bakery and hotels were his two main enterprises. He quickly changed the subject. "Wine?"

As much as Logan would like to tell Grace that the bakery business was one of the largest in the world and the boutique hotel he was talking about was just one more location in a string around Europe, he didn't want her to like him for his bank account. It really mattered Grace like the man first. What if she knew Aunt Flora's little shop was really the catalyst for Tartan Bakery and that his father had started what was now a billion-dollar company when he was a kid? Would things really go south?

Grace glanced at the menu and scanned the desserts.

"Everything looks amazing. It's too bad we can't order one of everything."

Logan poured the wine and held up a glass. "Let's toast to the first of many adventures."

She clinked his glass and took a sip. "Oh, this is good." She smiled. "Do you have any idea what you'd like to order?"

"Actually, I arranged with the chef to create a sampler platter for us." He gazed into her eyes. "I hope that's okay."

"Oh, sure." Teasing she said, "Did you do the same for dessert?"

He shrugged and said slyly, "Maybe?"

Grace's smile was a combination of sultry and amusement. She leaned back in her chair. "Well then, I leave our entire evening in your hands." In jest, she said, "But so that you've been warned, as a MacLellan, I really enjoy all food, especially desserts."

He found her enchanting. "I've given tonight considerable thought, and you can trust me when I say I'm prepared to delight your senses." Taking her hand and softly kissing the palm, he said, "All of them."

Grace didn't know what to make of Logan. He was charming and at times distant, like he was keeping her at arms-length and others decisive as if he knew exactly what he wanted. The way he'd kissed the sensitive part of her hand made her heart race. She had no business falling for a guy who lived in Scotland, no matter how captivating and gorgeous she found him.

A waiter approached their table with two plates and set them down in front of them. Three tiny cups of soup were artfully arranged on each one by color and texture. Unsure of what she was eating, Grace waited until Logan picked up his spoon.

With her spoon poised over the first cup, she asked, "Do I want to know what I'm about to eat?"

He dipped his spoon in the cup and his eyebrow arched. "Is it critical to your enjoyment?"

With a quick retort she said, "That's sounds a little like a challenge, and no, I can go into this blind." She dug into the mug that had corn niblets. At least it looked familiar. "Oh my, this is delicious. Is there shrimp in here?"

Logan laughed. "I'm not sure." He sampled the one that looked like it was tomato-based. "This is good too."

They made their way through several more courses. When it was time for dessert, Grace laid down her fork. "I'm not sure I can eat another bite."

He topped off her wine with the last of what was in the bottle. His brow wrinkled. "Surely there must be room for a little something?"

She smiled. "Well, maybe just a bite of the hot lemon pie."

The waiter approached and whisked away the plates. Logan asked, "May we have tea and dessert too?"

"Right away."

Grace glanced around the restaurant. The crowd had thinned. "How long have we been here?"

Glancing at his watch—Grace noticed it was a very expensive brand—Logan said, "Almost three hours."

"What? I've never lingered over any meal this long. They'd probably like to turn the table."

With a wave of his hand he said, "Please don't worry. We're fine. I made sure the staff knew we weren't in a rush tonight."

Worried, she glanced around. "Should we take dessert

to go?"

He laid a hand on top of hers. "Grace, please don't be concerned. Unless, of course, you'd like me to take you home?"

She squeezed his hand. "I'm having a wonderful time. There's no need to rush anywhere."

He nodded in the direction of the kitchen door. "That's good, because here comes dessert."

Grace's eyes bugged out when she saw a dinner-sized plate filled with petite versions of the entire dessert menu. "How did you…?"

Her voice trailed off as Logan chuckled and shrugged. "I have ways of making things happen."

He poured tea from the pot as he watched her. She could feel her cheeks grow warm under his steady gaze. She thought, *He's a bit mysterious, but I could get used to this kind of attention.*

Each dessert looked like it had exactly two bites, enough for them to share. She picked up a fork. "Are you going to join me?"

He picked up his own and dipped it into the pie. "We should do this together." He waited for Grace to get the last bite. "Ready?"

Grace's eyes closed and groaned. "This lemon pie is like nirvana or something close to heaven."

They savored each bite of the desserts, and over the last of the tea she said, "I've had so much fun tonight."

"And the night's still young. We could go listen to music and have a nightcap, or if you'd prefer we can take a walk.

Grace wiped her mouth on her napkin and laid it over the now empty dessert plate. "I would love to see some of the city."

Logan signaled for the check and handed the waiter his

credit card. After signing the charge slip, he pushed back his chair and then helped Grace up. Giving her his arm, he said, "Glasgow awaits."

The couple strolled down the sidewalk, and pinpricks of light up ahead caught Grace's attention. "What's that?"

"It's one of the gardens rumored to be populated by fairies. Would you like to stroll through?"

She tightened her hand in his. "I sure would."

They stepped into the garden through the ornate iron gate. "Oh, Logan," she said in a hushed tone, "can you feel the magic?" The garden was awash with small white twinkling lights. The path wound around the lush beds of flowers and greenery. White star shaped jasmine was running over an arbor. The sweet smell wafted around them. In the distance she could hear the low croak of toads that were somewhere in the park and the cricket chirps seemed to echo a reply.

"Aye, I've been here many times, but it does feel very different tonight." His lips brushed her temple. "I think I know why."

She looked up at him and waited.

"It's because I'm here with you."

Before she could respond, a drop of water landed in the middle of her forehead, and then another quickly followed.

"Logan?" She started to laugh. Unconcerned it was coming down in sheets, Grace swung him around. "Isn't it wonderful?"

With a stunned look on his face, he urged her toward the street. "Can you run in those shoes?"

"Why? Are you afraid you'll melt?" The rain was molding the dress to her curves and her curls were beginning to droop.

"Um, aren't you afraid of your dress or hair getting ruined?"

Grace laughed. "Are you kidding? I'm having a blast." She squeezed his hand. "Let's walk."

He gave her one last quizzical look as he leaned in, his lips almost touching hers. "Grace MacLellan, you are one in a million."

She leaned in and took what she longed for, his kiss, without a care that her emotions were running away with her heart.

Logan gathered her in his arms and sank into the kiss. Her lips were soft and yielding under the pressure of his mouth. Heat flashed through his body with surprising intensity. She moaned softly and took a step closer. His fingers twisted in her hair, pulling out the pins so the curls were free. He let his hands slide down to the small of her back and held her close. He wasn't going to rush. He was lost in the exquisite pleasure of her kiss.

She laid a hand on his chest and nudged a breath of space between them. His eyes sought hers. With a smoldering gaze she said, "Logan, we're soaking wet."

She stated the obvious with such humor he couldn't contain his laughter. "True. But if I recall correctly, you said you wouldn't melt."

"Since we now look like two drowned rats, I think we should skip the pub. But can I have a rain check?"

"How about the next time we bring umbrellas?"

Her smile took his breath away. Did she have any idea how absolutely alluring she looked, thoroughly kissed and rain-soaked? But as much as he'd like to stay right where they were, sensibility took over. He slung his arm around her shoulders and held her close as they strolled as one to the SUV. He kissed the top of her head and smiled to himself. Grace's curvaceous body fit his hard lines perfectly.

She looked into his eyes. "Next time, umbrellas."

CHAPTER 12

Grace watched as Logan's taillights disappeared down the drive. She was disappointed he hadn't tried to kiss her again, other than the quick brush on her lips with his at the door. On the way home Logan had held her hand as they made small talk for the quick thirty-minute drive. It was too bad the return trip was without traffic. It was way too short.

She could hear her cell phone ringing and she opened her tiny purse. She smiled when she saw his name on the display. "Hello, Logan."

"Miss me?" he teased.

Her heart skipped. "Did you forget something?"

"I did." His voice was husky. "I wanted to ask if you had plans tomorrow night. Maybe we could do a pub or a few of them. As we're on the cusp of the weekend, there are a lot of good bands playing."

"That sounds like fun. Shall I meet you in the city?" she asked.

"No. I'll come out to the farm, around six?"

"I'll be ready, and Logan, I had a great time tonight."

"I did too."

She didn't want the call to end, but she also didn't want to appear clingy, so she said simply, "Goodnight, Logan."

"Goodnight, Grace, sleep well."

The line went silent and she set it on the table. Too keyed up to sleep, she poured herself a glass of wine, filled the tub and sank into the warm, fragrant bubbles. *Two bubble baths in one day, this is living.*

She replayed the kiss in the rain and sighed. After taking a sip of wine, she thought, *that was one of the most romantic moments I've had. But I need to remember soon this will be over and I'll be home in Vermont.* She wondered if she could get time off at Christmas to come back to Scotland, and maybe she could see Logan too.

You're letting one kiss cause you to lose your perspective. The bubbles were fading as she sank chin-deep in the cooling water. When she finally pulled the plug, Grace felt she was relaxed enough to sleep.

Grace toyed with her coffee cup as she made a list of errands she needed to do. Talking to herself, she said, "Stop by the market and swing by MacMeekin's Bakery." After all, she was out of scones and shortbread, and a visit with Flora would be nice. They hadn't spent any time together since she was at the bakery with Tait. She rinsed her mug and set it in the drainer.

She stepped outside the back door and almost walked into Tait. "Hi." She took a step back. "This is a surprise."

"Hi, Grace." He shifted from one foot to the other. "Do you have a minute?"

"Do you want to come in?" She opened the door wider.

With a shake of his head, he said, "No. Can we walk

and talk?" He stepped off the stair and waited until she pulled the door closed behind her.

"I'm going to put my bag in the car." She zipped down the steps and tossed it on the passenger seat. Then she rejoined Tait, who was looking very uncomfortable.

"Um, I, um, was going to stop over last night to talk to you, and when I was pulling in I saw you leaving with Logan."

Grace didn't like where she thought this was headed. "He asked me to dinner."

Tait kicked the gravel as they walked, creating little clouds of dust that preceded them. "Gran-da and I had a talk yesterday. I'm hoping you might give me a chance and go on another date with me." He flushed bright red.

She stammered, "Tait. You're a very nice man. I don't want this to come out harsh, but no."

He dropped his chin and avoided her eyes. "You won't change your mind?"

"No, I won't change my mind about dating you." Guilty of being so direct gnawed at her. She never liked to be the kind of person who hurt others. To make up for it she asked, "Would you like to go for a horseback ride with me? I haven't been able to do that yet."

"I'm not much of a rider." He pulled himself up to his full height and said, "But if that's what you want to do, then count me in." His smile grew even broader.

"Just to be crystal clear, we're going as old friends, nothing more. Let's meet here at eleven?"

Tait started to walk away and said, "Grace, we're going to have the best ride."

She laughed. "If you say so." With a sinking feeling she watched Tait jog toward his truck. She hoped he understood when she said they were going as friends.

She hopped into her car and made the short trip to the

village, waving to various neighbors along the drive. There was a parking spot a short distance from the bakery, and she eased into the space. Out of habit she locked the car and then laughed at herself. In this town most people never locked anything; it was probably as quaint and homey as it had been years ago when her dad was a boy.

She peeked in various shop windows as she strolled, making a note to pick up some trinkets for the family before leaving. She squinted against the sun as she looked up at the sign above the bakery. How many years had Flora been located in this very spot, and what was she hoping the older woman would tell her about Logan?

Grace wasn't going to learn anything by lingering on the sidewalk. She stepped into the shop. Flora came out from the back, her smile welcoming.

"Good morning, Grace, it is wonderful to see you today." Beaming she said, "Would you like a cup of tea?"

Grace grinned. "Of course, and what are you baking? It smells divine."

Flora poured water into a pot and added the infuser. "A new scone for the holiday season with dried cranberries, orange and a touch of chocolate and cinnamon."

"Do you need an official taste tester?"

Without hesitation, Flora said, "Only if you promise to be brutally honest. I take a lot of pride in my recipes, and if it doesn't hold up to my customers standards I need to know." Her eyes twinkled. "Can you be objective, Grace?"

Grace took the pot of tea and grinned from ear to ear. "I will be honest but kind."

With a short nod Flora bustled into the kitchen and was back in a flash. On a matching plate sat two scones and a mini cup of butter. "Fresh from the oven." She handed it to Grace and asked, "Care if I join you? I've been on my feet all day."

"I'd be disappointed if you didn't." She waved the plate under her nose and took an appreciative sniff. "But we might need more scones."

Flora chuckled. "I've had my share, which is why I'm looking for a new set of taste buds."

Grace pulled out two chairs at her favorite table in the front window. "I'm so glad you have time for tea."

With a twinkle in her eye, Flora said, "I'm anxious to hear about your date with Logan. I hope you don't mind he told me you were going to dinner in the city."

Understanding that he and Flora were close made perfect sense she'd know their plans. "I'm glad he told you. We had a wonderful time. He arranged a special meal at a restaurant, and then we walked to a garden where it was lit up like fairies had been dancing." Dreamily, she said, "It was a perfect evening."

As Flora poured the tea, she asked, "Do you think you'll go out again?"

"Actually, we're having dinner tonight. But I think we're going more casual."

Flora smiled broadly. "That *is* good news, dear."

Grace leaned forward in her chair. Quietly she said, "He told me about his sister and parents. It must have been so hard for you both."

"We had each other to weather the storm." Flora's eyes grew misty. "You must be wondering a bit about our family."

"Well, I must admit I am curious. Aren't you around Gran's age?"

Flora smiled. "I am, and my sister was what we used to call a change of life baby. Eva was born when I was around twenty. Such a sweet and loving girl. She married Thomas Campbell right after university. They were quite a pair. Then they had Logan and Lisa, twins."

Grace said, "Logan never mentioned his sister was his twin."

"Aye." Flora's voice was pained. "They were very close, and it almost destroyed both Logan and Thomas when Eva and Lisa were killed." She picked up her teacup, her hand shaking, a few droplets fell to the table. "After the funeral Thomas and Logan spent more and more time at my cottage. As a way to cope, Thomas threw himself into his work, and the only way Logan got to spend time with his dad was to go to the office. So, at a very young age Logan grew into a man."

"How did Thomas die?"

"He had a massive heart attack, but I think it was his broken heart, leaving Logan in my care. I did the best I could. The business was being run by a couple of Thomas's most trusted friends while they waited for Logan to graduate from business school."

"And after graduation Logan took the reins?" Grace took a sip of her tea.

"He did, and devoted himself to growing the business. I think he's been trying to make his father proud of him."

"He seems to be a fine man. I don't know much about his work, but he did mention he was going to open a boutique hotel." Grace broke the now cool scone in half. She bit into the light and tender biscuit. She groaned. "Flora, this is unbelievable. The chocolate drizzle on the top and hint of cinnamon is the perfect combination." Closing her eyes, she savored another bite. "You have to add these to the menu for sure." When she opened them, she saw Flora was watching her intently. She picked up her napkin and sheepishly wiped her mouth. "Do I have chocolate on my chin?"

"Not at all. I was curious if Logan gave you any details on the hotel."

Grace said, "No. But we really didn't get into too much about his business. It was more like getting to know each other stuff." She shrugged. "Maybe we'll talk about it tonight."

Flora picked up the empty plate and said, "I'll be right back. There is a biscuit you should try too"—she smiled —"since you gave my scone a rave review."

Grace filled the cups and watched as a few cars drove down the street. Flora sat down after setting the plate in the middle of the table. "Enjoy. It's a new biscuit with a lemon filling."

Grace teased, "I'm going to gain ten pounds today alone being your official taste tester."

"Eva used to taste my new creations and, well, I've roped Logan into helping, but he's not big on sweets. He'd rather enjoy the savory varieties."

Grace toyed with a cookie and asked, "Does Logan date much?"

With a dismissive wave, Flora frowned. "He's never brought home a woman." With something that almost sounded like a groan, she announced, "He dates *airheads*." She patted Grace's hand and smiled. "Until you, that is."

"Flora, you do realize this is just a passing fling. We live over three thousand miles apart."

"I've been told long-distance relationships can work quite well, dear."

Her smile was purely angelic, and Grace snorted. "I would define a long-distance relationship by driving a couple of hours, not a transatlantic flight. Nor do I have the finances to support that kind of a romance."

Flora's eyes twinkled. "So, this is a romance?"

"You're incorrigible." Grace nibbled on the biscuit. "Oh, Flora, this is incredible." She took another bite. "It's light and the lemon filling doesn't overpower the cookie." She popped the last bit in her mouth. "So, when do you plan to introduce them to the shop?"

The older lady simply smiled. "I'm not sure."

Grace sat back in the chair. "These would sell like hotcakes."

"Maybe they'd be better suited for a larger bakery in the city with a broader reach," Flora said.

"What?" Grace searched for the right words so as not to offend Flora. "Your baked goods are the best I've ever had. You shouldn't give away your recipes to anyone else."

"Dear Grace, I'm thinking of retiring and letting someone else take over the bakery. I've been doing this for many years, longer than I care to count. It's time for fresh ideas." She patted Grace's hand. "But let's talk about your big date."

Ignoring her comment Grace cried, "Wait. You're going to close the bakery?"

"Dear, I'm not getting any younger and there is no one to take it over."

"What about Logan? Have you talked to him, maybe he has an idea?"

Flora patted her hand. "Logan has his hands full and besides; all good things must come to an end. Even a little bakery in Scotland."

Grace didn't know what to say. She couldn't imagine arriving in the village and not coming to the bakery as her first stop. "I still think you should speak with Logan."

"I'll give it some thought." Flora picked up her teacup. "Do you have any exciting plans for the rest of your holiday?"

"Did I tell you I'm going horseback riding with Tait tomorrow?"

Flora's eyes widened. "I thought you stopped seeing him."

Shaking her head, Grace said, "I've made it clear we're going as friends."

"Do you think he understands this?"

"Well, Tait didn't seem to get the message that I'm not interested in dating him, at first. But I think he does now." Grace toyed with her teacup. "Flora, there are zero sparks."

Flora giggled like a schoolgirl. "He's very handsome."

"Yeah, well, I'll give you that, but not my type." She reddened. "He's a nice guy, though."

"In my experience, just because a man is nice doesn't mean they give every girl butterflies." Slyly Flora looked at Grace. "And Logan?"

Grace felt the flush slowly rise up her cheeks. "He is a very handsome man." She hesitated. "Does he wear contacts?"

Flora laughed. "Not that I know of. Why do you ask?"

"His eyes are *so* green, almost to the point where he must wear colored contacts."

"I can assure you that he doesn't. He was born with them; they're like his father's."

"Interesting." Grace finished her tea. "I should get going so I can get ready."

"Where's he taking you tonight?"

"All he said was downtown. I'm going to wear comfortable slacks, flats for walking and take an umbrella. I don't want to get caught in the rain again."

"It sounds very romantic to an old woman."

"Flora, you're far from old." Grace picked up the dirty dishes and set them in the bus pan.

"Pack yourself some goodies for tomorrow." Flora watched Grace move around to the bakery cabinet.

Grace slipped a few items in a small white bag and closed it tight. She kissed Flora's soft cheek. "Dinner tomorrow night?"

Flora's eyes shone. "You might have other plans."

"I'll take that as a yes. In my short experience with men, it's good to not be available every time they ask."

Flora chuckled. "Oh, my heavens, Logan has met his match."

With a jaunty wave, Grace closed the door behind her, but not before calling back over her shoulder, "Dinner tomorrow, and I'll fill you in on my date with your nephew."

CHAPTER 13

Unsure what to wear for a pub crawl in Scotland, Grace eventually dressed in skinny jeans, a crisp white blouse, flats and a lightweight jacket with a floral scarf casually draped around her neck. She decided to leave her hair down and let the curls fly free. She chuckled to herself. *I hope Logan likes this version of me, casual and ready for fun.*

She rummaged around in Gran's closet and found a small handbag that would be just perfect with her outfit. It was large enough to hold her cell, some money and, of course, her lipstick. She wouldn't need more than that.

She was perched on the arm of a chair waiting when she saw Logan's car come down the driveway. Before he could get out, she bounced down the steps, smiling.

"Hello there!" She waved as he got out of the car. "Am I dressed okay?"

His gaze told her she looked more than just okay. "Hello, gorgeous."

He pulled her to his chest and thoroughly kissed her. She thought her toes actually curled in her shoes.

With the flush of heat high in her cheeks she laid her hand over his hammering heart and smiled up at him. "How was the drive out?" she asked.

"Uneventful, but it seemed to last forever." He held open her car door and waited until she was buckled up. He looked at her from the corner of his eye. A slow, sexy smile spread over his face. "I couldn't wait to see you."

A rush of heat spread through Grace, and all she could think to say was, "Oh."

Logan slid into the driver's seat, put the car in drive and with his free hand took hers. Interlacing their fingers, he said, "I'd thought we'd start in a little town about twenty minutes from here and then hit the one in town before calling it a night."

She teased, "You're already talking about bringing me home?"

His face flushed a deep shade of red. "Not like that. I'm not looking forward to the night ending."

Grace's breath hitched. She could think of one very tantalizing way for the evening to end. Pushing the thought aside—well, for the immediate future—she smiled and squeezed his hand. "I'm looking forward to our night."

She deliberately let the double meaning hover in the air.

Logan slowed the car as they arrived in the center of a small town. Grace had driven through it a few times but never lingered. There seemed to be a lot of people milling about the street.

"This must be a popular place," Grace said as Logan slipped his car into an open space.

"The food is fantastic, the beer even better." He turned the engine off. "The night is yours, so when you're ready to leave you give the word and we'll be off." He kissed the top of her hand and grinned. "Ready?"

Her heart skipped a beat or two as his lips brushed her skin. She beamed. "Absolutely."

The couple strolled hand in hand down the cobblestone sidewalk. Music was growing louder as they came within steps of their destination. Grace's pace quickened. She tugged Logan's hand. "Come on, sounds like we're missing out on all the fun."

He laughed as she opened the door. "If I had known coming to the pub would seem this much fun, we would have come last night."

She pecked his cheek and teased, "Everyone needs to blow off steam, even when one of us has been enjoying her vacation and the other half has been slaving away behind a desk."

Logan's expression became unreadable, but Grace took no notice. Stepping into the pub was like stepping back in time. There was a fire burning in the hearth across the room. A lively band complete with a fiddle, a couple guitars, an accordion and a small drum set was tucked into a corner, spilling out onto the dance floor. There was an empty table near the front window, and she said, "Do you think we can sit over there?"

Logan put his hand on the small of her back and steered her to the table. "It's typically first come, first serve."

She sat with her back to the window so she could people watch. A server hastened over, and Logan ordered them each a pint of ale. He accepted the single page of dinner specials and handed it to Grace. "If you want, we can share everything."

"Sounds good." She adjusted her chair so she could hear him over the music. Her finger drumming on the tabletop kept time to the lively song.

The server returned with their pints and Logan ordered several purported local favorites, including the house special, a venison platter. He picked up his pint. "Let's toast."

Grace held up her glass. "Let me."

He grinned. "Sure."

She chewed on her bottom lip. *Kenzie is always better at toasts than me.* She clinked her glass to his. Her hand trembled. "To the evening and wherever it takes us." Taking a sip of the ale, she said, "This is delicious."

Logan held his hand out to her. "Dance with me?"

Caught up in the energy of the room, she threw back her head and laughed. "I'm not a very good dance partner, but what the heck?"

He twirled her to the beat of the music. Grace found herself drowning in the deep green pools of his eyes. Her heart raced. She wasn't sure if it was the dancing or it was the man who held her securely in his arms. He held her close and she drank in the scent of his all male cologne. Lost in the music, they swayed. Unaware of their surroundings she only had eyes for Logan.

As the song came to an end, he lowered his mouth. She waited; his lips grazed hers. She slid her arms around his neck, pulling him closer.

Clapping around them caused Grace to pause. With a nervous laugh, she slowly stepped out of his embrace. She couldn't very well take what she wanted right here on the dance floor.

Logan nodded in the direction of their table. Several plates filled to the rims were waiting for them. Grace really didn't have an appetite for food but wanted something more. It was as if the ale and the atmosphere had altered her carefully controlled emotions, urging her to let go and just be in the moment with Logan. Was that what she really wanted?

She led Logan back to the table and slid her chair closer to his. He laid his hand on hers, his eyes glowed with happiness. "Are you having fun?"

"A blast. What about you?" She took a sip of her ale.

"I can't remember the last time I was in a pub and had this much fun." Letting go of her hand and picking up a fork, he transferred some venison and cheese to a smaller plate. He handed it to her. "Try the venison with the oatcake and brie." He pointed to a small cup of what looked to be jam. "Add the chutney too."

Skeptical, she did as he suggested. She wasn't a big fan of venison. All she could think of was those cute four-legged beauties grazing in an open field.

Her eyes widened after the first bite. "This is *so* good. And tender." She wiped her mouth with a napkin. "What should I try next?'

Logan walked her through each dish, and Grace was surprised that even with all the buzz around them it was as if it was just the two of them savoring their evening meal.

Stuffed, she pushed her empty plate toward the center of the table. She patted her midsection. "I'm full."

Logan drained his glass and set it aside before saying, "Let's go for a walk." He glanced out the window. "It's not raining." He signaled for the check.

She gave him a slow smile. "I'd love to."

After giving the server a few bills, he offered his hand. Grace took it, enjoying how natural it felt.

They strolled out the door. The night was cool and refreshing after the warmth of the pub. She shivered and pulled her jacket close, and rewrapped the scarf around her neck.

He said, "Are you chilly?"

Grace could see the concern in his eyes. She nodded. "A little."

Logan steered her toward the car. "We can walk another time. Let's get in and I can turn up the heat."

Grace looped her arm through his. Her voice dropped to above a whisper. "I have a better idea."

He studied her. "What would you like to do?"

"Take me home?"

Clearly taken aback, Logan stuttered, "If that's what you want, of course."

With a suggestive laugh, she said, "We can warm up together."

His brow arched. "Grace?"

She slid her arms around his waist and stood on tiptoes. Running her lips over his, she said, "I want to be completely alone with you."

He extracted himself from her arms and took her hand. They walked toward his car. Confused at the abrupt silence, she asked, "Logan, did I say something to offend you?"

"Not at all. I'm wondering how quickly I can safely drive to your house." He pulled her tight to his chest and kissed her, taking her breath away.

The farmhouse came into view as Logan tooled up the drive. Grace waited for him to open her car door. Her stomach was in knots. She had never been so bold with a man before, but this felt right.

Logan took the keys, his fingers lingering on hers. "Allow me." He eased open the door and stepped to one side.

She entered the hallway and flicked on a light. A stab of nerves washed over her. "Should we build a fire?"

He slipped off his jacket and dropped it on the chair. "I'll take care of that." His voice was soft like velvet on her skin. "Shall we have wine?"

Grace nodded and pointed to the living room. "Everything you need is in there."

She tossed her jacket on top of Logan's and hurried into the kitchen. Her fingers shook as she tried to open the wine. She gave up and grabbed two glasses, the bottle and corkscrew and went into the living room. The fire was beginning to crackle and the flames brightened the room. Logan stood with his hand on the mantle, watching the fire dance.

She cleared her throat. He turned and took two steps toward her. Taking the bottle and glasses from her, he set them aside.

"Grace." He cupped her cheek and tilted her chin up. The way he said her name was like a caress. He loosened her scarf, and it floated to the floor.

They sank to their knees, never taking their eyes off the other. Their connection was intense. Grace knew this was where she needed and wanted to be.

Physical space between the couple evaporated as they held each other close. She ran her hands down the length of his back, the fabric impeding her desire to feel his skin. She pulled the shirttails out of his jeans. Her fingers caressed his warm skin. She wanted to feel more of him.

She quickly unbuttoned and pushed the shirt from his broad shoulders. She sucked in a breath. She had no idea he was so muscular, so defined. Kissing the hollow at the base of his throat, she heard him groan. She let her mouth follow his hard, chiseled jaw to his lips. Her fingers slipped into his hair, pulling him to her. She demanded more as the kiss deepened.

Grace wasn't sure if it was the heat from the fireplace or the fire within her that made her blood thunder in her veins. She had to have more.

She moved slightly, giving Logan access to her blouse. His fingers grazed over the buttons and he hesitated. "Are you sure…?"

His simple question was sexy as hell. She sighed. "Yes."

He made short work of the blouse. His hand cupped her breast as his tongue followed the outline of the lace of her bra.

Grace leaned into him. The sensations that raced through her body were familiar but new and different. She eased him back to the floor. Bathed in the glow of the fire-light, she drank in the sight of his taut torso.

Laying her lips on his chest, she kissed her way to his belt buckle. She grabbed the leather strap and undid it. Next the button and zipper on his jeans. She hesitated. He stood and shrugged out of what was left of his clothing.

"Logan."

He pulled her to her feet and kissed her. She unbut-toned her jeans and shimmied out of them, leaving her wearing only a pair of lace panties and her bra. The look on his face told her he appreciated the matching set.

Grace slid her arms around his neck, and he lifted her as if she weighed nothing more than a feather. She wrapped her legs around his waist. Using his hand, he undid the clasp on her bra. She created a space between them so it hung loose. He slid one strap off one arm and then the other. They were skin to skin.

Where he ran his fingertips down her back, goose bumps followed. She savored each sensation, giving to him as good as she was receiving. She could feel him tremble under each stroke of her hand.

Logan reached for his pants, pulling out his wallet. He held up a foil packet. Grace was grateful he was prepared and laughed to herself—did he always carry protection?

The thought vanished as he reached out and caressed her breast. His hands and fingers continued their journey over her body, leaving her quaking for more. She could feel the center of herself tingle, but before she would allow release she wanted Logan to have the same response.

Laying him back against the floor, she mirrored each of his strokes and caress. In triple slow motion, she touched his body. From the way his eyes closed and he moved ever so slightly under her fingers, she knew just how he felt. His breath came in deep gulps.

Grace picked up the square packet and ripped it open. Logan's eyes opened with a slow and lazy look, and he smiled. "Shall I?"

Grace whispered, "Yes."

She sat astride him. He lifted her hips, and slowly slid into her as they became one. They moved in unison, Logan and Grace taking pleasure in each sensation.

She tensed. With the way her body was reacting to his, it wasn't going to take long before she exploded. Her tongue plunged into his mouth, desire pushing her higher with each thrust. Their breath came in deep, ragged gasps until at last, they couldn't hold back the tide and let go. With one final thrust and shudder, they held each other close, as their hearts returned to normal.

Logan kissed Grace's brow tenderly. "Are you okay?"

She snuggled in closer, her head on his chest. She smiled. "Never better."

CHAPTER 14

Wearing jeans, riding boots and a cotton shirt with a fleece tied around her waist, Grace waited for Tait in the driveway.

Her cell buzzed. She glanced at the text. It was from Logan. *Last night was unforgettable. Dinner tonight?*

Regretfully she shot back. *Sorry, I have other plans. How about tomorrow night? I'll cook.*

Buzz, buzz; *I'll call you.*

Grace stowed the cell in her pocket and crossed to a small stone bench under the birch tree. The sun filtered through the branches, making it the perfect spot to get lost in the memory of last night. From the moment Logan picked Grace up until this morning when he left, it had been the single most emotionally charged experience of her life. It made her nervous to think of how much fun she had with Logan.

But remember you're going home next week, and nothing can come of a relationship with an ocean between us. Closing her eyes, she sighed. But oh, how that man could kiss, and so much more.

His arm slid around her waist, pulling her close. She looked into the pools of deep green, and goose bumps slid over her arms. She waited, and his lips touched hers. Standing in his warm embrace, she slid her arms around his neck...

"Grace?" The sound of Tait's voice stopped her from relishing the memory.

She jumped to her feet. She could feel the heat flood her face. "Tait, I was enjoying listening to the sounds of nature all around me." That sounded stupid even to her ears. "Shall we saddle up?"

"I mentioned to my dad we were going, and he volunteered to saddle the horses for us." He held out his hand, but Grace hesitated, so he dropped it to his side. She could see a cloud cross his face. They walked to the barn, the tension thick between them.

"Maybe this isn't a good idea," Grace began. "You seem to be annoyed and I really don't want to start off on the wrong hoof." She attempted to use humor to change his melancholy mood.

Tait gave her a half-hearted smile. "I'm sorry."

Grace stopped mid-step. She had to clear the air one final time. "Tait." She looked him directly in the eye. "I value your friendship, but if you still hold out hope that something might change between us, I think it best we skip our ride and go our own ways."

Tait looked stricken. Grace felt horrible for being direct again, but she didn't want there to be any misunderstanding.

"You said you didn't want anything long distance, so why are you dating Logan Campbell?"

Grace heard the distinct tone of jealousy in his question. "Tait." This time her voice was sharp. "I don't need to explain to anyone where I go and who I choose to spend my time with, but if you must know, just as I'm having fun with you, I'm enjoying Logan's company."

Her mind shifted to the feel of Logan's lips on hers, but she pushed the memory away.

His voice dropped and he looked at her with puppy dog eyes. "I'm sorry." He stuck out his hand. "Friends?"

Grace took it and smiled. "This is the last time we're having this conversation."

His head bobbed. "Agreed. Now how about the ride through the hills." He pointed to the horses, who were tethered to the fence. "And for good measure I packed a light lunch."

She withdrew her hand. "That is a very nice *friend* thing to do."

With a sweep of his arm, he said, "After you."

With a slight roll from side to side, Grace had a firm seat in the saddle. The temperature was perfect with just a hint of crispness in the air under a warm sun. Tait seemed fairly comfortable in the saddle. However, it was obvious to Grace he would have chosen a different activity if left up to him.

"I haven't had a chance to wander around this part of the farm." Grace pushed her sunglasses up her nose. "It's beautiful, as always." The heather was beginning to bloom and the fields seemed to sway in the light breeze. A faint earthy-herb smell floated on the air. "This is what I remember when I think of Scotland. The smell of heather."

Tait chuckled. "It doesn't have much of a smell, Grace."

She looked over at him and laughed softly. "I think you need to be around it more to appreciate its subtle scent."

The horses climbed the hill with ease as they crested

the ridge. Grace pulled her mount to a halt and stood in the stirrups. "Will you look at this view? The valley goes on for miles. I love the rich colors of the Highlands, with the deep green mountains stretching up. They seem to poke the puffy white clouds, lazily floating in the pale blue sky." She could hear the excitement in her voice, but she didn't care. What she was looking at was purely spectacular. "And will you look at the way the sun seems to touch small sections of the valley?" Drinking in a deep breath of air, she exhaled. "I need to come here more often."

Tait said, "Now that would be nice, to have you around more."

Grace smiled. "I'm afraid that's a dream." Her horse nickered softly. "I think she's ready to get to the stream. How about we eat there?"

"Sure."

Using her heels, Grace nudged the horse down the side of the hill. As if knowing something wonderful was in store for them, the horses moved at a brisk but steady pace with Grace taking the lead.

They rounded the final bend in the trail and the stream was just up ahead. The sound of gurgling water was music to her ears.

The horses broke into a gentle cantor with little urging from Grace and Tait. Gliding to a halt under the canopy of trees, Grace dismounted and Tait jumped to the ground. Taking both sets of reins, she walked the horses to the stream's edge to let them drink. Once they were done, she tugged them toward the tree line, removed a lead rope from the saddlebag and clipped it to the halter under the bridle, then tied each horse securely to the tree.

After double-checking that they were secured, she was surprised to see Tait sitting on a fallen log watching her. "You're good with animals."

"There's a stable not far from our house, and as kids we spent a lot time there. Now Kenzie is married to Robbie, whose family owns it."

"You know, I always envied how you and your sisters are so close. When you'd come on holiday, it always looked like you had so much fun."

Grace's eyes grew misty. "It was Gran. She made every day an adventure and she instilled in us a strong sense of family." She sighed. "We always said it was like magic, our trips here."

He held up a sack. "Are you hungry?"

She smiled, grateful he was changing the subject. It was amazing how sometimes the pain of losing Gran was as fresh as the moment her father told her. "Absolutely."

Tait held up containers.

"That looks like quite a feast." She popped open one. "Everything looks delicious."

"Nothing but the best for you."

Grace said, "I appreciate the effort." She sat on the ground and leaned back on the log. "This is nice."

Birds chirped in the trees and a few bees lazily drifted by to gather nectar from the nearby heather. Pleasant conversation flowed. In the distance Grace could hear the drone of an all-terrain vehicle.

"Why do you suppose someone is on our land with one of those gas hogs? It certainly isn't your dad rounding up sheep." She hopped up and walked toward the sound.

"Maybe they're lost?" he said simply.

"We own almost ten thousand acres, and aren't we posted as private?"

"Aye." Before Tait could continue, the sound grew closer.

She held tight to her temper. Hands on hips, Grace was ready to stand in the way of the ATV and the path. A rider pulled up and the engine died. With a flick of a hand, the visor went up and Grace's temper spiked.

"Logan. What are you doing here?"

"After our conversation this morning, I stopped by to see you. Patrick told me you and Tait had gone for a ride, so I thought I'd catch up with you." With a cocky grin he said, "Surprise."

With a frosty voice she said, "On one of those? Did you ever consider that you might spook the horses?"

Immediately contrite, Logan said, "Ah, no, I didn't. I'm sorry, Grace, and Patrick said they were used to the sound."

Tait had joined her with a steady gaze on Logan. "Campbell."

Logan met his gaze and growled, "Dennie."

The testosterone sizzled. "Now that we've established we know everyone's name, gentlemen"—she looked at Tait—"can I have a moment with Logan, alone?"

Without a word Tait stalked away. Grace waited until he couldn't hear what she was going to say, lest he get the wrong idea.

"Logan, I really don't know what you're doing here." She folded her arms across her chest. "We didn't have plans for today, so why did you really come looking for me?"

"Would you believe me if I said I missed you?" He flashed a grin, which would have made her weak in the knees if her temper weren't running hot.

"Why aren't you at work?"

He took off the helmet and swung his leg over and got off the machine. Reaching out for her, he said, "Walk with me, for just a minute, and then I'll leave."

Unable to resist, she allowed Logan to take her hand. She walked with him toward the stream.

"I didn't mean to upset you, but in full disclosure, I

was jealous when Aunt Flora told me you were spending time with Tait." He ran a finger down her cheek and brushed a stray curl back from her face. "I left the office and drove out here hoping to find you. When I didn't, I started to wander around and bumped into Patrick." He searched her eyes. "I'm sorry, really. When he offered to lend me the ATV, I jumped at the chance. Tait had told him where you would be, so I took off in search of you both." As an afterthought, he said, "Tait's got a thing for you."

She pulled her hand away and stuck them in her fleece pockets. "We talked about it, and Tait knows we won't be more than friends. Besides I'm going home in a few days."

"I wanted to talk to you about that." Logan reached for her hand again. "Is it open for negotiation?"

Grace chuckled. "No, I have a job to get back to and a cottage to decorate." Her face dropped. "But maybe when I come back for the holidays we can spend time together."

"I don't think I can wait five months to see you." He pulled her close and brushed his lips over hers. "Stay." It came out as a whisper and a plea.

"Logan." She pushed herself away and glanced in Tait's direction. "We need to have this conversation later."

"But Grace…" Logan said.

Firmly, she said, "I'll talk to you tomorrow." She steered him toward the ATV. "And do me a favor, don't gun that stupid machine when you leave it will scare the horses. I don't need a skittish mount for the return trip."

He kissed her cheek. "I am sorry I upset you." Logan glanced at Tait. "But I think I made my point with him."

"And what was that exactly?" Grace asked.

He cocked his head and winked at her. Once again, his charming smile played about his face. "That you're my girl."

She groaned. "Logan, we've had a few dates and I've really enjoyed them, but don't get all territorial on me."

Logan's green eyes locked on her. In a low, serious voice, he said, "I've been waiting for you my entire life. You're a special woman, Grace MacLellan." He took a step closer and bent his head, claiming her lips with a tender kiss. Grace melted.

Logan stepped away from her. "I will call you tonight." He waved to Tait. "Have fun."

Tait hopped up and strode over. "Will you be waiting for us when we get back to the farm?"

In a steady voice, Logan said, "No, I'm driving back to Glasgow."

With a curt nod Tait said, "You don't need to worry about Grace. I'll make sure she gets back safely."

"Guys." She wanted to stamp her feet and break this up. "I'm standing right here, and for the record, I'm not a fragile china doll in a display case. I'm perfectly capable of taking care of myself."

Logan winked. "You are more than capable." He slipped the helmet over his head and hopped into the seat. "Talk to you later." He blew her a kiss and the engine roared to life. Slowly he drove away, leaving Grace watching Logan and Tait watching Grace.

"I thought he'd never leave," Tait muttered.

Grace sighed and glanced up at him. "Let's finish lunch and then we can resume our ride. I have dinner plans tonight."

"With him?" Tait growled.

"No. Not that I need to explain anything to anyone, but I'm having dinner with Flora and Simon."

Tait brightened. "Can I join you?"

"No." She laughed. "It's dinner for three."

His face fell. "Maybe next time."

Grace gave him a playful punch in the arm. "I'm starving."

"Then by all means, let's eat." He didn't try to take her hand or arm like he had earlier as they walked back to where they could sit down. "And then it's a short ride back to the farm."

Tait stopped her mid-step. "Grace, if I was super rich like Logan, would you be interested in me?"

"What do you mean?" Shock filled her face. "He runs a small family business."

With a snort Tait said, "Is that what he told you? Maybe you should ask him about Tartan Bakery and how it was launched from the kitchen at MacMeekin's Bakery. In fact, Flora is always creating new recipes for the company. She tries it out here, and if something gets an overwhelming response from customers, she transfers it to Tartan."

Her face pale, Grace stuttered, "Logan would have told me."

Tait's eyebrow shot up. "Are you sure?"

CHAPTER 15

Grace studied her reflection and wondered how she could have been so wrong about Logan. He'd lied to her.

It all made sense now. The traveling he did for work, being able to take off whenever he wanted. But Flora—why wouldn't she tell her the truth about the bakery? *I can ask her tonight.*

Grace finished getting ready and made the short drive into town. Her head was still reeling with Tait's announcement that Logan was more than rich. And the sad thing was, he'd seemed pleased he was the one who told her.

She needed to talk to her sisters. Grace pulled to the side of the road and sent a quick text. *Skype tonight—6 your time*

After hitting send, she finished the rest of the drive to Flora's. She half expected to see Logan's SUV in the driveway. But why would he be there? As far as he was concerned, everything was fine.

~

Flora heard a knock on the back door and called, "Come in!" Her words rolled off her tongue.

She heard, "Flora. It's me, Grace."

She entered the heart of her home, the kitchen. "Come in, dear." She kissed Grace's cheek and placed the back of her hand on Grace's forehead. "Are you sick?"

Grace's shoulders slumped. "How come Logan didn't tell me who he is and the real connection to your bakery?"

Flora pulled her into her arms. "I'm sure he had his reasons."

Grace murmured, "Was it because he thought he could toy with my emotions and that I'd be gone in a few weeks, so it just didn't matter?"

Flora's heart broke for the girl. "He's not that kind of man, but you should be having this conversation with Logan, not me."

"Why didn't you tell me about your recipes?"

Confused, she said, "What do you mean, recipes?"

Grace's tone was accusatory. "You're the creative genius behind Tartan."

Flora led her to the table. "Sit down, Grace."

Grace stood like a statue.

"Please?" Flora pleaded with her.

The wooden legs of the chair scraped over the tile. Grace flopped down. "I'm listening."

Flora folded her hands on the table top. Very softly she said, "When Eva died, I wanted to help my family, give Thomas and Logan a reason to get up in the morning. A goal, so to speak. That's when I approached Thomas about using some of my recipes. At first, he balked at the idea, but I persisted. We started with a couple of items and sales soared. After that, things took off. I never wanted to be part of the bigger picture. I love my little bakery right here in my hometown."

"I understand all of that, Flora, but why did Logan hide the truth?" Grace hopped up and paced the cozy kitchen. "What was the big deal?"

"Dear, you need to ask him. It's not my place to explain his actions."

Grace leaned down and kissed Flora's cheek. "I'm sorry, but I can't stay for dinner. I hope you understand."

Flora stood and hugged the young woman. "I'm here whenever you need me."

Grace stumbled out the back door. Flora watched her drive away. Closing the door, she picked up the phone receiver and dialed. After patiently listening to it ring, she heard, "Hello."

"Logan, its Aunt Flora."

"I wasn't expecting to hear from you tonight." She could hear the lightness in his voice.

Her voice flat, she said, "Grace just left."

"Dinner's over already?" He chuckled. "You sure did eat quickly."

"She knows about you."

"What do you mean? What does Grace know?"

With a heavy heart she said, "About Tartan Bakery and your role."

She heard a thud, which made her conclude his fist had connected with the desk. "How?"

"I have no idea, but you should give her the night and call her tomorrow. You'll need to explain everything or risk losing the finest woman you'll ever meet."

"Aunt Flora, it's more than dating. I know it hasn't been that long but I've fallen in love with her."

She could hear the anguish in his voice. "Then, dear boy, you need to talk to her and tell her why you kept that side of you a secret."

"It wasn't a secret—I wanted to make sure she fell for

me as a man, not as someone with a few Pounds in the bank."

Flora laughed. "That is an understatement. But as I said, call her, or better yet, go see her before the damage is irreversible."

"Thanks for calling, Aunt Flora, and don't worry. I can be very persuasive."

After saying their goodbyes, Flora hung up. She called Simon and postponed their dinner. How she wished she could talk to Arabel. All of their hopes of a future between Logan and Grace were evaporating.

Logan twirled in his office chair and then leaned forward, hunched over his desk, clasping and unclasping his hands. All he had wanted was Grace to fall for him as a regular guy. He was like a magnet that seemed to attract the wrong women. When he thought he found someone special it turned out to be about expensive dinners, gifts and dreams of a walk down the aisle.

Cursing a blue streak, his brogue grew thick. He stared out the office window at the immense skyline. If he simply explained why he hadn't been more transparent, would she understand? Pacing in front of the large window, he thought it was going to take more than a conversation to help her see his point of view. Grace expected complete honesty. She was open, and, well, sweet was the best way to describe her. He had never met anyone like her, and wasn't that why he was attracted to her?

Flowers! That was it, he'd send her flowers. With a slow shake of his head, he perched on the edge of the desk. He could pick wildflowers and take them to her with a heartfelt conversation. That was the right thing to do. He smiled to himself. Grace MacLellan was not a woman who would be thrilled to be showered with gifts when she was furious at him.

He flipped open his laptop and sent an email to his assistant, clearing his schedule for tomorrow. He addressed a few urgent items in his inbox, satisfied he would be able to show Grace he was a stand-up guy. He called the bakery and left his aunt a message, asking for an assortment of teacakes and scones, all of Grace's favorites. Flowers and sweets, what could go wrong?

Grace slammed the front door and flung her handbag on the table. Muttering, she stomped into the kitchen and put the teakettle on with a clang. "He just works for a good company, right. He owns the whole damn thing. That explains why he could breeze in and out of the office at will. And why the restaurant was bending over backward—he's a frequent diner." She groaned. "How many other women has he taken there and done that same date?" She smacked the palm of her hand against her forehead. "I am *so* gullible."

While waiting for the water to heat, she took a cup from the drainer and without even looking grabbed a tin of tea. She really needed to talk to Jamie and Kenzie; they'd know just how to handle this. They had so much more dating experience than she did.

She glanced at the clock and realized she had a few hours to kill before she could talk to them. How was she ever going to keep her mind occupied while waiting?

A sharp rap on the back door distracted her. In a few steps, she flung it open. "Tait, what are you doing here?"

He dropped his head. "May I come in?"

She left the door standing open and took the whistling kettle from the stove. "Tea?"

He nodded and closed the door behind him. Despite his tall frame, Grace thought he seemed to want to sink into the woodwork.

Her voice frosty, she said, "Have a seat."

Without looking up he did as she suggested, and finally gave her a half-hearted smile as she set a cup in front of him. Breaking the uncomfortable silence, Grace said, "I have to say I'm surprised to see you here."

"I had to come to apologize. What I told you today, about Logan, was mean-spirited and it's not like me."

She waved a dismissive hand. "I'm glad someone thought to tell me the truth." She looked at him through narrowed eyes. "But what did you hope to gain?"

He stared at the cup as he slowly swirled the spoon around. "This is going to sound very high school, but I was hoping if Logan wasn't a part of the picture you'd look at me in a new light."

Grace slumped in the chair opposite to him and sighed. "Tait, I'm not the grand prize at the county fair that you two can wrestle over. I'm here on vacation looking to have some fun."

His eyes met hers, and slowly he said, "I see the way you look at him."

Uncomfortable under his gaze, she said, "I have no idea what you're talking about."

"You have strong feelings for him."

She let out a strangled laugh. "No, I don't."

Tait said, "Well, it doesn't matter what you say to me, but you should think about it. If I were Logan Campbell, I would be showering you with gifts and flowers to win you back."

"Oh, Tait, that's not how to win a girl's heart."

His brow furrowed. He said, "But I thought girls liked that kind of stuff."

"Maybe some do, but any woman worth having is more interested in the man, not what he can give her." She thought for a moment before saying, "With one exception…if he gives his heart freely, that is the most precious gift of all."

Looking hopeful he said, "But—"

Grace didn't want to dash his hopes, but he needed to understand one critical point. "You also need chemistry."

Softly he said, "And we don't have it, do we?"

"No. I've been trying to tell you that for days. You're a sweet man and there is a very special girl waiting for you to sweep her off her feet, and you will." She laid a hand on his arm. "Tait?"

He looked into her eyes. "I thought I would have found her when I was at the university. But my head was always buried in a book, studying."

With a gentle smile she said, "Now it's time to open your eyes and see who keeps crossing paths with you. I'll bet there is someone who would love to date you, a girl you see all the time and maybe just really haven't looked at her."

He laid a hand on top of Grace's. "When do you leave for America?" He released it.

"In a few days." She picked up her mug and took a sip. "There are a couple more things I want to do, and then I'll be ready to go home."

"When will you be back?"

"My family is planning on the Christmas holiday." She swirled the liquid in her cup, then set it down. "We haven't spent the holidays here in years. It will be nice."

"Aye, there's nothing like the Highlands in the winter."

He stood and set his mug in the sink. "Would you like to have dinner before you leave?"

Grace winced. He just wouldn't give up. "I don't know if that's a good idea."

Grinning he said, "I thought it'd be nice for two old friends to grab a pint and a platter of fish and chips."

Grace hopped up and flung her arms around Tait. "Thanks, and yes, old friends can share a platter and a pint."

He kissed her cheek and said, "You should talk to Logan. From what I know of his reputation he's not all bad, and you can't really hold his money against him."

She looked up into his eyes and asked, "Do I dare ask?"

Tait chuckled. "That's a question for him, as I have no idea how rich he really is."

"I'm glad you stopped so we could clear the air. I'll call tomorrow and we'll set up which night we'll go out to the pub."

His face grew a nice shade of pink. "I'm looking forward to it," He held up his hands and finished, "as friends."

With a sigh of relief Grace said, "Me too."

It still wasn't time to Skype, so she texted Jamie to see if they could talk sooner.

While Grace waited for a response, she brewed another cup of tea and went into the living room. Within a few minutes her phone pinged.

Give us an hour? Kenzie is finishing a spin class.

Sure, I'll be waiting.

Grace set her phone aside and then curiosity got the best of her. If Logan Campbell was a big shot, everything he was involved in would be a few key strokes away. Wondering why she hadn't thought of this sooner, she retrieved her laptop, opened a browser, and searched for *Tartan Bakery* and *Logan Campbell*. The page loaded and she was shocked with the number of results along with links to a ton of images, the women he dated and businesses he owned.

Clicking the first link, she saw the article about losing his mother and sister and then Logan assuming the reins of the company. At that time, it was a nice size business on the brink of a major acquisition. There was little mention of MacMeekin's Bakery, which she was sure was by design.

The next link included a picture of Logan standing in front of the restaurant he took her to on their first date. "What, he owns the restaurant? No wonder we got special treatment and a table so quickly."

Next, she read an article about a string of boutique hotels around Europe. "So much for him thinking about a new business venture, when he's knee-deep in hotels. He's like his own Monopoly game."

The final article she opened was about Tartan Bakery expanding to the Americas. "Well, that explains why he was on my flight last year."

Her mouse hovered over the word, images. Sucking in a deep breath she clicked on the link. Instantly thumbnail pictures covered the screen of Logan with a variety of gorgeous women on his arm. "He's dated half of Europe and they all look like models."

She sagged against the cushions. *Why does he want to go out with me? I'm just an average girl. I'm a plain Jane compared to some of those women.* She snorted. *Who am I kidding, all of those women. They look like they could give most women a good case of insecurity.* She copied the link and sent it to Jamie's and Kenzie's emails.

Her cell phone pinged. "Jamie." She signed into Skype. Her sisters' faces appeared on the small screen. "My favorite sisters." Her smile was tight. She could tell they were at Kenzie's gym.

"For the record, we're your only sisters, but hi, Gracie." Kenzie smiled at her.

Jamie's eyes were bright. "Hey, kiddo, what's going on?"

"You'll never guess who I've been dating."

Jamie and Kenzie looked at each other, and Jamie said, "Logan."

"Check your email. I just sent you a link." She waved her hand. "Go on, I'll wait while you do."

Kenzie asked, "What's the problem? I thought he was a businessman."

"Yes, he is a businessman, but he is uber rich and he lied to me." She blinked back a flood of tears. "I'm not going to see him again. Ever!"

CHAPTER 16

Kenzie studied the email on Jamie's laptop. "He's gorgeous."

Exasperated, Grace rolled her eyes. "I never said he wasn't hot. But he never told me he was like a billionaire or something, and for that matter I'll bet Flora is rich too."

Jamie snapped the lid shut and asked, "So he's got money. That's not a crime, is it?"

"In the last two weeks, we've seen each other several times, bumping into each other and a few dates. He's never said a word about how extensive his business really is. He said he was thinking about opening a hotel when he already owns a string of exclusive properties. He took me out for the most amazing dinner and he owns the damn restaurant too."

Jamie looked off into the distance and said, "He was treating you like a man who's interested in you. I don't understand, what's wrong with that?"

Grace squeaked out, "Honesty seems to be low on the a la carte menu, like he can pick and choose what to tell me.

If we start out being selective with the truth, there isn't a possibility for something more meaningful, right?"

Kenzie poked Jamie and winked. "I thought this was a vacation fling."

Grace reddened and groaned. "Of course it is, but we've been having fun and now he's ruined it."

"Squirt," Kenzie said affectionately. "Maybe he doesn't think it's relevant."

Grace snapped, "If I didn't tell him important stuff about me, wouldn't that be relevant?"

"If he asked you, and you deliberately lied, yes," Jamie said. "But have you considered you might be making a mountain out of a molehill?"

"Why would I do that?" Grace asked. "Besides, I did ask him and he didn't tell me the whole truth."

Kenzie looked at Jamie. "I'll take this one." She gave Grace a grin. "Have you forgotten whose sister you are?"

With a laugh, they said together, "Ours."

Kenzie continued, "We're the sisters who claimed we'd never get married. We had a pact, we were going to remain happily single. And now look at us, we did everything we could to chase away the men who love us and now we're happily married."

Grace sputtered, "That doesn't mean I want to marry Logan."

"Before you get your shorts in a knot, why don't you talk to him?" Kenzie suggested. "Ask why he wasn't completely honest with you."

Slowly Grace said, "I suppose I could..."

"Before you waste another minute, shoot him a text." Kenzie waggled her finger. "I'm sure your phone is right next to you."

Grace's smile was tight. "What will I say?"

Jamie suggested, "Ask him for a drink. You'll be on your turf at the farm."

Kenzie leaned toward the screen. "Nope. Neutral territory. This way if you want to leave, you can. Ask him to meet you at the pub in the village."

Grace picked up her phone, finger poised over the keyboard. She chewed on her lower lip. "Are you sure I should do this?"

Kenzie nodded. "If I had talked to Robbie instead of pushing him away, we might not have spent three agonizing months apart when he was living in Burlington. Remember, I ran away from my feelings for a long time until I was forced to face the truth. I was in love with him, and now look, we're happily married."

"Yeah, for all of, what, six weeks?" Grace was annoyed. Her voice betrayed her true state of mind, mildly jealous that her sisters had what she longed to have too. She needed to talk to Logan.

Kenzie's voice softened. "Gracie, if you think you could have any serious feelings for Logan, don't walk away. You might be missing out on something wonderful."

Grace dropped her head and her eyes rose to the screen. "Hang on. If I send the text while you're with me, you can help me write it." Talking out loud, she said, *"Logan, will you meet me at the pub tomorrow around seven?"* Grace paused. "How's that?"

Jamie said, "Hit send."

Kenzie followed up with, "Straight to the point. I like it."

Grace's phone went *bloop*. "That's done."

Before she could set the phone aside, it buzzed. She wasn't sure if she was happy or nervous. She glanced down and a slow smile spread across her face. "He said that he'll see me there."

With a brisk nod, Jamie and then Kenzie grinned. Jamie said, "It's like ripping off a Band-Aid. It only hurts for a second."

Grace couldn't help but smile. "Using a medical simile on me."

Jamie tapped her watch. "I need to run, but we'll see you in a couple of days."

Kenzie teased, "Unless she decides to change her ticket and stay a little longer."

Grace frowned. "If I want to come back with the family in December, I need to get back to work and accrue more vacation time. That's how it works when you're employed by someone else. Unlike the two of you, I'm not my own boss."

"Ouch," Kenzie said playfully. "Despite the perks of being our own boss, we do have customers and obligations."

With a sniff and then a chuckle Grace said, "And I have patients." She blew a kiss toward the screen. "Love you guys."

Jamie and Kenzie did the same. They both said, "Love you too."

Jamie reminded her, "Call if you need us."

She forced herself to give a half-hearted smile, "I will." Grace closed the program down.

Logan sat in his car outside of the pub waiting for Grace. He wasn't sure, should he be inside waiting or let her go in and find a table? He felt like this was his first date ever. Cursing he hit the steering wheel with his fist. *Why didn't I tell her about my business? Then we wouldn't be in this mess.* He looked at the bunch of wildflowers and box from

MacMeekin's on the passenger seat. He would give them to her when they came out, together.

Her rental car pulled up in front of the pub. He watched her get out and lock the car, then look up and down the street. He sank low into his seat. She was breathtaking. The way she carried herself spoke of her inner strength. The evening sun glinted off her copper-streaked curls. Her jeans hugged her curves as she walked with a slight sway into the pub. He was entranced. Waiting until the door closed behind her, Logan wiped damp palms onto his jeans. Grace was one in a million.

He gathered his courage—it was time to face the music.

He hurried across the street. The pub was lively with early diners and groups of people enjoying adult beverages. His eyes sought Grace's. When they met, he felt her icy anger pierce his heart. How he could read her so well was a mystery to him. Even after a couple of weeks, he could tell by a toss of her hair, a look or even her silence just what emotions were coursing through her.

He crossed the room. "Hello, Grace." He lightly kissed her cheek. "You look lovely."

"Thank you, Logan."

He didn't miss that she failed to smile or say hello as he slipped into the booth. He caught the waitress' attention. Grace ordered whiskey neat and Logan asked for the waitress to make it two.

He leaned forward, his elbows on the table, wanting to touch her hands but stopping as she tucked them under the table. "I was glad to hear from you last night."

Her eyes bored into his soul. "I'll be honest..." She frowned. "My sisters encouraged me to give you a chance to tell me why you lied to me."

"Grace," he said softly. "I never lied to you. I just didn't give you complete details about my life."

She hissed, "That's the same thing to me." She glanced around the pub and lowered her voice. "When you date someone and you talk about things, letting little things slip like, 'Oh, I'm thinking of buying a hotel,' but you actually own a string of them is, what, a minor detail?"

He took a deep breath. "In my defense, women usually date me for my bank account and don't take any time to get to know the man." He paused as the waitress set two glasses on the table. She moved away and he continued, "How is it a lie if for once in my life I just wanted to go on a date with a beautiful woman as just Logan? Not the CEO of a global corporation."

He watched her eyes pop. "I can't believe you really own Tartan." She shook her head. "And Evangeline Hotels."

His eyes never left hers as he nodded. "I do."

She slapped her hand to her forehead. "I just got it—Evangeline, Eva, you named the hotel chain in honor of your mother."

"And I have a few other businesses tucked under Lisa Enterprises, my twin sister."

She toyed with her glass. A tear clung to her lower lashes. "I think that is very sweet, but Logan, you could have talked to Flora. She would have told you I wasn't a gold digger." Color flamed her cheeks. "You lumped me in as just another girl, and that hurts."

He clasped his hands over hers. "Grace, I know you're not like anyone I've ever met and definitely not interested in me for my bank account. I've gotten used to protecting my privacy, and it was my issue, not yours."

"I'm sorry too." She withdrew her hands. "I liked you." She dug in her handbag and withdrew a few Pounds. Tossing them on the table, she slid from the booth. "Next time you might want to give people you meet the benefit of the doubt. Not everyone is after you for your money—someone might just like you for you. I know I did." She hurried toward the door, dodging around people and tables.

"Grace!" He raced after her. "Wait!"

He was a half a second too late. She jumped into the car and raced off, tires squealing against the pavement.

He stood on the sidewalk and watched as the car disappeared around the corner. He didn't know if he should go after her or wait until tomorrow. With a sinking heart, he realized she had one full day left before returning to her home. Making a snap decision, he ran to his car and hopped in. Aunt Flora would know what to do.

Grace brushed the tears from her cheeks. Why was she so upset over what Logan Campbell did or didn't tell her? What was the big deal? They went out a couple of times, hiked and basically had fun. She groaned, "But the way that man makes me feel things."

She ran her finger over her lower lip, remembering how it felt to have his mouth claim hers. She had never felt her blood race in her veins like that before. *I should never have agreed to go out with him. It was trouble from the moment at Rosemarkie.* She admonished herself, *It wasn't like I invited him to meet me there or knew he was coming. Heck, other than his name I didn't even know a single thing about him.*

She slowed the car and pulled off to the side of the road. In the early evening light the old stone church seemed to beckon to her. Hesitating, she shut the car off and walked into the graveyard.

Brushing a stray leaf from the hard granite bench, Grace sat down. "Hi, Gran."

She dropped to her knees and knelt on the dew-damp grass. After pulling a couple of stray weeds from around the rosebush in front of the headstone, she sat back on her heels. The wind rustled the leaves overhead.

"I'll be going home soon," she said. "I went on a few dates with Logan, Flora's nephew." She sighed. "He's funny, smart, and those eyes. But, Gran, he can't be the guy for me—he lives here, and you know how much I value honesty. Sadly, he withheld information about himself and I don't know if I could ever trust him."

The wind teased her curls. It almost felt as if Gran was twirling a tendril around her finger as she often did when Grace was a child.

"Is that what you wanted, for us to meet? Did you and Flora hope something would develop? Well, it can't." She kissed her fingers and laid them on Gran's name. "I have to go now, but I'll see you at Christmas." She stood up. Her throat constricted. "I miss you so much."

With fingers trailing across the headstone, she walked back to her car as if the weight of the world were on her shoulders.

CHAPTER 17

Grace flipped the covers from her head, annoyed at the sound of insistent knocking. Pulling on her robe as she lumbered down the stairs, her irritation built.

"Can I help you?" she called through the door.

"Delivery for Ms. MacLellan."

She groaned, flipped the lock and pulled the door open a crack. "You have a delivery for Grace MacLellan?"

A young man stood on the walkway and held out a square, nondescript box. Suspicious, she looked from the box to the boy to the white van in the driveway. The side sported a logo—*Wee Delivery Service.*

She pointed at the van. "Cute name."

With a shrug he said, "Mum's sense of humor. We deliver small things."

Grace gave him a tentative smile. "Do I need to sign?"

He handed her the small box and thrust a pad of paper with a pen to her. "Yes, please."

Grace scrawled her name and said, "Hold on a minute and I'll get you a tip."

With a shake of his head, he back-stepped. "No need, it was pre-tipped." He grinned. "No one ever does that."

Scowling, she muttered, "Logan."

"Excuse me, miss, did you say something?"

"No, thank you. Drive safely."

She hovered in the doorway until the van was headed down the drive. She shook the box. It was light as a feather. Carrying it inside, she set it on the kitchen counter. Coffee—she needed a large, strong cup. Her head was pounding. She thought, *It's going to be a long day.*

She didn't want to open it, certain Logan was trying to buy her affection with something extravagant. Curiosity won out. She pulled the top back and discovered tucked inside was one cream bun.

She breathed in the aroma. "Fresh baked." She was pleasantly surprised to discover it was still warm from the oven.

She laughed to herself. "Nice touch. I can see Flora had a hand in this one."

Setting it on a plate, she waited for the coffee to finish percolating and then took her mug and bun to the back terrace. The morning was cool, and she tightened the belt on her robe. Holding the mug in two hands, she savored the quiet. The sounds of daily farm life were humming in the distance. She could see sheep grazing in the hills. It was a perfect moment. She was alone but reveling in the solitude. She felt very close to Gran this morning. Grace half expected her to walk out of the kitchen door with a cup of tea.

Sipping her coffee, she wondered, *Should I acknowledge the gesture?* Grace reached into her deep pocket for her cell phone. She sent Logan a short text: *Thank you for the bun.*

Satisfied she had done the right thing, she set her

phone aside. It buzzed with an incoming message. *You're welcome. L*

She savored each bite of the bun and took the dirty dishes in the house, pausing for a refill of caffeine. Making a snap decision to stop by the bakery, Grace cleaned up the kitchen. Flora could give her directions to Logan's office. She was going to drop in and say...well she wasn't sure, but at least to say goodbye.

Who was she kidding? She needed answers. Time was wasting. She still needed to pack and empty the fridge before leaving in the morning.

Logan looked at the clock for the twentieth time in the last hour. Once Aunt Flora had called to let him know Grace was on her way, he hoped it would be good news. He was prepared to tell her how easy a long-distance relationship would be and that he'd be happy to move her to Scotland.

His intercom buzzed. "Logan," Tracey said, "Grace MacLellan is here."

"Thank you, Tracey, please escort her in." Logan waited behind his desk. If she wanted to know the real man, here he was.

Grace walked in, her mouth agape obviously awestruck at the simple but elegant office with enormous windows overlooking the city. He held out his hand to her. "I'm happy you're here."

"You don't seem surprised." A knowing look came into her eyes. "Flora."

With a small smile he said, "Of course. I think she called before you even got back in your car."

A soft tap on the door, and it opened. Tracey came in

carrying a small tray with a coffeepot and two cups with the Tartan Bakery logo.

"I thought you might like a cup." Logan gestured to the leather chairs near the windows. "Please sit." His heart raced. He reminded himself to let Grace set the tone of their conversation.

She sank into the chair and swiveled her neck to look out over the city. "Your view is magnificent."

Blithely, he said, "You get used to it." He handed the first mug to her. "Cream and sugar?"

"Um, sure."

Logan smiled and sat back in the chair. "I've never seen you at a loss for words."

In a small voice she said, "It's one thing to know you're rich"—her gaze roamed the room—"but it's another to see you surrounded by such understated elegance."

"Just trappings for business meetings." He took a sip of coffee to steady his nerves, again reminding himself this was Grace's meeting and she needed to say what she needed to say.

Crossing her ankles, she began, "I'm not sure why I wanted to see you, but I didn't like the way I left the pub last night. I was rude."

"It was understandable. I was"—the palms of his hands upturned—"we were...oh hell, I don't know what happened." He scooted forward in the chair and took her hand. "Grace, I'm glad you're here. I've come up with a solution to our problem."

Her brow arched, her blue eyes wide. "I don't understand."

"I know the distance between us seems difficult, but I'll buy you a plane ticket any time you want to come over, and when you're ready I'll pay your moving expenses."

Her mouth dropped open. "What?"

Without considering what the fast forming plan in his brain might sound like, Logan continued, "You won't need to work, unless you want to, of course. I have plenty of money and I'll give you a credit card, whatever you need." He failed to see the flash of fire in her eyes. "It'll be great."

Grace jumped to her feet, her face beet-red. "I'm not one of those women who want anything to do with your money. I can buy my own plane tickets to wherever I want to go." She turned on her heel and strode to the door. "And for the record, you deserve those gold diggers since you seem to be under the mistaken impression that throwing your money around was the way to—to—well, to ruin a perfectly wonderful vacation." She flung the door open and it made a resounding thud as it hit the wall.

Stunned, Logan watched as Grace, the woman who had captured his heart, ran out of his office and his life. "Wait!" He raced after her. He was a moment too late as the elevator door shut. Should he go after her or give her time to cool off? And how the heck was he going to convince Grace that he was totally smitten with her if they weren't even on the same side of the ocean?

Grace could feel her cheeks were burning. Clutching the steering wheel, she expertly navigated Glasgow traffic. How on earth could he think offering to support her financially was the way to her heart? Until she learned he had been keeping parts of his life shrouded under a cloud of mystery, she thought he might have been the one for her.

A horn blared, startling her. Grace looked for the next exit. She was in no mood to be driving on the highway—she needed the slower pace of quaint towns and side roads. She had nowhere to be until tomorrow so she could afford the time to meander. She wiped the tears from her eyes and flicked on her blinker.

The narrow country roads wound around a few small villages. Grace found a café and stopped in to get lunch. She juggled a small bag containing a meat pie and a hot tea while turning up the collar of her rain jacket against the chill. She strolled down the street to a park. Spying a bench near a pond, she made a beeline for it. It was partially under a tree, so if it rained she'd be protected from the drizzle.

Her gaze wandered. This was a lovely town. She didn't think Gran had ever brought her here, at least not from what she could remember. She watched as a small gaggle of geese glided over the mirror-like water. She felt herself relax and her thoughts wander.

What did any of this really matter? Trying the wedding dress on in Scotland didn't show me what lies ahead. Even Gran was concerned about the dress being in the States. I'm going to go home, do a little painting in my new cottage, dig in the dirt and plant a few bulbs, and work my butt off so I can earn PTO to come back with the family in December.

Satisfied with her plan, she took a bite of the savory meat pie. After washing it down with the tea, it was time to make one last stop and then back to Gran's to finish packing. With a sigh, she took one final look at a pair of geese. They were head to head, their necks shaped into a lopsided heart.

She murmured, "That's exactly how my heart feels, a little bit wonky and not quite whole."

CHAPTER 18

Grace was seated next to the window and watched as land appeared in the distance, growing closer as they prepared to land. Soon she'd be on the ground in Boston. And then after the long drive to Easton she would be home. The landing gear clunked and it seemed like moments later they bumped along the runway. With a heavy heart, she gathered her things, ready to disembark once the doors opened.

She turned on her cell phone and several messages popped up. She smiled. She really did have the best sisters. The three of them were going to enjoy a glass of wine with a light late afternoon snack and her refrigerator had been stocked for the week. She texted them: *On the ground, see you soon.*

The last message was from Logan. It simply said, *I'm sorry.*

She paused, wondering if she should respond. With a shake of her head, she slipped the phone into her bag. She had said all she needed to say. It was a nice diversion for a couple of weeks and now back to her reality.

~

Grace watched as her garage door slid open. It gave her a thrill to know she was the proud owner of this cottage. But before she could open the car door, Jamie and Kenzie were standing there, with cheek-splitting grins.

"Welcome home, Grace!" Kenzie and Jamie said together.

"Good flight?" Jamie asked.

Grace leaned her head out the window and laughed. "Can I get out of the car, please?"

Kenzie said, "Pop the trunk and I'll grab your bags."

Grace did as she asked and rolled up the window before shutting the car off. It was good to be home. The moment she was out of the car, her sisters pulled her into a bear hug.

She smiled. "Hey, be careful, you're going to hug the stuffing right out of me."

"We missed you, squirt," Kenzie said. "It was weird—we were here and you were there."

Jamie was nodding in agreement. "Let's not vacation apart too often."

Grace held them tight. "You do know your husbands may want to vacation without family, specifically your younger sister tagging along."

Jamie stepped out of her arms. "Ha!" She smirked. "If he thinks he gets me all to himself all the time, we'll be having a talk."

Kenzie was studying Grace. "You don't look any different."

Grace was puzzled. "Why would I?"

Kenzie snorted. "Falling in love and all. I thought it might change you."

"Who said anything about love? I just had a bit of fun.

Nothing more." She hoped her eyes wouldn't betray the sadness she felt. Anxious to change the subject she linked arms with them. "Let's forget about the luggage—you said something about wine and food?"

Jamie laughed. "We have plenty of wine to loosen your tongue so you'll tell us everything that happened. You've been uncharacteristically silent." She steered Grace through the kitchen and out the back door.

Grace's mouth formed an O. Tears pricked her eyes. Her sisters had hung twinkling lights and placed potted flowers around the perimeter of the patio. The wrought-iron table was set with a platter of appetizers, three wine glasses and two bottles of red wine. "You didn't need to do all of this."

Jamie pointed Grace toward a chaise. "Have a seat. After the last few days, you needed a really nice welcome home."

"I need to run inside. I'll be right out." Grace hurried into the house and kicked off her shoes. Her sisters were right, this was exactly what she needed. Time with them always helped her.

Grace freshened up and was walking through the kitchen when she stopped to listen to Kenzie and Jamie. She had to strain as their voices were low.

Jamie said, "I'd like to wring his neck."

"I can't believe Mrs. M's nephew would turn out to be such a jerk. She's so sweet, and didn't she have a hand in raising him?"

"She did," Jamie said, "but obviously he missed something to be so cavalier with the truth."

Kenzie agreed. "Why do you think she wasn't interested in Tait?"

Grace had heard enough. She pushed open the back door and saw the look on their faces. Pure guilt. She decided she was going to pretend she hadn't been eaves-dropping.

"No one's poured the wine yet?" Despite her fatigue, she was looking forward to the next few hours.

Jamie popped the cork. "I'm on it."

Kenzie placed a few snacks on smaller plates and handed one to Grace. "Go stretch out. You look exhausted."

Grace sank to the lounge chair. "The trip coming home always seems shorter with the time change and all, but wow, I'm wiped out."

Jamie handed her and Kenzie half-filled glasses. "There's plenty more."

Grace let the bouquet of the wine fill her senses. Taking a sip, she said, "Smooth."

Kenzie took a drink and leaned back in her chair. "This is nice."

Jamie said, "It reminds me of the times before we got married." A small smile played over her face. "Who would have thought we'd have fallen in love and married two great guys?"

Grace frowned and ate an olive and some pepperoni before responding. "Kenz, how is married life? You haven't said anything."

Kenzie laid a hand over her heart and beamed. "Robbie is absolutely the best husband for me. I'm living a dream, being married to my best friend who knows me better than I know myself."

Grace chuckled. "Well, he should, since you've been BFFs since you were in diapers."

Kenzie's head bobbed. "I know, but I was worried about living together and having to share things like closets and, well, working together too. We're always together."

Grace's eyebrow shot up. "I never thought about that.

But it's good?"

"Better than good." Kenzie's eyes twinkled.

Grace was happy to see Kenzie actually blush. "And you, Jamie? Married life still agreeing with you?"

"Blissfully happy." She nibbled on a cracker. "And it doesn't hurt that he does most of the cooking."

Grace teased, "It's self-preservation. You can only cook two good meals, roast chicken and burgers on the grill."

Jamie laughed out loud. "Don't forget I can toss a mean salad."

Grace grew thoughtful. "Do you think I'll find it?"

Jamie looked at Kenzie and was quick to respond. "You will when it's the right guy."

Kenzie asked, "Do you want to talk about Logan?"

"I feel like I've talked this to death." She stared at a hummingbird at the feeder. "I went to see him yesterday."

Kenzie prodded, "And?"

"He said he'd set me up with a place to live and money to live off of if I wanted to move to Scotland."

"What?" Jamie demanded, sitting up straight. "You're joking, right?"

Grace shook her head slowly. "Nope."

Kenzie's face betrayed her anger. "I'm sure you set him straight."

"Ha! You could say that. I told him in no uncertain terms that he had no idea what kind of person I was. How could he even think of making such a suggestion?"

Jamie leaned over and laid a comforting hand on Grace's arm. "I'm sorry, Gracie."

"Yeah, me too." She dropped her eyes. "I really cared for him."

"Well, I say good riddance." Kenzie's voice was sharp. "Although I still can't believe he'd be so dumb. I thought he was some hotshot businessman."

"He is. He owns Tartan Bakery and Evangeline Hotels. But I guess when it comes to people he's not so smart." Grace held out her empty glass, and Kenzie picked up the bottle to refill it. "I think he dated me because I had no idea who he was—he could be anonymous."

Jamie's face lit up. "Maybe it's like the romance movies on television. You know, where the handsome prince pretends to be an average person so the girl falls in love with the man and not the title."

Grace gave a wry laugh. "This isn't a made-for-TV movie, Jamie. It's real life and people don't do that kind of stuff."

"What about all the stars who dress up in disguise to avoid being recognized? Isn't that kind of the same thing?" Jamie looked at Kenzie. "Don't you think that's possible?"

Kenzie shrugged. "How should I know? I've never met anybody who's super rich or famous."

Grace interjected, "It doesn't matter. I won't see him again. It's not like we live in the same town." She yawned and stretched her arms overhead. "When are we getting together with the rest of the family for dinner?"

"Whenever you're up for it," Jamie said. "I told Mom I'd give her a call."

Grace pulled herself to a sitting position and slung her legs over the cushion. "I could go for a good burger."

"How about the Roadside Shack?" Kenzie suggested. "We haven't been there yet this summer."

Jamie pulled her phone from her pocket. "I'll send a text and tell everyone to meet us in, what?" She glanced at Grace. "Thirty minutes?"

"Sure, that'll give me time to unpack the trip gifts I picked up for everyone." She looked at Kenzie. "Do you mind driving me and then bringing me home?"

Kenzie grinned. "Jetlag kicking in?"

"Between that and the wine, I'm a little tired." Her smile drooped. "It's been a long day."

"Squirt, we can skip dinner tonight," Jamie said as she stood up and draped her arm over Grace's shoulders.

Grace looked up at her sister. "If we eat out I don't have to worry about cooking or cleaning up the kitchen."

Kenzie said, "I'll get your bags." She hurried from the patio, giving Jamie and Grace a few minutes together.

"Jamie, I thought Logan might be the guy," Grace confessed softly.

Jamie dropped a kiss on her sister's head. "I know you did, Gracie, but I get the feeling this isn't over, at least not yet. Who knows what will happen in December? Logan may stop by the farm and try to make amends."

Grace pulled herself up to her full height and straightened her shoulders. "It'll take more than apologizing to make up for how I felt."

"He's already tried that, I gather?"

"He texted an apology." Grace took a step toward the back door. She looked at Jamie and stated, "He is an amazing man, just not for me."

"Is the issue he lied to you and assumed you move to Scotland and live off him?" Jamie's face was serious. "Or is it because if you let yourself fall for him, and you want to be with him your living situation changes?"

Grace walked inside with Jamie trailing her and said, "Maybe the latter." Her eyes scanned the kitchen, dining and living room areas. "I have a home of my own that I love, and my family is here. I couldn't leave any of this."

Kenzie walked in with a suitcase in each hand and said, "Where are you going?"

With a shake of her head, Grace took the bags. "Nowhere." She headed down the hall to her bedroom. "I'll be right back."

~

Kenzie looked at Jamie and waited until Grace was out of sight. "She has it bad for this guy, doesn't she?"

Jamie grinned. "Heck yeah. Love looks good on our baby sister." She rubbed her hands together. "Now what are we going to do to help things along?"

Kenzie's eyes lit up. "Are we going to call Mrs. M?"

A grin spread across Jamie's face. "I think that's a good place to start. I trust her that if Logan isn't good for Grace she'll tell us."

Kenzie glanced down the hallway before continuing. "For what it's worth, I checked him out already and he seems to be a good guy. Financially he's sound and does a ton of charity work. But, I mean, I still want to kick his butt for hurting Grace."

"That's what I'd expect you to say." Jamie's eyes popped open. "When did you do a search?"

"Last night." Kenzie leaned in and whispered, "I didn't have to dig deep to find out the really important stuff."

"You didn't find anything that would indicate he's a horrible boss or person?"

With a quick shake of her head, Kenzie said, "Not even a whisper from the women he's dated." A door slammed in the bedroom. She put a finger over her lips. "We'll talk later."

Jamie winked at her as Grace appeared, oblivious to what she'd almost walked in on.

"I'm ready." She had a tote bag over one shoulder. She patted it and grinned. "No peeking. Everyone gets their gifts at the same time."

Kenzie said, "Robbie's hoping for shortbread from MacMeekin's."

Jamie laughed. “It would be broken into bits.” She pulled at the bag, trying to peek inside.

Grace clutched it to her side. “Hey. Patience,” she teased.

Kenzie looked at Jamie and winked. “We could just tickle her and she’d cave.”

Grace took a step back. “All right, if I tell you, can you act surprised?”

Jamie crossed her hand over her heart. “I can. Kenz?”

“Me too.”

Grace set the bag down on the coffee table. Pulling out bubble-wrapped objects, she set them out one at a time. She held up heather honey, fruit wines and malt whiskey. “I have three jars of each one for every household.”

Jamie picked up the honey. “This is going to be so yummy on toast in the morning.”

Kenzie grabbed a bottle of wine. “To heck with breakfast, I’m thinking we have beverages for a night cap.”

Grace snorted. “You can drink it at your place. Immediately after dinner I’ll be crawling into bed. I’m back to work in the morning.”

“Understandable.” Jamie put the rewrapped packages back into the bag. “These are wonderful gifts, Grace. Thanks for bringing them home.”

“You may have been here, but in spirit, you were right there with me while I shopped.” Grace pulled her sisters in for a hug. With a lump in her throat, she said, “Thanks for understanding that I had to go by myself this time.”

The girls held tight as Kenzie said, “You’ve always been the most independent of us. We have to follow our own path, but we’re always here for each other.”

Grace gave them one last squeeze. “After all, we *are* the MacLellan sisters.”

CHAPTER 19

Grace sailed through her parents' back door. Their laughter drifted down the hallway. They were lucky they had each other. Her shoulders sagged. She was the only one in the family without a partner.

She stopped in the archway, plastered a smile on her face and called out, "I'm here."

Dad opened his arms. "There's my lass." He set down a glass of wine and pulled her in for a half hug. "You look tired."

Mom shushed him. "She's a working woman and has been back only for a few days. You know how jetlag can linger." She handed her a glass of wine.

Grace gratefully took the wine. Brightly she said, "I'm fine, really. But starved." She looked around the kitchen. "What's for dinner?"

"Grilled chicken and salad," Mom said. "I thought after all the great food you had on vacation, something basic would hit the spot."

Grace took a sip of her wine. Her brows shot up. "Wow,

this is good." She looked at the bottle and noticed the label. Evangeline? It couldn't be. "Where did this come from?"

A funny look crossed Dad's face, but it was gone as fast as it came. "The store."

Too tired to care, Grace decided to let it go. She was sure there were a lot of companies using women's names. It had to be a coincidence.

Mom handed her the salad bowl. "Will you take this outside?"

Grace pushed the sliding door open and then took the bowl. Mom hadn't asked her any questions about Logan. Her stomach flopped. Did this mean Mom and Dad were going to grill her, no pun intended, over dinner? What had Jamie and Kenzie told them?

Dad was right behind her with a platter of chicken, and Mom carried out a tray with everything else. "Can I cook, Dad?"

He pointed to a cushion-covered chair. "Have a seat and keep Mom company while I do the honors."

She kicked off her flip-flops and settled back. "So, what have you two been up to lately?"

Mom's eyes sparkled. "I'm trying to talk Dad into redoing a few rooms in the house. You know, fresh paint, window treatments and such. It's been quite some time, at least ten years since we've done anything."

"The last time you did was when I moved to college and you repainted my room and the bathroom upstairs."

Mom smiled. "I thought it was time to get rid of the bunnies on your walls."

Grace's smile filled her face. "I loved them. But it *was* time."

Dad interjected, "I remember trying to talk you into

letting me paint just as you became a teenager, and you told me you liked them and they were staying. I think you kept them all those years because you were stubborn."

With a small shake of her head, Grace said, "I watched Jamie and Kenzie grow up and change. I loved being the baby of the family. I thought, in some small way, if the bunnies were painted over then I'd have to grow up and my life would change too."

Mom tucked a wavy lock behind Grace's ear. "Change is a part of life, sweetie."

Grace laid her hand over her mom's while holding it close to her cheek. "I outgrew that fear."

"Do you want to talk about what happened in Scotland?"

Grace pulled away and picked up her glass. "There's not much to tell." Her hand had a slight tremor. "I took the dress back, found another journal Gran wanted me to read, spent time with Flora and wandered around taking in the sights."

She knew Dad was hanging on every word. "I heard from Patrick that you and Tait spent some time together. He's a fine man, Grace, and quite taken with you."

Grace rolled her eyes. "Dad, really?"

He held up his hands. "What's wrong with pointing out a few harmless facts?"

"James." Mom's voice held a familiar warning tone. "Grace is allowed to choose how and with whom she spends her time."

Grace started to speak, but Mom continued. "Maybe she and Tait didn't have enough in common."

"Mom!" Her voice was sharp. "You're talking like I'm not even in the room. Did you invite me to dinner to talk to me or about me?"

Mom fell silent and looked at Dad. "Sweetheart, I'm sorry. I didn't mean anything."

"I know, but we don't need to talk about the absence of my love life."

Dad opened his mouth and shut it. Grace caught the look he shot Mom before he turned his attention to the grill. Quietly she said, "I'm sure the girls told you. I did meet an amazing man in Scotland."

Mom perked up in her chair and to her credit didn't ask any questions. Yet.

"You may know him: Logan Campbell. Flora's nephew." Mom nodded and waited. Grace's eyebrow arched. "Aren't you going to ask any questions?" she teased. "I'm sure your interest has been piqued."

"Grace, I want to know everything, but only what you want to tell me." She grinned. "And I have met him once or twice. He is very good looking."

"Did you also know he's extremely wealthy?" Grace asked.

"I know he works hard, but the subject of his bank account never came up."

Dad turned a chicken breast and grumbled, "You're going to hold that against the man?"

Hurt filled her voice. "What do you mean? He wasn't forthcoming with that very important detail."

"And why did he need to tell you? Did you tell him how much money *you* have in the bank?"

"How is that relevant? And aren't you supposed to have my back?"

"That is the point, Grace. I do. I happen to think Logan is a good man."

"Besides, he knows what I do for a living; you don't get rich in my profession." Grace noticed Mom let the conversation flow between her and Dad.

He reminded her, "You and your sisters all have trust funds."

She jutted out her chin. "They're small by comparison and that's hardly the same thing. We're not millionaires, and my sisters and I agree we're saving them in case of an emergency. We haven't touched a penny."

"You've missed the point, Grace. When you begin dating someone, there are things you don't talk about, and one of them is money."

The air seemed to escape from the balloon of indignation Grace had been carrying since Tait told her about Logan. Dad had a point. Maybe she had judged Logan unfairly. She rejected him because he had money. No, it wasn't that he had money, it was because he hadn't told her.

Clasping her hands together, she knew Dad was right. She picked her head up and her blue eyes caught his. "Dad, should I call him and apologize?"

"That's up to you, lass. Have you heard from him since you've been home?"

"With the exception of an apology, not a word about anything else."

"And Tait?" he asked.

"Yes, he's sent a couple of texts. But I don't feel that zing inside I did with Logan." Her eyes clouded. "Does that make me a bad person? To be keeping in contact when there isn't anything more that will come of it?"

He held the tongs aloft as the chicken popped and sizzled. "Did you give the lad hope?" he asked.

With a shake of her head she said, "Not at all. We parted as friends."

Dad gave her an encouraging smile. "You're a kind-hearted girl, Grace."

She turned to Mom. "What do you think, should I call Logan?"

"You need to think about what message you'll be sending. Do you want to have a long distance relationship or are you proposing to be friends?" She searched Grace's eyes. "Do you think you're falling in love with him?"

"I'm attracted to him, but I'm not sure what love should feel like." She felt bad for not admitting the truth about the depth of her feelings. She reasoned it was easier to skirt the truth.

Dad set the plate of chicken on the table and sat down. "Love is defined by the two people involved." He looked lovingly at Mom. "Take your Mom and me as an example. Who would have thought we'd have lasted all these years? We're so different, but our hearts beat as one." He leaned over and pecked her lips.

Anxious to lighten the mood, Grace said, "Yuck. Get a room."

Mom winked at Dad. "The best thing about being a parent is when your kids move out and you suddenly have lots of rooms."

She groaned. "Mom. Dad. Stop."

Dad chuckled and tweaked Grace's nose. "That's love for you."

She smiled. "You know all of this is your fault. You guys made it look so easy to have a loving partner in life. It's a lot for any guy to live up to."

"Happy to have given you and your sisters a good example. And from the looks of the glowing faces when I see them, your sisters married well." Dad grinned. "When the time is right, you will as well."

~

Grace lay in bed staring into the darkness. Dad was right, she had jumped to conclusions without really talking about things with Logan. Just as she was drifting off, she bolted to a sitting position.

Wait just a doggone minute. He started throwing his money around the last time we talked. He is all about his money and what it can do for him.

She lay back down and pulled the blanket over her shoulders. After tossing and turning for over an hour, she finally gave up and padded barefoot down the hall to the kitchen. The cool wood floors didn't register. Tea was needed to soothe her jangled thoughts.

After going through the routine of heating the water, she rinsed out her favorite mug. Looking but not really seeing out the window, a filmy moving shadow seemed to be lit from within like an orb. It caught her attention.

What the heck?

She hurried to the back door and flung it open. She caught a whiff of Gran's perfume, lilacs, and could swear she was standing in the yard. Stepping out into the cool night air, she wrapped her arms around her. Her thin pajamas weren't warm enough to keep the midnight chill away.

The glow of light seemed to illuminate a semitransparent version of Gran that she saw from the window. Grace boldly crossed the patio while the shadow seemed to wait for her. It seemed to settle into a chair. Grace hesitated and then did the same. Facing what looked to be her beloved Gran, she waited for several long minutes. "I'm not afraid of you." The trill of the kettle pierced the night. The shadowy figure of Gran pointed toward the house.

Unsure what to do, Grace said, "I'm making tea."

The figure pointed again. Grace rose and said, "I'll be right back."

She ran into the house, hurriedly turned the stove off and sloshed water over the infuser. Picking the mug up, she started to go back outdoors and stopped just outside the doorway. The moon bathed the patio in brilliant light. The space was empty.

Grace dropped the mug and it shattered, splashing hot tea on her legs. She cried out in pain and hopped around on one foot. After bringing it down on a shard of ceramic, tears sprang to her eyes. Hobbling into the house, leaving a trail of blood on the floor, Grace grabbed a towel and wiped off the side of her foot.

"Damn it!" She examined where the tea had hit; her skin was red but wasn't blistering, so that was a good sign, but her foot needed attention. Hopefully the shard wasn't in too deep.

She grabbed the first aid kit from the kitchen cabinet, soaked a clean towel in water and sank to the floor. Between the reddened towel and the wet one, she was able to clean her foot and inspect it. She was relieved to find nothing lingering in the cut. After it was dried, she added antibiotic ointment and a bandage.

She leaned against the cabinet. This reminded her of last fall during Jamie's wedding when Kenzie cut her foot open and Robbie came to her rescue. She closed her eyes and imagined what that would be like, to have someone ready to lend a hand in situations like these.

Logan's handsome face came to mind. With a shake of her head, Grace reminded herself that bridge was closed, permanently.

Looking at the mess on the floor, Grace stood up and balanced on one foot. She grabbed a mop and cleaned up. She thought about that cup of tea that started this series of events. Crossing to the window, she looked out. The patio was empty.

With a heavy heart Grace tossed the dirty towels in the sink and made her way back to bed.

As she lay down, a whiff of baking shortbread comforted her. Her last thought before drifting off was, *Gran, what are you trying to tell me?*

CHAPTER 20

Grace walked into Kenzie's gym to find her sisters were hovering over a laptop. "Hey, guys, what are you doing?"

Kenzie slapped the lid shut and looked at Jamie. Guilt written all over her face. She eked out, "Shopping?"

"Uh, okay." Grace suspected they were up to something, and from prior experience she knew eventually she'd find out. Kenzie was never great at keeping a secret. She glanced at Jamie. "Is that your story too?"

Jamie grinned. "Yup, and sticking to it."

Kenzie pushed back from the desk. "Did you come to work out or chitchat?"

Letting it go for the moment, Grace said, "I'm up for some cardio." She looked at Jamie. "And you?"

"Sounds good. If I keep eating everything Caleb cooks and not exercising, I'm going to gain ten pounds before the end of the year."

Kenzie looked at the clock. "I have a spin class in fifteen minutes if you want to join us."

"Sure, we'll change and meet you inside. Jamie, are you coming?"

"Right behind you."

Jamie winked at Kenzie, and Grace said, "I saw that."

She held up her hands. "What? I didn't do anything."

Grace crossed her arms. "You didn't need to. The looks on your faces tell me you're up to something."

Jamie twirled Grace toward the locker room. "Let's get changed, squirt. Kenzie's been itching to get us in the bike saddle and make us sweat since you got home."

Grace let herself be gently guided into the other room. "I'll find out you know." Her voice held a hint of warning and laughter.

"Maybe, maybe not," Jamie said as the door closed behind them.

Grace labored through the last minutes of spin. Kenzie, who was in top condition, pushed the class to the point of utter exhaustion. Swiping sweat from her brow, Grace breathed a sigh of relief as the music indicated it was time for cooldown. Slowly peddling, sitting tall in the seat, her heart rate began to descend to normal. She stole a glance at Jamie, whose face glistened with a fine sheen of sweat too. Smiling at Jamie, Grace mouthed *dinner?* A curt nod answered her, and Jamie jerked her head toward Kenzie, who caught the gesture. Grace mimicked bringing a utensil to her mouth. Kenzie gave a thumbs-up.

Grace wanted to talk to them about what was going on in their lives. Since she had been home, she had been so busy at work she felt out of the loop.

After going through a stretching routine, Grace and

Jamie hit the showers. "Jamie, what time do you think Kenz will be able to get out of here?"

Towel-drying her hair, Jamie said, "I saw her talking to Robbie, so I'm sure he'll close up so we can have some sister time."

"Will Caleb mind?" A flash of worry stabbed at Grace.

Picking up the blow dryer, Jamie grinned. "He might actually like the quiet time. Every night I've been showing him decorating ideas for the house. I'm sure he would rather I pick out the window treatments and he'd happily take care of outfitting the kitchen.

"It must be nice to have someone to go home to," Grace said, talking above the blow dryer.

Kenzie burst through the door. Obviously spin class gave her an energy boost as opposed to leaving her drained. Grace turned her head in the whirlwind's direction. "Kenz, how do you do it? You look like you could conquer the world after that class and at the end of a long day of many classes."

Kenzie brightened. "I love what I do. Helping people work on their health pumps me up." She twirled the padlock on her locker. "I need to dash through the shower and then I'll be ready to roll." Grabbing her toiletry bag and a large white towel, she headed into a private stall. She called over her shoulder, "Where are we eating tonight?"

"The bistro? I'm not in the mood for Italian."

Grace buckled her sandal, and Kenzie popped her head around the corner of the stall as Jamie laid the blow dryer aside. "Does that sound good, Jamie?"

"Sure." She ran a brush through her hair and said, "I'm going to call Caleb and check email. I'll wait out front."

"Use my desk if you want."

Jamie slung her bag over her shoulder and asked, "Is Cheryl still here?"

Grace liked Cheryl. She had been with Kenzie for almost a year as the newly promoted gym manager and really pitched in when Kenzie had broken her ankle and wrist.

"Nah, she had a date with her cute mechanic." The shower turned on, ending further discussion.

Jamie asked, "Did she seem annoyed?"

Grace grinned. "You know Kenz, straight to the point."

Jamie pushed open the door and turned to look at Grace. "I'm glad you're a combination of both of us, with a dash of Gran thrown in for good measure."

Grace trailed behind her, curious to discover what Jamie meant. "I'm nothing like either of you."

Jamie's laughter lightened Grace's heart. "I'm happy to point out you're like us in some ways and different in many others."

Grace and Jamie were alone in the lobby. They sat on clear plastic chairs. "Do tell," Grace said.

Jamie set her bag aside after she pulled her cell phone out and laid it on the table between them. "Well, we are all driven to be the best we can be, but you're organized and detailed like yours truly. You can be as stubborn as Kenzie, but you have a softer side, like Gran. You believe all things are possible. However, the most significant difference between us is that you're brave. Blazing your own path."

Grace's forehead wrinkled in confusion. "How am I brave?"

"Your Scotland trip, for one. You read Gran's letter and did as she asked. You didn't even think to ask Mom and Dad to go with you or, for that matter, me or Kenzie. You packed your bags and went on an adventure."

With a wave of her hand, Grace brushed it off. "We've been there tons of times. It's not like I went off on safari alone."

With a slow shake of her head, Jamie said, "I respectfully disagree. You walked into a house full of memories, with a wedding dress that seems to hold magic…at least I know it did for me and Kenz."

"Does Kenz feel the same way?" Grace was curious.

There was a pregnant pause before Jamie tented her fingers and said, "It doesn't matter what we think. It's how you see it."

Grace started to open her mouth when Jamie said, "Let's talk about it over dinner with Kenzie. I think it's important for you to understand how proud we are of you."

Kenzie came bobbing out of the locker room and glanced their way. She grinned. "I'm going to track down my husband for a smooch and then we can walk to the restaurant."

Grace's eyes followed Kenzie. "She really is happy, isn't she?"

Jamie got a little choked up. "Once she realized Robbie was the love of her life and she didn't have to give up her independence to have it all, it was like she found her groove."

Grace's head swiveled toward Jamie. "Is that how you feel? Like you found yourself?"

A slow smile spread across Jamie's face and happiness filled her eyes. "That is a great way to describe it."

"You didn't call Caleb." Grace handed Jamie's cell phone to her. "We'll wait."

Jamie took the phone and hit a couple of buttons. "Grace, you will find the man who fills your heart with joy." She held up a finger. "Hi, handsome."

Grace rose from the chair and wandered across the room giving Jamie privacy. She wondered, *Am I brave or just doing what Gran asked of me?* She stared out the window and could picture Logan helping her out of the stream. That was after she tried the dress on and Gran wanted her to go to Rosemarkie. *Was it possible I was supposed to meet Logan that day?*

"Earth to Grace…" Kenzie had come up behind her. "Where were you just now?"

With a smile, Grace said, "I was thinking about Rosemarkie. Gran sent me there, and that's when I met Logan. Well, I had bumped into him before, but that time we really talked."

Kenzie gave her a knowing smile. "And let me guess, you're trying to dissect Gran's motive for sending you there. But she would have had no way of knowing you'd bump into Logan."

"Guilty as charged and you're right. Seeing Logan was by chance." She stretched her hands toward the ceiling. "I'm a hopeless romantic."

"That is one thing you have that Jamie and I never did." Kenzie's voice softened. "Until now. We have taken a page from that particular book."

Grace laid a hand on her sister's shoulder. Giving it a squeeze, she said, "You wear marriage like a fine leather glove that was made for you."

Kenzie glanced over her shoulder to where Robbie was working with a client. She sighed. "I'm so lucky."

Grace laughed. "I'm not sure how many guys would spend a lifetime waiting for one woman, to almost lose her to stubborn pride. And then show up to support a hare-brained idea like running a half marathon literally just out of a cast mere weeks later."

With a nonchalant shrug, Kenzie said sheepishly, "The old saying is true—love does conquer all."

Grace looked down. "How's your foot feeling these days?"

Kenzie held out her left leg and said, "I get a tiny bit of

swelling after a long day on my feet, but it's getting stronger all the time. I'm still doing the exercises Ally gave me."

"Speaking of Ally, is she still coming in?"

Kenzie grinned. "Yes, she is still a member, and I introduced her to a couple of the single guys around town who I thought might be good dating options."

With a snort, Grace said, "Sounds like you've become a matchmaker since your nuptials."

Kenzie slipped an arm around Grace's waist, steering her back to where Jamie was wrapping up her phone call. "I am a firm believer in a happily ever after." She tugged Grace closer. "And that includes one for my baby sister."

Jamie hopped up. "I'm starving. What about you guys?"

"We've been waiting for you to stop saying sweet nothings into the phone," Grace teased.

Jamie blushed. "I just can't help it. He's so darn cute, and the way that man can..." She fanned herself.

Grace shook her head. "Way too much information, you'll make me lose my appetite."

Kenzie laughed and said, "Then we'd better get going."

Grace said, "Lead the way."

Swirling the wine in her glass, Grace studied it thoughtfully. With a full stomach, she knew it was time for her sisters to poke at her about Logan.

"I think I saw Gran last night." Grace thought she could hear a pin drop. Her gaze slid from Kenzie to Jamie. "And I smelled shortbread baking."

Jamie looked at Grace. "Do you want to tell us exactly what happened?"

Grace took a sip of wine. "I was having trouble sleeping

and decided to make tea. As I was waiting for the kettle, I could swear I saw her standing on the patio."

Jamie was nodding. "The same thing happened to me. But she never spoke."

Grace's eyes met Jamie's. "When I went outside to talk to her, I had just sat down and the kettle started whistling. Gran pointed toward the house. I rushed inside to take care of it and when I came back out she was gone."

Kenzie said, "There were times I thought she was prodding me, but I never saw her." Her eyes were downcast. "Why do you think I didn't?"

Jamie said, "I don't have any answers. But you said you always felt her presence. I never did except for the time I thought I saw her."

Grace interjected with a shrug, "Maybe like so many things, Gran reaching out is different for each of us."

The girls were quiet, sitting in companionable silence. Grace was sure her sisters were remembering special moments they had with Gran. She had been thinking how Gran sent her to Scotland. More than likely she had been in cahoots with Flora hoping Grace would meet Logan and maybe even Tait.

"Girls, do you think Gran would somehow finagle it so I'd meet Tait and Logan?"

Kenzie slowly looked up, and Jamie chuckled. "I wouldn't put anything past her if she were alive. You know Gran was a romantic," Jamie said.

Kenzie's eyes lit up. "That would definitely be something she'd do. Maybe she had talked to Simon and they came up with the idea when you went to Scotland he was to make sure you two met again."

"Just because Tait and I were friends as children how could Gran have thought we'd have romantic feelings for each other?"

Jamie tapped the wine glass with her fingernail. "She knows he's a good guy and he's kind-hearted. And don't forget, he's Scottish. That would be a winning combination for our grandmother."

Laughing, Grace said, "True. But Logan also fits that same criteria."

Kenzie leaned back in the chair. "Let's think about the sequence of events. Gran knew everything would start when she passed away. Dad shipped the box containing the dress to us. Jamie tried it on, found her letter from Gran and got married. She passed the dress on to me and I tried it on, found my letter and ended up falling in love. Finally, I gave the dress to you, and Gran left you a letter asking you to take it back to Scotland. Then the dress is almost stolen and Logan gets it back for you. Tait shows up at the farm. Maybe the whole point was to show you their differences."

Grace mulled over this idea. With a shake of her head, she said, "I have no idea what Gran might have been thinking and we'll never know for sure. What do you say we forget about all of this and enjoy spending time together?" She caught the look between her sisters. "Stop. I'm not doing what you think I am."

Jamie said, "What, pray tell, are you talking about?"

"Burying my head in the sand about the men in my life." She snorted. "Listen to me, the men in my life. It's just my luck I date a guy on the opposite side of the Atlantic Ocean and develop some feelings for him. But can I find a nice guy to date here, nope. On top of all of that, the wedding dress is in Scotland, just as Gran requested."

Kenzie opened her mouth and then closed it.

"What were you going to say Kenz?"

With a shake of her head she said, "Nothing."

Grace reminded her, "You're a terrible liar. Fess up. What were you about to say?"

Kenzie hesitated. “Maybe if you want to find love you need to live in Scotland.”

“That’s crazy. I’m not moving to Scotland just to find a husband,” Grace stated with indignation. “I plan on growing old right here in the good ole US of A. With or without a husband.”

CHAPTER 21

Logan looked at his phone for the umpteenth time today. Why hadn't she at least sent him a text?

"Aunt Flora, I still haven't heard from her." He looked at his aunt as they shared a pot of tea. "I know our last conversation didn't go so well, but I thought she wouldn't stay mad. I had hoped she'd think about everything and realize I was trying to come up with a solution for us. Why wouldn't she reach out so that we could at least talk?"

"Logan, have you put yourself in her shoes for one tiny moment? I was friends with Arabel MacLellan for many years, so I know honesty is the most important quality to Grace."

"In my defense, most women I date know exactly who I am, including the fact that I have financial security."

His aunt admonished him. "Do you hear yourself? If you sounded this obnoxious with Grace, I can see why you haven't heard from her."

His face fell. "You know it's all a façade. I'm not proud of it but acting like an arrogant jerk is the way I keep people at a distance. You should know that better than anyone." He toyed with his cup. "I was hoping she'd want to stay with me, move to Scotland, and together we could do great things."

"What I understand is losing your mum and sister and then your dad a short time later broke your spirit. You were left with a family of one, and I'm not going to live forever."

He clasped her hands. His voice trembled. "Don't say that. You're going to be with me until I'm an old, gray-haired man."

"My dear boy, we all have a time to go. We just don't know when it is. Which is why I feel compelled to point out you'd be a fool to let Grace slip away from you. She is one in a million."

Earnestly he said, "How do I reach her?"

"I find a simple, heart-felt gesture always works best." Aunt Flora patted his hand. "Put your thinking cap on and I'm sure you'll come up with something."

"I could fly over there and surprise her?" He grabbed his phone. "I'll ask Tracey to book me on the first available flight, and then Grace'll see how much she means to me."

As his fingers flew over the keyboard, Aunt Flora said sharply, "Logan."

Without looking up he said, "Hm?"

"Logan!"

The sound of her voice had him look up, mid-text. "Yes."

"Flying over there is a grand gesture. I would encourage you to think smaller. How about sending her flowers?"

"Anyone can send flowers." He began to text again until his aunt pulled the phone from his hands.

"The difference is they'd be from you. Flowers show you're thinking about her. It's not over the top, it's not extravagant, it's romance in its pure form."

His eyes brightened. "I could send wild orchids."

With a shake of her head, Aunt Flora said, "I really don't think you're listening to me at all. Think simple. Romantic. What's wrong with a classic, like roses?"

"Anyone can send roses." Slowly a smile spread across his face. "But what if I sent one exquisite long-stemmed red rose?"

Beaming she said, "That is a lovely idea. I would include a short note. Something sweet and endearing."

Drumming his fingers on the tabletop, he gazed out the window. "What about '*Thinking of you*'? It's simple, to the point and honest."

"I like it." Aunt Flora slowly stood. Logan reached out a steadying hand. "Would you like to stay over tonight or do you need to get back to Glasgow?"

"I can stay."

"Then help your favorite aunt close up for the night. You know the routine—tables need a final wipe, check the napkins, and we'll work our way back to the kitchen. And then you can escort me home."

Impulsively he dropped a kiss on her cheek. "What would I do without you?"

She patted his face. "Lose the most perfect girl, I suspect."

He slung an arm over her thin shoulder. "Will you dance at my wedding?"

"You can count on it." Laughing, she wandered into the kitchen.

Logan watched his beloved aunt leave the room and couldn't help but notice she was moving slower these days. Maybe it was time they hired some extra help in the bakery. Aunt Flora could concentrate on what she loved most, creating a new twist on old favorites. He'd talk to her about it tonight.

~

At the end of a long, hectic day Grace pulled in her driveway. A white box was leaning against the back door. "What the heck is that?"

Parking her car, she pushed a button and the overhead door slid closed. She picked up the box and noticed it was from a florist in Burlington. After opening the back door, she clicked on the light in the kitchen and took the lid off the box. Nestled in tissue paper was a single long-stemmed pink rose. Inhaling the subtle fragrance, she closed her eyes. She loved roses.

Grace marveled at the velvety petals, and then curiosity finally won out. She picked up the small white envelope and read the card.

Thinking of you—LC

She smiled. Logan. This definitely deserved a text.

Digging through her handbag, she paused. What should she say? *Keep it simple, Grace.*

She took a picture of the flower and sent it as a text with just a thank you. Hitting send, she wondered if Logan would text back.

Disappointed she didn't get a response, she realized it was almost midnight in Scotland. Then her phone beeped. *You're welcome. L*

She picked up the vase and set it on the coffee table where she could see it from the kitchen too. Her cell rang. "Hello."

"Hey, Gracie, are you up for a run after work tomorrow?"

Grace sank to the stool. "Kenz, please don't tell me we're in training again. I think running the Shamrock Race was enough for one year." She laughed. "Even though I did beat the rest of the family in the 5k…bragging rights were nice for a while."

"Ah, come on." Grace could hear the smile in Kenzie's voice. "I thought you had fun."

Grace grinned despite herself. "I did, but I have a sneaking suspicion if I give you an inch you're going to take a mile and we'll be entering all kinds of races."

"Well, you can relax. I really just want to go for a run." Kenzie hesitated. "Are you in?"

"Yeah, I'll swing by the gym. Are we going to run outside or on the treadmill?"

"We're busting out." Kenzie chuckled. "Robbie's going home to cook dinner and Cheryl's going to close up. If you want you can come for dinner too."

"Sounds like a plan." Grace waited a few moments before saying, "Logan sent me a long-stemmed pink rose today."

A low whistle was Kenzie's response. "Just one?"

Grace walked into the living room and picked up the slender vase, relishing in the thoughtful expression. "It is beautiful."

"Did you call him?"

"I sent him a text." Grace set it back down and flopped onto the couch.

"Does this mean you're thinking of calling him?" Kenzie asked.

"All it means is Logan sent me a flower and I thanked him. We live very different lives." She sat up straight. "Kenz, am I being unreasonable?"

"Grace, what I think doesn't count. If there is one thing I learned last year, it didn't matter what anyone else thought regarding my relationship with Robbie. I had to figure out how I felt and what I wanted out of life. Thank heavens I didn't lose him in the process. I'm pretty sure Gran would tell me it's the power of love."

Grace sighed heavily. "It is so inspiring to hear you talk like this. You and Robbie always belonged together."

Kenzie asked. "What is the biggest stumbling block with Logan?"

In a small, quiet voice, Grace answered, "I'm not sure."

The sisters sat in silence for what seemed like a very long minute. Grace finally said, "All right then, I'll see you around five tomorrow."

Before Grace disconnected, Kenzie said, "If you want to talk later, give me a call."

"Thanks, but I need to do some soul searching." Grace hung up with the promise to call if she needed to, but really she longed to talk to Gran.

After dinner she hurried to clean up the kitchen, Grace wanted to read the journal she brought from Scotland. She brought it to show Jamie and Kenzie, but maybe there was something that would help her figure out what she needed to do.

Grace took the journal and went out to the patio. Looking toward the sky, she said, "Gran, if you can hear me, tell me what page I need to start reading first."

She sat down in the chaise and held the book in her lap. She waited. Absentmindedly she tapped the cover of the journal, she wondered should she just open the book and pray that was where she needed to start.

Flipping it open, she closed her eyes and leaned her head back, resting it on the cushion. *Gran, I'm so confused. I feel like you put both Tait and Logan in my path. But Logan makes my heart soar. I have a strong idea that you and Flora discussed us and hoped we would meet. But how can it work when we live in different countries? Besides, he enjoys making money and I want to help people, to give back. We have different ideas about life.*

A breeze fluttered, turning the pages of the journal.

Grace smiled. *Thanks Gran.* She opened her eyes and started reading.

My loving husband Rory is dealing with missing his family. Although Scotland is a small country, travel is difficult as this winter the cold and snow have been severe, the worst in history. I'm very fortunate he's never asked me to leave my home and go to the Lowlands to his family's farm. I've spent time thinking what I would say if he asked. I'm torn. I'm the only child, so if I were to leave the farm it would be a hardship on my parents. I must talk to Rory and discuss our options.

Grace turned the page.

Before I broached the subject of moving, I came to a decision. If it was very important to my husband, I would move, with the concession that when we started a family we could return to Mackenzie land. But my dear Rory surprised me. He brought up a possible move first. He is ready to assume more responsibility at the farm and he asked for us to make the trip to see his family in the summer months. It will be well past the birth of the lambs and before the harvest. I was so relieved I almost felt guilty. But I was willing to make the change for the man I love.

Grace closed the book. Would she have done the same if she had been in Gran's shoes? It was something to think about.

A cool breeze teased her unruly curls, just like when Gran used to tug on one to get her attention. Under her breath she said, "I'm trying Gran."

Another sleepless night. Logan sat on the edge of his bed and looked at the text from Grace. He was thrilled to receive the brief message. Should he wait a few days before sending her another flower? Or wait, maybe he should send something else. *Chocolates? From Switzerland? Perfect!*

He shook his head. No, he would see what he could find local to her. That way it wouldn't be over the top, just thoughtful.

After opening his laptop, he searched for the best chocolates near Easton. He found one with a five-star rating, Lake Chocolates. Making a note of the phone number, he set a reminder on his phone to call as soon as they were open. He smiled to himself and wondered, what other simple gestures would Grace enjoy? A basket of apples and cheese? Fine hand soap or lotions? A book? A photo of Rosemarkie Falls? All great ideas.

Logan got up from the bed and watched as the city slept. Tiny pinpricks from the streetlights dotted the streets. The vast star-filled sky would soon be streaked with the fresh blush of dawn. He yawned. When he got to the office he'd check his schedule and make plans to fly to America.

But not right away. First, he would send a few more gifts and definitely more flowers. He would show Grace that he had a soft, unassuming side.

He padded back to bed. It was time for a couple of hours of much needed rest if he was to have the ability to think clearly and select a few perfect items to send to the woman he loved.

CHAPTER 22

Logan tapped the lid of his laptop closed. For the next two weeks, on Monday, Thursday and Saturday, Grace would receive a small token of his affection. It would be a mix of delectable treats, flowers and perfume. He took one final check of his calendar and called to Tracey.

She walked at a sedate pace into the room. "Do you need something?"

He snickered at her tone, impatient, like he had interrupted her doing something important when he knew she had been dying for him to ask for her help. "But of course. I've been checking my meeting schedule and I don't see any free time for weeks. Is it possible you can clear my schedule for a week or so? Two, no more than three weeks from today?"

Tracey's eyebrow shot up. "Is the trip for business?"

He waggled a finger at her. "You know better than that. If it was for business I wouldn't have asked you to clear my schedule. I'd be asking you to shuffle it."

Her face wore a bland expression. "How should I know what your motivation is? You're being very mysterious."

"Since I tell you almost everything about my life, I might as well confess now so you can get to work." He struck the desk with his hand and announced, "I'm going to pay a surprise visit to Grace in Vermont."

She crossed her arms and bit back a grin. "Are you now?"

"I am. And what's more, I'm going to enlist the help of her sisters to pull it off."

"What makes you think her sisters will help you?" Tracey leaned against his desk with an amused expression on her face. "You do realize that sisters stick together through thick and thin. If they think you have hurt Grace, they might not be inclined to help you skulk into Vermont."

"As a matter of fact, I was going to send an email today."

"Interesting," was all Tracey had to say.

Feeling a tad smug, he leaned back into a chair. "Don't you agree that is a brilliant idea?"

Tracey didn't answer.

Logan shifted in his chair, feeling restless. "I know it's not. I really screwed this up."

Slowly, she nodded, encouraging him to keep talking.

"But how could I have guessed that not telling her *all* about me was a bad idea? And in my defense—"

Tracey interrupted him. "Don't go down that path. You care for this woman and you're determined to win her back. The first step is to let go of what happened and build on the good moments. You don't need to defend yourself. Can you imagine how hard it must have been to hear, as an independent woman, that some man you were dating offered to set you up and give you a credit card as long as you dropped everything and moved to a foreign country?"

Logan protested, "She's half Scottish."

"Who was born and raised in America," Tracey pointed out.

Logan crossed the room and stared out the window. "I've known a few women who would have jumped at the chance."

"Grace isn't most women. Which is why she has captured your attention."

Softly he said, "She texted me."

"For no reason?"

"She was thanking me for the rose I sent to her." He looked at Tracey. "If you were a girl..."

She chuckled. "You do realize I am, right?"

"Tracey," he laughed, "think like the girl I'm trying to woo." He grinned.

Tracey picked up a pad and pen from Logan's desk. "I'm assuming I'll be doing a little research for what you want to come next."

"You know me so well, and I would appreciate the help." He strode to his desk and opened his laptop. Striking a few keys, he brought up the website for Lake Chocolates. "I'm thinking of ordering a box of candy for her." He glanced up, "Do you think that is too cliché?"

"Most women love chocolate. So it would be very sweet of you." She made a note. "What else were you thinking?"

"I'm going to send something three times a week."

Tracey shook her head. "Wow. Too much. You could send a card, but as far as gifts are concerned, you don't want to overwhelm her and seem too pushy, or worse, like a man who is showing off his money."

He tapped his finger on his chin. "I never thought of it that way. I'm still going to do the chocolates at the end of the week, and what if I went out to Rosemarkie and took some pictures? Had one framed and then sent it to her?"

"Are the waterfalls special to her?"

"It was one of the places I bumped into her; we spent time there roaming around. We even shared her lunch." His face lit up. "It was something special, at least to me. Maybe it will help her remember how much fun we had there."

"That is a wonderfully romantic gesture." Tracey picked up his keys from the desk and tossed them to him. "I happen to know that, as of this moment, your schedule is clear for the afternoon and it's a lovely day. A perfect day for photography."

He grabbed his cell phone. "In that case I'm taking the rest of the day off." He grinned. "I'm going to play photographer at all the places we went and have photos I can send to her." Logan hurried to the door. "You can reach me via cell."

With a wave of her hand, she called after him, "Take your time, and most of all, have fun."

Logan could hear her laughter follow him as he stepped onto the elevator. He wasn't sure why he was in such a hurry, but he felt like he needed to get to Rosemarkie as quickly as possible and take the perfect photo. Too bad he wasn't a professional photographer; it would be *so* much better.

As the elevator doors closed after him, he thought maybe he should buy a photo at an art gallery and send it to her. He quickly dismissed that idea. Anyone could buy art. For the first time since he was a boy, he was going to make a homemade gift. He smiled to himself—he'd make something just like he did for his mum.

He felt like he was walking on air as the elevator

whooshed open. Today was the best day he had had in a very long time.

The week had been hectic and Grace was happy it was Thursday. The weekend was on the horizon. She had her feet propped up on the coffee table, relaxing when the front doorbell rang. "Who could that be?"

She pulled open the door and a delivery truck was pulling away from the curb. Perched on a small table on the porch was a medium-sized box. She carried it inside. "I'm not expecting anything." She gave it a shake. "Kind of light." The return address was surprising. "Lake Chocolates?"

She carefully cut the packing tape and sliced the bubble wrap. Nestled in the protective wrapping was a one-pound box of assorted truffles. She opened the card and smiled.

For the sweetest girl I know. L

Grace picked up her phone. Her fingers hovered over the keys. *What should I say? Something clever or just a simple thank you?*

How did you know? They are my favorite chocolates. You're very sweet… G.

She hit send and then took a picture of the box along with the rose and sent it to Logan too. *Thank you.*

Grace wondered if she should tell Jamie and Kenzie. Before she could fret too long, she forwarded the picture to her sisters. She texted *From Logan* with a smiley face.

A reply came back from Kenzie. *I'm coming over, wine open?*

Grace chuckled. She texted back a picture of an empty wineglass. She knew what to expect next, a message from

Jamie saying she was coming too. She waited before putting the phone aside. Blip: *Me too! J*

Grace unlocked the back door for her sisters and went to get two more glasses and a bottle of red uncorked. This tidbit was far too juicy for her sisters to take their time getting to her place.

It seemed like only seconds passed before the back door banged and Kenzie rushed into the kitchen. Grace was casually leaning against the counter and held out a glass of red wine. "What did you do, fly?"

"Jamie was just pulling in too."

With a smirk Grace gave an almost imperceptible nod. She picked up the next glass and could hear Jamie's high heels clicking against the tile floor as she hurried down the hall. She burst into the kitchen and, beaming, took the wine and pulled out a stool, her eyes never leaving Grace. "Well? So, what's going on?" she demanded. "Logan sent you another gift?"

Drawing out the suspense for her sister, Grace smiled and said, "It seems so. The chocolates just arrived."

Kenzie pulled the box to her and announced, "He's got good taste." She picked one out and nibbled on it. Closing her eyes, she said, "Velvety soft, and orange liqueur."

Grace pulled the box back. "Do you mind if I have one too?"

Kenzie waved her hand and looked at her as if she wondered what the big deal was. "By all means."

Grace chose one and slid the box to Jamie. "Help yourself."

With a shake of her head, Jamie said, "I really want to hear what you're thinking about regarding these little gifts he sent. You have to admit it is very sweet *and* romantic."

With the truffle poised at her lips, Grace said, "I'm not

sure what to think other than it's nice to know he's thinking about me."

"True," Jamie said. "And I can assume you've been gracious and thanked him for both gifts?"

Grace rolled her eyes. "I was raised with good manners. I replied with appropriate appreciation." She bit into the confection and sighed. "He does know how to weaken my defenses."

"Aha!" Jamie exclaimed. "I knew it. He's starting to soften your tough shell."

Grace shrugged. She finished the candy and wiped her fingers on a napkin. "Just because he's sent me two little tokens doesn't mean I'm ready to pack up and move to Scotland." She took a sip of her wine and her eyes twinkled. "But I do like knowing I'm on his mind."

Kenzie popped another truffle in her mouth and mumbled, "Do you think Mrs. M is helping him with the ideas?"

Grace shook her head. "I don't think she'd help him. She knew I was pretty upset about the whole thing."

"Mrs. M is Logan's aunt; she would want what is best for him." Kenzie leaned back in the stool and studied Grace. "What are you going to do if the gifts keep coming?"

"That's where I was hoping I could count on the two of you for advice. I don't have a lot of experience with this kind of attention." Grace looked from Jamie to Kenzie. "What would you do?"

Kenzie said, "Well, I guess I'd wait to see what comes next, if anything. Maybe he's done and this was his way to smooth things over with you."

"Maybe." Grace frowned.

Jamie swirled the contents of her glass and avoided looking at Grace.

"Jamie, what do you think?"

Jamie was quiet for a minute and then said, "Enjoy it. Don't read too much into the gifts, like some grand hidden meaning. It seems to be a sweet, old-fashioned way of courting you, and I find it refreshing."

Kenzie piped up, "Jamie's right. It's not like the man can ask you to dinner or a movie or to go for a stroll through the hills."

"I guess so." Grace selected another chocolate. "But he sure has me pegged. The single pink rose and now my favorite truffles." She looked at her sisters. Her gaze sliding from one to the other. "Unless..." She straightened. "Have either of you been talking to him and telling him what my favorite things are?"

Looking sufficiently irritated, Jamie said, "No."

Kenzie followed up with, "Absolutely not."

Jamie continued, "I've never told anyone your weakness for these specific truffles."

Kenzie said, "I thought daisies were your favorite flower, so it's not like I blabbed."

Grace closed the box of candy. "I'm sorry for being so suspicious. It's just that for Logan to have chosen two of my favorite things is uncanny." She cocked her head. "Don't you think?"

Jamie set her glass aside and said, "You spent a lot of time with him; you must have said something."

Grace stared into space. Her forehead crinkled. "Well, he knows about my love affair with all things chocolate, so zeroing in on truffles must have been a fluke. And who wouldn't love a long-stemmed rose? It's so romantic."

"Right now, I'd say he gets my vote for Mr. Romance." Kenzie snickered.

"You should plan on seeing him at Christmas," Jamie suggested.

Grace's head snapped up. "Jamie, is there something you're not telling me?"

"What are you talking about?"

"That tone in your voice is the one you use when you think I should be doing something you feel is best." Grace's eyes narrowed.

Smoothing her long hair off her face, Jamie said. "Not at all. We haven't had Christmas at Gran's house in a long time and while we're there you could spend some time with him."

Kenzie's face fell. "Do you think we'll ever stop calling it Gran's?" With a catch in her voice she continued, "It's been almost two years that she's been gone, and the pain is still sharp."

Grace clasped hands with her sisters, forming a circle. "We will carry her with us forever. One of the things I discovered as I was reading her journals is we are her living legacy."

Jamie squeezed her sisters' hands. "Grace is right, the best way to honor her is by living our best lives. We've made a good start by trying on Great-gran's wedding dress, and two of us have married wonderful men." She beamed as she looked at Grace. "Soon it will be your turn. Then we'll start thinking about the next generation of women who will wear the dress."

Kenzie pulled her hands away. "I wish there was something in Gran's journals that revealed what the next part of our future holds. Something I've been wondering about a lot is, will we have children?"

Jamie's eyes twinkled. "Caleb and I decided after the first of the year we're going to start trying!"

Grace squealed, and Kenzie jumped up and hugged her sister. "That is great news! When can we start talking about cribs and all the stuff that goes with having a baby?"

Jamie laughed. "Girls, we're going to start *trying*. Who knows how long it's going to take to actually get pregnant?"

Kenzie was grinning. "You know what would be totally cool?" She waited half a beat and then said, "I can't believe I'm about to say this, but what if we had babies around the same time and they were girls who could grow up together, like sisters?"

Grace chuckled. "If you don't mind, I'd prefer to be married before having a baby, and I'm missing one crucial component. I kind of need the right guy in my life to even get pregnant."

Kenzie sat down, not defeated, but that familiar look told Grace one thing: she was focused. "Then we need to have you find your happily ever after and get married to the third best guy in the world."

A knowing look came into Jamie's eye. "Grace, we've found the first two, and we're going to make sure you find the third."

Grace couldn't believe that her sisters were so sure she would actually find true love. "Let's not rush things. When it's time for me to find Mr. Right, I will." Her eyes were bright. "After all, I believed in the dress before either of you, and I've looked in the mirror while wearing it."

She felt at peace. "He's coming as fast as he can, but he must have a long journey ahead of him."

CHAPTER 23

Grace walked into her parent's kitchen and discovered Jamie and Kenzie had their heads together over a laptop. Once again, they looked guilty when they saw her. Jamie closed the lid when Grace crossed the room. "What are you two up to?"

Jamie held down the cover and smiled sweetly. "Nothing?"

Pretending to be annoyed, Grace said, "I get the feeling you two are conspiring against me."

Jamie pulled her into a hug. "Never."

Deciding this line of conversation wasn't worth pursuing, Grace said, "What's for dinner?"

Mom came in through the sliding glass door. "We're barbequing, but we'll eat inside. It's going to get chilly later."

"Sounds good." Grace picked a slice of cucumber off the cutting board and popped it in her mouth. "Need any help?"

"Not unless you want to pour drinks." Mom pointed to the refrigerator. "There's iced tea, beer and wine."

Grace opened the cabinet and took down glasses, assuming what everyone's preference would be. "What time are the guys getting here?"

Jamie glanced at her watch. "Caleb should be here in a few minutes." She picked up a stack of plates. "And Robbie will be over soon after. He had to finish up with a client."

Grace leaned against the counter, her arms folded across her stomach. She watched Dad fussing with the grill. "Mom, has Dad ever made you so angry you wanted to spit nails?"

Mom laughed. "Recently or over the years?"

Jamie piped up, "Guess that answers your question, Grace."

"I mean in the early days, when you were getting to know each other."

"Is this about your young man in Scotland?" Mom asked.

"Logan?" Grace asked.

"Yes. Logan." Mom stopped chopping and wiped her hands on a towel. "Grace, sit down. We need to talk."

With a shake of her head, Grace said, "There isn't really anything to talk about. I was curious more than anything."

Mom set the towel on the counter and looked at Jamie and Kenzie.

"Kenzie, we should help Dad." Kenzie followed Jamie out of the kitchen, leaving Mom steering Grace to the table.

"You still think about Logan, don't you?"

Looking glum, she said, "I haven't heard from him in three days. Not a text, a call or email since he sent the chocolates. I thought he was different from other guys I've dated. Then he turns out to be a bigger jerk than most."

"Is it about Logan suggesting you move to Scotland or is this really about your conflicting emotions?"

Grace lifted her face. "I'm not sure what you mean."

"If you fall in love with a man who lives in another country, the only hope of it working out is one of you has to move. From what I've been able to learn, he has several businesses in Europe, and yes, you have a wonderful job, but he suggested you make the sacrifice and move." Mom took her hand. "Leaving your home and family."

Slowly Grace nodded. "That was never part of my plan. I wanted to get married, have my children live in the same small town as I did and grow old here, with my family."

Sympathetically Mom said, "And your feelings about him have changed that mental picture?"

"Yeah, you could say that." Grace looked out the window toward her sisters. "They got lucky, marrying guys who want to live here."

Gently, Mom said, "Dad moved to Vermont to be with me."

"I know, but he's a guy."

"He still loved his hometown and left his family and friends to marry me, and it worked out."

"Don't you think it's easier for a guy? Aren't they expected to strike out on their own and find their path in life?"

"No, I don't think it was easier for him, but we compromised by spending our summers at the farm. I always knew that one day, after retirement, we'd spend more time in Scotland, and I'm okay with that."

"What about when we start having kids? Won't you miss out on important milestones?"

"For all the important things we'll be there." Mom patted her hand. "Grace, only you'll know if you can move from this town and, more importantly, from your sisters."

Grace's shoulders slumped. "It's just hard to think of

not seeing them whenever I want." She brightened. "Maybe everyone would want to move."

Chuckling Mom said, "That would be convenient, but not practical."

"Well, he did send me a long-stemmed rose the other day, and then the truffles."

Mom's eyes widened. "Now that is very romantic."

Their conversation was cut short as the kitchen door burst opened and Caleb and Robbie came in, talking like they had been best friends for their entire lives. "Hey, Liv," Caleb said. "Where are the girls?"

Mom pointed out the back. Hurrying out onto the deck, they swooped their wives off their feet with laughs and kisses.

Grace sighed wistfully. "That's what I'd love to have."

"You will, Grace."

Dad called out, "Dinner's ready."

"Let's continue this conversation later, but are you okay for now?"

Grace gave her mom a half-hearted smile. "I'm fine. Don't worry."

"Telling a mother to not worry is like asking the sun not to shine." She gave Grace a quick peck on the cheek. "I always find the best way to discover my heart's desire is to really listen to what it's trying to tell me." Mom patted her on the shoulder. "Now help me get dinner on the table."

Grace had a pen poised over a pad, ready to take down the details of their holiday vacation. "When do we plan on leaving?" She didn't ask anyone in particular. "Christmas is on a Thursday, and I have call the previous weekend until Monday at six."

Jamie had the laptop open, ready to start looking for flights. "AM?" she asked.

Grace chuckled. "I wish, but sadly PM."

Kenzie and Robbie looked at each other. She said, "We were planning on going over the Sunday before Christmas. We want to do some hiking."

Dad beamed, his brogue pronounced as he said, "That's a good Scottish lass and lad. It might be a bit wet as typically there is a fifty percent chance of rain every day. We don't see the sun pretty much the entire month."

Robbie pushed back the chair to get another cup of coffee. "I told Kenzie we'd hike at least one day. Hopefully we'll get lucky and that will be the day it doesn't rain." He grinned. "And I've been told we'll be taking a side trip to Rosemarkie and a few other destinations. I'm not sure how we're going to fit in any holiday festivities with Kenz's itinerary."

"I want to show you all the most important spots to me." Kenzie pretended to pout and Robbie relented with a grin.

"We'll go wherever you want, my darling wife."

She perked up and said, "Jamie, do you and Caleb want to go over with us?"

Jamie was tapping the keyboard. "Caleb and I will fly over with Grace." She looked at Grace from the corner of her eye. "Is that okay with you?"

"Sure. Mom, when are you and Dad flying over?" Grace asked, turning Jamie's laptop in her direction.

"We've talked about going over after Thanksgiving. We're going to give the house a thorough cleaning and stock the cupboards and fridge. Also, I want to get a few batches of cookies baked."

Kenzie piped up, "We can get whatever we need from MacMeekin's."

Grace smacked the table with the palm of her hand. "Absolutely not. We have to have all our traditional cookies and breads, otherwise it won't feel like Christmas."

"But," Kenzie sputtered, "We love all the special Scottish goodies too. Especially Ecclefechan tarts, with all those nuts, dried fruit and a buttery pastry shell." She smacked her lips. "I can taste them now, and Mrs. M's are the best ever. Well, except for Gran's."

Caleb held up his hand. "Why don't I take on the task of a few specialty items? If you tell me what you have to have, I'll try them here. When I get to Scotland, I'm sure your grandmother has the recipes written down. While Kenzie and Robbie are doing their thing, Jamie and I can shop and get what we need."

Mom got up from the table and hurried over to a cabinet. Over her shoulder she said, "Caleb, Arabel gave me some recipes when James and I got married. I'm a terrible baker, but maybe there's something that might help you."

She pushed aside a few cookbooks and found a soft leather-bound book. She flipped open the cover and smiled. "I stand corrected, it's not Arabel's, it was your Great-grandmother Anne's." She handed the book to Caleb. "I'm sure there's gold tucked in between those covers."

Carefully he opened the first page. "This has to be over a hundred years old." He turned the yellowed pages, pausing to scan the handwritten notes. He looked at Liv. "Do you mind if I take this home tonight? I'll bring it back in a couple of days, after I copy over some of these ideas."

James cleared his throat. "I think you and Jamie should take it now. After all, a professional chef should be the next custodian of our food heritage."

Caleb looked at Jamie. With a laugh he said, "It's your book, but do us all a favor and let me do the actual cooking."

Warm laughter filled the room. Jamie said, "We all know I'm not the cook in the family." Worriedly, she looked at Kenzie and Grace. "Do either of you want the book?"

Kenzie shook her head. "Not me. I can cook, but I'm happy to let Caleb do it."

Grace looked at her sisters. "Maybe I could have a copy of a few recipes, like the tarts and cream buns?"

Relief washed over Jamie's face. "Of course. We'll copy whatever you want."

"Then I'm fine with Caleb being the family chef."

He chuckled. "Seems I was just appointed to keep this family fed in good Scottish tradition."

Robbie piped up, "Better you than me. But while you're becoming proficient in your technique, maybe you could try your skill at cooking the traditional *tipsy laird* served in honor of the first Robbie Burns, the Scot poet."

"Yeah, I can definitely do that." Caleb bent his head low over the book and was instantly captivated by the notes written in the margins. "Jamie, your great-grandmother had to have been very busy perfecting each recipe."

She nodded appreciatively. "Caleb, let's finish making our plans before we lose you entirely into that cookbook." Teasing, she added, "I know how you love to read anything to do with food."

Reluctantly he closed the cover and looked around the room with a sheepish grin. "Sorry."

James said, "Son, I'm glad you're interested in our past."

Grace rapped on the tabletop with her knuckles. "If we're all finished talking about what we're going to be eating during the holidays, can we get back to the plans of actually getting there? Flights, rental cars and the like. It's all about logistics."

Jamie smiled. "You're right. What do you see for flights for the three of us?"

Grace clicked some keys and said, "There's a late-night flight out of Boston and returns on the third of January. Price isn't bad either."

Kenzie said, "Can you check for me and Robbie?"

With a few key strokes Grace said, "If you were to leave late on Friday, it's a lot cheaper than waiting until Saturday."

Robbie pulled his wallet out of his back pocket and said, "Book it. Arriving a day earlier would be perfect."

Kenzie winked at her new husband. "A little extra time before the bustle. Maybe we could spend the night in Glasgow before heading out to the farm. A mini honeymoon night."

Grace snorted. "Isn't every night like a honeymoon for all of you?" She jabbed a finger in both Jamie's and Kenzie's directions.

The girls pretended to swoon and everyone chuckled. A stab of longing hit Grace hard. Was it more than luck? It had to have been the magic of the dress. Maybe she should have brought it back to the States with her.

No, Gran specifically stated I needed to take the dress to Scotland. If she had wanted me to bring it home she would have told me.

As Grace was sipping tea, her cell rang. She glanced at caller id. "Hi Mom."

"Hi Grace. You rushed out of the house after dinner before we could finish our conversation."

"There isn't much else to talk about." Grace's eyes drifted to the rose, the edges of the petals were beginning to turn brown and curl just a bit. "He was being thoughtful."

"I agree, but what do you think is next?"

"Who knows? Maybe I'll see him when we're in Scotland. I could ask him to come out to the farm for a little party." Warming to the idea Grace asked, "Could we have something on Boxing Day?"

When Mom didn't respond immediately, Grace said, "Do you think that's a bad idea?"

Hurriedly Mom said, "No, in fact I think it is a great idea. We can invite Patrick and his family, Flora and a few other neighbors. It will be a wonderful way to keep the festivities rolling right to the New Year's Eve celebration."

Grace relaxed. "I'll text Jamie and Kenzie to let them know about the party, and I'll even put together a formal invitation to send."

"Let me know what you need from me."

Grace could hear the excitement in her mom's voice. She always loved a good party. "Well, I was thinking when you and Dad get over there, could you mail them? And I'll list Gran's phone number for RSVPs."

"That's a great idea."

"I'll keep it on the smaller side."

"We have plenty of room for people to mingle, so let's plan on having a great party." Mom laughed.

Grace smiled into the phone. "Hey, Mom?"

"Yes?"

"Thanks for calling tonight. I was feeling a little blue, and now that I can invite Logan out to the farm for the party, well, who knows what will happen?"

CHAPTER 24

It seemed like everyone in town had some sort of nasty cold or flu bug. Grace had spent most of the weekend working at the hospital. Since it was Sunday afternoon she hoped for a little respite from running to the hospital, at least for a couple of hours.

Before kicking back on the sofa, Grace saw a box on the kitchen counter. She had gotten a text from Mom saying she was dropping it off. Curious, she popped open the top and discovered Mom had found a classic invitation for Boxing Day. Grace smiled to herself. They were perfect right down to the MacLellan plaid, but the downside was that the interior was blank. Grace would have to handwrite each one. She had a light bulb moment—she would pick up some fancy paper, print the details off the computer and paste them inside.

Her cell phone buzzed with an incoming text. Expecting to see a group message from her sisters, a slow smile spread across her face.

Thinking of you—L

She hugged the phone to her chest and grinned.

Looking at the message again she wondered, *What should I text back?*

She tapped out *Thank you* and studied the screen. "Well, that's not quite enough."

She deleted it, set the phone down and yawned. Going through the motions, she made a pot of tea, all the while glancing at the phone. She had to say something, right? Otherwise he'd think she was being rude.

She picked up the phone again. "I don't want it to seem like I'm just waiting for a text." She did some shoulder rolls, as if preparing for a boxing match. Laughing at herself, she typed *Hope you're doing well.* Before she could change her mind, she hit send.

Whoosh. An incoming text. *All is good from across the pond.*

With a soft laugh she responded, *Here too. Long day at work, going to take a nap.*

A quick whoosh again. *Sleep well.*

"Someone is sitting by the phone." The kettle on the stove whistled and Grace put the phone aside. She was dragging. Hopefully the chamomile tea would send her to dreamland for a short while, and with any luck she wouldn't be needed at the hospital any time soon.

It was midday when Logan strode into his office, a man on a mission. He connected his laptop to the dock station and attached the cord from his camera to the computer. He had spent the morning getting the last photos for the book he was working on.

Pulling on the zipper, he flipped open his laptop bag and pulled out a slim hardbound book. He opened the cover and lightly ran his fingertips over the words he had written so many years ago. How could three chance meetings and a couple of weeks change how he viewed the world around him? To open his heart to a new possibility was terrifying. Especially after the overwhelming losses he had suffered. But Grace was worth the risk.

Closing it, he called out, "Tracey? Can you come in here, please?" He laid the book aside along with an envelope with Grace's name scrawled boldly across it.

"Logan, I didn't know you were here. Is everything okay?"

"You weren't at your desk when I got in." Beaming, Logan said, "Everything is fantastic. I've been roaming the spectacular Highlands taking pictures for a book I'm making for Grace. After that I swung by Aunt Flora's house." He held out the book and envelope to Tracey. "Would you mind sending this for me, express?"

Tracey looked at the well-worn book. She looked into Logan's eyes. "Are you sure you want to send this book?"

His head bobbed. "I do."

"All right then, I'll get it out and she should have it in two days." Tracey turned to leave and paused mid-step. "This is the most heartfelt and personal gift you could send to her."

A lump lodged in his throat. "I know she'll enjoy it."

Without another word Tracey left the room, softly closing the door behind her.

Focusing on the task at hand, Logan began the difficult process of selecting a few of the best photos he had taken and saved them to his hard drive. "This will make a wonderful Christmas gift." His office phone rang and he answered. "Hello?"

An unfamiliar female voice asked, "Is this Logan Campbell?"

"It is, who's this?"

"Jamie MacLellan Sullivan. I'm..."

Logan interrupted, "Grace's sister." He stood up. "Is she okay?" A vise constricted his heart.

"Yes, Grace is fine, and for the record she doesn't know I'm calling you. I'd appreciate it if you'd keep the conversation strictly between us."

Curiosity piqued, he said, "I won't make any promises until I know why you're calling me."

A soft laugh, which sounded just like Grace, answered him. "I can live with that," Jamie said.

Logan dropped to his chair. "So, tell me, how can I help you?"

"I think the better question is how can I—well, we, my sister Kenzie and I—help you get back into Grace's good graces?"

Logan could swear he could hear the laughter in her voice. "I think I'm doing just fine on my own."

"I'll admit you're making a bit of headway with her, but wouldn't you like to know what makes Grace tick?" Jamie's voice held a hint of a challenge.

"What exactly do you know about our relationship?" He leaned back, settling in for what promised to be a most interesting conversation.

"We know that you tried to throw your bank account around and convince Grace to drop everything and move to Scotland." She cleared her throat and continued, "Which I have to ask, do you know *anything* about women?"

He bit back a sharp retort and said, "The women I usually meet would jump at the chance I gave to Grace." He shook his head, not believing what had just come out of his mouth.

She laughed. "And that tells me a lot."

"What?" he snapped.

"Logan, relax. We're on your side."

This woman was exasperating. "Good to know." He sighed. "Jamie, I'm sorry I've been curt. Please, do tell me why you have called."

It sounded like she clapped her hands together. "Okay, so here's the upshot. The rose and truffles were a nice touch. She really thought they were sweet, but how do you plan to follow up on them?"

He hesitated. "Would you support a future between your sister and me, even if it meant her having to live in Scotland part of the time?"

Slowly she asked, "So, you were serious about her moving?"

"Aye, my business is here." The silence became extended, Logan wondered if they had been disconnected. "Jamie?"

Finally, he heard her say, "Do you have strong feelings for Grace?"

He wasn't sure why, but he felt compelled to speak his truth. "I've never felt about another girl the way I do for Grace. I know it makes no sense, but the very first time I saw her on the plane and our eyes met, it was like—oh hell, it's not something I can explain."

"Maybe I can," Jamie interjected. "It was like an unbreakable invisible thread connected you to her."

He knew his mouth gaped open.

"And once you started to get to know her you just knew you had to know more?"

"Did Grace tell you that?"

"No. It's how I felt the first time I saw my husband. My sisters and I were having dinner and he came into the same restaurant. We didn't speak until later that night, but I was instantly drawn to him."

It was Logan's turn to be silent.

Jamie continued, "For Kenzie it was different. She and

Robbie, her husband, have been best friends since they were babies, but for my parents, that's how they knew."

"Knew?"

"The person their heart searched for."

Jamie stated with simplicity, but it scared the hell out of Logan. He protested, "I didn't say I wanted to marry her, I just want to spend time with her, get to know her."

Soft laughter answered him.

"Jamie?"

"Logan?"

In his soul he knew Jamie spoke the truth. He wasn't ready to admit it to her before he made peace with his feelings. "I'm sending her a book of poems."

"She'll love it," Jamie assured him. "But what else do you plan to do? Keep sending her small gifts in hopes that will win her back?"

"No," he stated. "I have a plan."

"Good! How can we help?" Jamie asked.

"At the moment I'm going to keep my cards close to my vest, but if I do need something, I'll be sure to let you know."

"Well, if you say so."

Logan could hear the hesitation in her voice. "Jamie, you'll need to trust me."

"Let me give you Kenzie's and my cell phone numbers. Just in case."

With a wry shake of his head, he picked up a pen, poised over paper. "Go ahead."

She rattled off the two phone numbers. "Call any time."

"Thank you, Jamie. And I promise this conversation will stay just between us."

"Logan, Grace has a huge heart, and that means it bruises and bleeds. Please don't hurt her."

In a deep, strong voice, he said, "I would never do anything to hurt Grace."

He disconnected the phone and pushed his chair from his desk, lacing his fingers behind his head. He leaned back. Grace's face danced in front of his closed eyes. He longed to let his fingers follow the curve of her cheek, tilting her lips toward his.

"Logan?"

He snapped out of his daydream. "What's up, Tracey?"

She held out a small slip of paper. "I thought you might like the tracking number for the package."

Logan took it and tucked it into his jacket pocket. "Thanks."

She studied him. "I know you're scheduled to leave on Thursday for Boston, but don't you think we should get a few pesky details about the new hotel wrapped up before you leave?"

He ran his hand through his hair. "Are you trying to tell me in the nicest way possible to focus on the business at hand?"

She shrugged one shoulder. "If you keep busy, the time will go by much quicker."

"You are a very wise person." He got up. "Coffee first, and then we'll get down to business."

With a smirk, she nudged his shoulder. "Are you buying?"

"Nah. I think you're buying." He draped his arm around the older woman's shoulder. "You know, if it wasn't for you and Aunt Flora, I would have become totally self-absorbed after Mom and Lisa died, and then losing Dad too." He shook his head. His voice thick, he said, "That just made losing them hurt all the more."

Tracey looked up at him. "Your mother was one of my

best friends, and I know she would have done the same if our roles had been reversed."

They waited for the elevator. His voice was filled with nostalgia, he said, "Instead of coffee, let's have lunch. Mum always said if you had a lot of work to do it was best to be well nourished; it helps the brain cells or something."

They stepped in the elevator, Tracey and Logan rode in silence. As the elevator came to a halt Tracey said, "Eva would have approved of what you're doing regarding Grace."

Logan gave her a one-armed hug. "Lisa and Grace would have been great friends and Mom and Dad would have loved her."

CHAPTER 25

The start of Grace's week was uneventful. If her sisters had asked she would never admit it, but she was disappointed she hadn't received another gift from Logan. It wasn't the gifts themselves—they showed the very handsome Scot was thinking of her. She had wondered if she crossed his mind as many times in the course of a day that he did for her.

A large brown delivery van was pulling away from her house as she drove down her street. Her heart quickened. She wasn't expecting anything. Could Logan have sent her another little something?

Hurriedly she parked and without bothering to grab her bags she half ran to the back entrance where a small box leaned against the door. Her breath caught as she looked at the return address. Scotland.

Standing on the back step, she ripped open the box. Nestled inside was a slim, bubble-wrapped item. She tore at the tape and folded back the plastic bubbles. It was an old, well-loved book. She opened the cover and read the inscription.

To Lisa, who's always quoting her favorite poet, Emily Dickinson. Logan

Her mouth fell open. Who was Lisa and why would Logan send Grace this book? She marched back to her car, resisting the urge to fling the book on the ground. Grabbing her bags, she slung them over her shoulders and went toward the door, her steps slowing. Wait, wasn't that the name of Logan's twin? It was too late to call Flora, so how else could she confirm this was his sister's book?

She pushed open the back door and placed her bags on the table. She turned on a few lights and hurried into her office. She could do a quick search on the internet of Logan and his sister.

She hesitated. She should just go with the idea that he had sent her something that was dear to him. Mom would know what to do.

She rushed from the room and grabbed her handbag and book. It was almost dinnertime, but her parents wouldn't care if she dropped by. Besides, this was important.

Breezing in the back door, she caught her parents in a lip lock. "Mom! Dad!"

They pulled apart and Mom laughed. "Grace, we didn't know you were stopping by."

With a snicker she said, "Obviously."

"Lass, come in. We'll have tea." Dad pecked Mom's lips before taking the kettle to the sink for a fill up.

Mom grasped her hand and pulled her toward the table. "Sit." She flashed Dad a look.

"I saw that," Grace said. "You don't need to worry. I'm fine."

Mom set up the infuser and teapot, and Dad waved her toward the table. "I'll make the tea. Liv, you sit and see to Grace."

"Why do you think I have something to talk about?" Grace's eyes slid from her father to her mother.

"You've always worn your emotions on your face. Which is why you're no good at poker." Dad wagged his finger at her. "When your eyebrows have that crinkle in them, it's a dead giveaway you've got a bee in your bonnet."

The kettle began to sing. Grace decided to show Mom the book. "I got this today." She passed it across the table.

Mom read the inscription on the cover and her brow arched. "Lisa?"

Grace stated, "I think it might be his sister's. She died in an accident with his mom when he was a teenager."

Mom set the book on the table. "This is a very special gift." She patted her hand. "What are you thinking of doing?"

Her heart thumped. "I should send it back to him. He needs to keep it."

"Why?" Dad cleared his throat. "He obviously wanted you to have it."

Grace looked at him. "Dad, what do you think?"

"He wouldn't have sent it to you if he didn't want you to have it." He busied himself with pouring water over the tea. "Did you call him to say thank you?"

"It's close to midnight there. I'm not going to wake him up."

Mom suggested, "Grace, what about sending a text? At least this way when he gets up he'll know you received the book."

She said slowly, "I could, but the book is very special. I feel like I should speak with him."

Dad set the pot on the table. "Good manners are always appreciated, just as a thoughtful gift is as well."

Grace poured the hot liquid into the mugs. Satisfied she

had a plan, she said, "I'll send him something when I get home. We can enjoy our tea and then you two can get back to smooching."

"No need to rush off, lass, stay for dinner. Mom and I can lock lips later."

"No, really, I need to get home. My PJs are calling me." She took a sip of tea and smiled. "Chamomile. Perfect choice."

Dad grinned. "I always know what my girls need and maybe even sometimes before they know themselves."

Mom picked up her teacup, did the cheers gesture and said, "It's years of observation, my love."

Dad chuckled. "You don't need to burst my bubble. I was kind of hoping I had gotten more in tune with my daughters."

Grace laughed. "Oh Dad."

Curled up in soft cotton pajamas, Grace snuggled under an afghan with a glass of wine and the book of poetry. They were poems of love. Based on the inscription, Emily Dickinson must have been Lisa's favorite and it certainly was very sweet of Logan to give it to her. Grace guessed the random thoughts scribbled on some of the pages were Lisa's. They gave her a glimpse into what the teenage girl was thinking, hope of finding love as it was described by the poet.

Grace's cell phone sat on the table. It was as if it was calling to her. She didn't know what to say to Logan. Sharing this book with her was so unexpected and *very* personal. Her heart was filled with love from this simple gesture.

She picked up the phone and wrote a new text. *Logan,*

Sharing Lisa's book of poetry has left me speechless. Thinking of you. G

She reread the message and hit send. Setting the phone aside, she toyed with her wine glass. If she had been in his shoes would she have told someone on the first few dates she was wealthy? Probably not. Maybe she really had misjudged him. He was just being cautious. She couldn't wait to send the invitation for the party and hoped he'd agree to come.

I really want to see him. It would be so much simpler if Logan lived at least within driving distance. I wonder what Gran would say if she was here.

She opened the first page and started to read the poem before her thoughts drifted to the day when she had fallen into the waterfalls. Gran had written she needed to go there, but why was Logan there too? She knew he was a workaholic, so to play hooky from work to go traipsing on the trail…had it been a mere coincidence that he appeared? And what about the airport and the market? Maybe once was by chance, but all three? Could Gran have been an angel pushing things around to suit what she had wanted? After all, Grace got the distinct impression from Flora that the two old friends had longed to have them get to know each other. No, it was the dress that held the magic, not Gran.

But Gran hadn't interfered like this with Jamie and Kenzie. Could there have been more to Gran's individual letters to her sisters, like hers it was specific to go back to Scotland? Grabbing her cell phone, she sent a group text.

J, K. Do you still have Gran's last letters to you? Can I see them?

She hit send and waited. Maybe there was a clue in their letters that would help her piece some of this together.

The responses came in one right after the other. Both said yes and yes.

Let's meet at the gym tomorrow after work and bring them with you.

They answered with thumbs-up emoji's. Grace tossed her phone on the sofa and took a sip of wine. Could the letters be the key that would unlock what she would need to do next, or would they be just another puzzle piece in this already intricate and mysterious journey she was on?

Sighing, Grace knew she would have to wait less than twenty-four hours to see what would come next.

With pep in her step, Grace pulled open the heavy glass door at Mac's Gym. Kenzie was sitting behind the counter, totally engrossed in whatever was on her computer screen.

Grace knocked on the counter "Earth to Kenz."

Kenzie held up a finger and grumbled, "Hold on a sec."

Being ever cheerful, Grace prodded, "What are you working on?"

Finally, Kenzie looked up and frowned. "A spreadsheet. My accountant wants to file my quarterly taxes and I have a few more items to tally up before she'll do her portion."

Grace's brow crinkled. "Don't you use Jamie?"

"Of course I do. But she insists I do part of the tedious work—she says it will help me understand where my money is going and some other BS."

Grace could hear the frustration in her sister's voice, and she could empathize. Jamie made her suffer through taxes every year, just so she understood about her money too. "Sorry, sis."

With a dismissive wave of her hand, Kenzie pushed back from the desk. "Are you going to work out tonight?"

"No. I'm exhausted. I thought I'd grab the letters and head home."

Kenzie draped an arm around Grace's shoulders. "Some light cardio is just what the doctor ordered." With a smirk, she said, "Or I could always do a spin class for you and Jamie."

With a shake of her head, Grace groaned. "Heavens no. That'll put me over the edge." She looped her arm through Kenzie's. "Is Jamie here yet?"

"She's changing. I've already convinced her that we should do spin." Kenzie laughed. "But considering you're seriously tired, we can do some light biking or the treadmill."

With a snort Grace said, "I appreciate that you're taking pity on your baby sister."

Kenzie held open the locker room door and gestured for her to go inside. "Meet you in the cardio room."

The door softly whooshed closed behind her. Jamie was securing her hair into a high ponytail. Grace dropped her bag on the bench.

"Jeez, you look whipped," Jamie said as she crossed the small room, pulling Grace into a quick hug.

Surprised, Grace said, "What was that for?"

Jamie tugged one of Grace's curls. "You look like you could use one."

"I could use more than that, and now Kenzie insists I work out. How do I let the two of you talk me into so many different things when I don't want to do them?" She pulled her top off and tossed it on the bench in a heap. Jamie picked it up and folded it. "It's been that way since we were kids. When either of you come up with a bright idea, there I am, following along."

"You've always known how brilliant the two of us are, and to go in a different direction would just be a waste of time as you'd eventually follow us anyway." Jamie smirked. "It really is easier this way."

Grace finished changing as Jamie put her folded clothes on top of her bag. "You don't need to pick up after me."

Jamie's brow shot up. Quietly she said, "Just being nice, squirt." She picked up her water bottle and said, "Ready?"

Annoyed with herself for snapping, she grabbed her bottle and followed Jamie. "As ready as I'll ever be." She paused at the water bubbler to fill up her bottle. Jamie handed Grace her bottle for a fill-up too.

Kenzie waved at them from inside the cardio room. As Grace secured the top on her bottle she said, "Once we get going, I want to talk about this idea that's been running through my brain about Gran and her plans for our futures."

Jamie cocked her head. "Like how much of our lives it seems she tried to plan out for us, and you in particular?"

With a quick nod, Grace said, "How many times do things happen where they're no longer by chance or were somehow planned?"

Jamie's eyes grew wide. "She can't do anything from beyond the grave."

"Well, how do we know for sure what she can do? The woman was a force of nature."

Jamie laughed. "That's the pot calling the kettle black."

The sisters walked through the door and Kenzie stepped on a treadmill, starting at a slow, steady pace. "What took you two so long? I could have walked a hundred miles while waiting for you."

"Ha ha. Such an exaggeration." Grace grinned. "You do have a flair for the dramatic." She hopped on a bike and punched a few buttons on the keypad. "I'm doing the level one and nobody pick on me either."

Kenzie held up her hands. “We wouldn’t dream of teasing you. I’m just glad you’re moving.”

Jamie began a brisk walk and glanced at her sister. “Are you going to keep us in suspense or tell us what’s on your mind?”

Grace hesitated and took a drink before placing it in the holder in front of her. “Well…” Her thoughts fell into sequence. “What if somehow Gran orchestrated some of what happened to each of us, more specifically me and Logan? I know she and Flora had their heads together before Gran died. Maybe somehow she’s the real magic and it doesn’t have anything to do with the enchanted thread used to sew the wedding dress.”

CHAPTER 26

Kenzie snorted. "Like a puppet master? You're giving Gran far too much credit from beyond."

Grace's curls bounced as she increased the speed on the bike. "Well, maybe for you two—other than sending the dress—but I really feel that she has done something more when it comes to me and Logan." She glanced at Jamie. "You're pretty quiet. What do you think?"

Jamie kept her pace on the treadmill. "You said that in your letter Gran insisted you try the dress on over there. What is your working theory?"

Grace stated, "I think the magic was limited and I needed to take it back to Scotland, to Gran's house."

"How on earth did you come up with that idea?" Kenzie asked.

With her head held high Grace stated, "Everyone knows magic is based on energy. Stands to reason. There is more magic in Scotland with the fairies."

"I don't think the magic can be drained, as you put it, from the dress. It was all about the thread and Great-gran

Anne sewing it." Stifling a laugh, Kenzie said, "But Gracie, I can see you've given this a great deal of thought."

"Of course I did. I had a long flight to think about why on earth Gran wanted me to go to the farm, and it's the only thing I could come up with."

Jamie mused, "You said she and Flora were probably hoping that you would run into Logan." She took a drink of water. "Did Gran say anything else in her letter, at least what you can remember?"

Grace paused, then haltingly said, "She did say I needed to follow my heart and that I had always followed your path. It was time for a change."

"And?" Jamie prodded. "That is something Gran would have seen."

Grace cast her a blank look. Mildly irritated she said, "So?"

"What happened when you got there?" Kenzie asked.

"Um, well, let's see. I almost had the dress stolen."

"Which led you to who?" Kenzie pushed.

"Logan?"

"Exactly, and then you get to the farm and what happened?"

Jamie remained quiet.

"I ran into Tait?" Grace's brow wrinkled. "Is that where you're going with your questions?"

"Yes. Maybe Gran hoped you'd meet a nice man in Scotland and fall in love." Kenzie concluded, "You did meet two very different men. The first person you see is Logan and you happen to have the dress with you. The second is Tait, who has always been a friend. Maybe having spent time with both of them was a way for you to open your eyes and see who really melded with your heart."

Exasperated Grace groaned, "Girls, the bigger point is they both live in Scotland."

Jamie said, "They do, and Gran said you needed to step out of our shadow and into your very own spotlight. Maybe that's what she meant."

Grace's eyes grew wide and in a hushed tone asked, "Move to Scotland?"

Jamie gave a little laugh. "You make it sound like it's the end of the universe."

She blinked hard. "I always thought we would be the Three Musketeers forever. We'd be the kind of sisters who live near each other, go to get their hair done and shop for orthotic shoes and stuff, just always be together."

Kenzie grimaced. "I don't want to think about us getting really old and decrepit for a very long time." She brightened. "However, I'm looking forward to when we have kids. They'll play together and go to school together. A nice big extended family."

Grace's face fell. "See, if I were living anywhere but here I'd miss out on spending time with your kids."

Jamie slowed the treadmill to a stop. "Grace, it won't matter where we live, we will always be close. Geography won't change that. You need to remember how close we were to Gran. It didn't matter she lived in Scotland."

Grace stopped pedaling. Pushing her frizzy curls from her face she said, "I'm just not going to think about it." She slid off the bike and grabbed her water bottle. "If I can take your letters I'm going to head home. This conversation has put me in the dumps."

"Grace, give us a few minutes to get changed. We'll reconvene at your place," Kenzie suggested. "We can read the letters together and see if we can come up anything new."

With her eyes downcast, Grace said, "No. You go home to your husbands. I'm going to get a pint and dive in."

Jamie's eyebrow arched. "A pint of?"

Grace looked up. "Ice cream. Of course."

"Better make it three if you're stopping at the store. And no frozen yogurt either. I want the premium brand with all the yummy add-ins." Jamie licked her lips. "Now that is what I call a treat."

Grace could tell by the look on Kenzie's face that she was trying to pretend she was against the idea of pint diving, but the twinkle in her eye gave her away.

Kenzie made sure the door was closed before asking Jamie, "So what do you think this all means?"

"Are you asking if I think magic had something to do with Grace running into Logan?"

Kenzie nodded and, in a rush, said, "Yeah. I mean, I know—well, I think—it's not possible, but I've been more open-minded about things I don't understand since the dress arrived. You met Caleb and fell in love. I opened my eyes and discovered the love of my life had been by my side forever."

Jamie listened as Kenzie rambled on without taking a single breath. Needing to be productive, Jamie grabbed a cleaning cloth and wiped down the sinks while Kenzie spritzed the shower stalls with vinegar. She measured her words carefully. "In my opinion we should read the letters together. I never read Grace's; I only know what she read to us. There might be a few key phrases she's overlooked." She rinsed out the sink. "But if I was to guess, I'd say Gran and Flora put their heads together and hoped, at some point, Logan and Grace would meet. After all, Logan is Flora's nephew. And the dress gets us to see a different future. That is Great-gran's legacy."

Kenzie leaned against the wall pondering what Jamie was saying. "But how could they have arranged for Grace and Logan to bump into each other at the market, or the attempt to steal the dress and Logan running after the thief and finally the whole adventure at Rosemarkie?"

Shrugging Jamie said, "I haven't a clue. I was trying to be logical, but you make a good point. There is no way Gran and Flora could have arranged all of that before Gran died."

Kenzie rubbed her hands over her arms. "I just got goose bumps."

Scooping up the spray bottle, Jamie said, 'I'm going to get going and I'll meet you at Grace's soon, right?"

"I'm ten minutes behind you," Kenzie reassured her.

"Where is Kenzie?" Grace demanded of Jamie. "I thought you said she was on her way." She glanced at the clock and then peered out the front window, growing increasingly concerned. "It's not like her to be thirty minutes late and not call." Before the words were even out of her mouth, Jamie's cell rang.

"Hello?" Her brow furrowed. "Is she all right?"

Grace pulled on Jamie's arm, mouthing the word *what?*

Jamie held up a finger. "We're on our way." She nodded. "Grace will call Mom and Dad." She grabbed her bag. "That was Robbie. Kenzie is being taken to the ER—she hit a deer."

Grace was right on her heels. "How bad is she hurt?"

Looking over her shoulder, Jamie said, "I'm not sure. I'll drive. You call Mom and Dad."

They hopped in the car, and as Jamie was backing down

the drive Grace was talking to Mom. "Kenzie was in a car accident. Meet us at the ER. We're on our way."

She hung up and called Caleb, explaining to him what had happened.

"Caleb said to drive carefully and he'll meet us there too." Without looking at her sister Grace said, "There's one thing about our family—when something happens, we're there for each other. No questions asked."

Jamie glanced her way. "It's what family does."

The large glass doors opened and Grace strode in. She glanced around the room and didn't see Robbie. Approaching the desk, she said in a clear, commanding voice, "Joyce, I'm looking for my sister, Kenzie Burns."

"Hi Grace, she's inside and her husband is with her. Take a breath, it looks like she has a small laceration on her forehead from hitting the side window but otherwise just a few bumps and bruises."

Grace turned to Jamie. "Wait here for Mom and Dad. I'm going to check on her and I'll be right back."

She pushed open the swinging door and her gaze roamed over the cubicles. All were empty except for one. Kenzie's sneakers were barely visible, but she could see Robbie standing at the end of the bed.

Her heart rate slowed. Since the staff wasn't rushing around she knew, based on experience, Kenzie's injuries weren't serious. She stepped around the privacy curtain and didn't disguise the relief she felt. Keeping her voice light, she said, "Kenzie, it's not deer season yet."

Kenzie kept her upper body rigid as she turned around. "Stupid deer. Jumped right out in front of the car and hit the windshield." Her fingers grazed the bump on her head, careful not to touch the bandage covering the laceration. Tears welled up in her eyes. "I don't think the deer was lucky. She wasn't moving."

Robbie rubbed her hand. "The important thing is you're okay."

Grace stepped around the bed. "Mind if I take a look?"

Kenzie tipped her head back slightly and looked at her sister. "The doctor just left. I think I'm getting a couple of stitches."

"I'm going to wash my hands and get a penlight." Giving Kenzie a bright smile, she said, "I'll be right back."

Joyce was waiting in the doorway and handed her a lab coat. "I figured you'd want to examine her."

Grace gave her a smile. "Thanks. You know me so well." She slipped the coat on and went to the hand-washing station. After lathering up and rinsing thoroughly, she grabbed a penlight and hurried back to Kenzie.

Grace slowed as she walked toward the couple. Their voices were low and Robbie seemed to be reassuring Kenz. She stopped. Like a ton of bricks, it hit her. This was why she couldn't pick up and move to another country—her family needed her, for these kinds of emergencies. Who could they count on when they had kids, or as her parents got older? It was going to happen and she was the only family member with the expertise to take care of them.

Straightening her shoulders, she pushed all thoughts of Logan from her mind. Her place was here.

"I'm back." Kenzie was lying back on the pillows with her eyes partially closed. "Is anything wrong, Kenz?"

With a rueful laugh, she said, "The lights are so bright. I need sunglasses."

In an imitation of the Big Bad Wolf, Grace teased, "The better to see you with, my dear."

Kenzie scowled. "You are *so* not funny."

Turning to the business at hand, Grace requested Kenzie sit up. Robbie slipped his arm behind Kenzie's back.

"Any dizziness?" Grace clicked the light on and flashed it in each eye and back again. She gently prodded the bump on Kenzie's head. "Does this hurt?"

Kenzie grimaced. "Only when you touch it."

Grace swallowed her laugh. "Can you squeeze my hands?" Kenzie did as she asked. Grace winced. "You don't need to break my fingers."

"I thought you were trying to see how strong I am." A twinkle appeared in Kenzie's eye.

Grace went through the remainder of the exam. "Based on my assessment, you don't have a concussion, and once you're stitched up I'm sure you can go home."

Robbie exhaled. "Thank goodness. We've seen enough of hospital rooms for a long time. Remember she's a terrible patient, which I learned firsthand last year when she broke her wrist and ankle."

Kenzie groaned. "Don't remind me."

Grace spritzed her hands with sanitizer. "I'll see how long before someone will be in to stitch you up and release you. I'll run out front and let the family know you're going to survive."

She started to walk away when Kenzie called, "Grace?"

"Do you need something?"

Kenzie shook her head. "I wanted to say thanks for coming. I feel better knowing you've taken a look."

Quietly she said, "It's what we do; we take care of each other." She pointed in the direction of the waiting room. "I'll be back in a few minutes."

As she was turning, she witnessed Kenzie pull Robbie's hand to her cheek. A pang of longing thumped in Grace's chest. Pushing it aside, she went in search of her family.

Before leaving the hospital, Kenzie and Jamie had given Grace their letters from Gran. Grace took them promising they would talk about the contents soon, but she had already made her decision. When the time was right, she'd tell her sisters.

CHAPTER 27

She drove home. She was no longer looking for clues, but curiosity was getting the best of her. She decided to read the letters tonight.

She settled into the chaise on the patio with a blanket tucked around her legs. She carefully unfolded Jamie's letter. Grace smiled as she saw Gran's graceful, flowing handwriting. She angled the paper toward the lantern light.

Dearest Jamie,

I hope you don't mind that I went into your room so I could slip a wee little note into your suitcase as a surprise for later. When you find this, don't tell your sisters, as I did the same for them. On second thought, I'm sure they're with you now, so it's no longer going to be a surprise.

During our visit I wanted to tell you about a very special dress that you will receive after I'm gone. After giving it much thought, I've come to the conclusion that will be my last gift to you, my beautiful, strong and independent granddaughters. Each one of you reminds me of myself when I was a young woman. Oh, you're all individuals, but there is something that connects you to me: love and blood.

I hope your father has found my journals to pass on to you. There are so many stories untold and so much I still wanted to teach you. But time is dwindling. Now, don't cry, I've been blessed beyond my wildest dreams by growing up on this farm and then having the opportunity to meet and marry your grandfather, who understood why I could never leave this land. When my son James went to America I thought my heart would shatter like glass. I missed him so much. But instead of heartbreak, he met your mother, Olivia. She became the daughter I always longed to have. They went on to have the three of you. Jamie, Kenzie and Grace, you are my legacy.

Many times, the four of us have talked into the wee hours of the morning about your desire to never marry. I'd like for you to keep your hearts open to the possibility of love and continuing the legacy of our family.

Jamie, this is for you specifically. Please don't read this aloud, but if you wish you can tell Kenzie and Grace what I wrote later.

Grace smiled, nodding as if she could hear Gran's voice. The next sentence was one she hadn't known about.

There is a tall, dark-haired man who will come into your life, a twin to an Irishman. Keep your heart open and love will find the path to your heart.

My darlings, it's time for me to finish my letters and turn in for the night as tomorrow is our last day together, and what plans we have. A hike along the waterfall and the heather is in full bloom, and as a surprise I'm going to show you the secret place where my dear Rory picked white heather for me.

Until we meet again, all my love, Gran

"I wonder how she got any sleep that night, writing our letters and then sneaking into our rooms." Grace clutched the letter to her heart and looked at the pinpricks of light that dotted the night sky. She sighed. "Oh Gran. I wish you were here."

She unfolded Kenzie's letter next. It began the same as Jamie's. Grace scanned it until she read:

I wonder, how did Jamie look in our dress? I'm sure she was radiant. Each one of you reminds me of myself when I was a young woman. You're strong-willed and stubborn. You're the most like me in temperament, so I understand your reluctance to let go and fall in love.

There are so many stories untold and so much I still wanted to teach you. But time has passed us by. I need for you to understand that marrying your grandfather was the best thing I ever did, and I wouldn't have wanted to miss a single minute of our life together. My cup runneth over when I had a son, and my three sweet granddaughters were truly beyond my wildest dreams. You are the MacLellan future.

Kenzie, true love is waiting for you. Open your heart and a lifetime filled with joy will follow. To take the first step is to wear the dress, look in the mirror and be honest with yourself. Who do you see standing next to you? A man you can love with all your heart, who will stand beside you through good times and bad? He is the one for you.

Grace set the pages on top of Jamie's letter and wiped the moisture from her cheeks with the back of her hand. She hadn't realized she was crying until the night air cooled her face.

"Gran, you keep saying we need to keep our hearts open to the possibility of love and a future. Jamie and Kenzie did what you asked, but why did you send me to Scotland, with the dress? Was I supposed to meet Logan and fall in love with him?"

Grace's thoughts turned over and over and she cried, "I'm so confused, Gran!"

She shivered. The blanket was growing damp and the pricks of light now glowed bright. The full moon had risen and it was time for Grace to call it a night. She had never felt more alone than she did in this very moment. Would living the single life be something she could do forever?

With slow, halting steps, she walked toward the house. Each step felt as if the weight of the world was on her slender shoulders. After locking the kitchen door, she picked up her cell phone, checking in case Robbie had called and Kenzie needed her.

There was a message from Logan. *Hi, have you read the book?*

He had never asked about the other gifts. Well, the others hadn't been this personal either. Carrying the phone into the bedroom, she picked up the book, took a picture and sent it to him. *I'm thoroughly enjoying the poems. Thank you again, and if you want it back please don't hesitate to let me know. It is very special.*

She didn't expect an answer as it was before dawn in Scotland, but an incoming text bleeped. *Lisa would be happy to know you have it.*

Grace sat on the edge of the bed. Unsure how to answer him, she simply said, *Thank you again.*

Laying the phone facedown, she wandered into the bathroom to get ready for bed. Tomorrow was going to be another long and lonely day.

Logan boarded the plane and patted his briefcase again. Safely secured inside was an opal-and-diamond necklace that was reminiscent of a waterfall in Rosemarkie. The strands of diamonds seem to flow over the large opal on slender threads of gold. His intention had been to pass it off as a piece of costume jewelry, but it was time Grace understood that if he wanted to buy her something special, he would. Tracey had been direct when she said Logan should be honest if Grace asked, but he was praying she would accept it as a thoughtful gift.

He buckled his seatbelt and waited for the pilot's announcement that they were pushing back from the gate. Closing his eyes, he could picture Grace wearing the necklace.

Then the doubts started to creep in. What if she wasn't as amazing as he remembered? Or worse, what if he couldn't bear to leave her and Grace didn't really want anything to do with him and the texts had been merely the polite thing to do? Was he about to make himself out to be the biggest love-struck fool on the planet?

His heart pounded in his chest. He pulled his cell out and dialed. On the second ring he said, "Hi Aunt Flora."

"Logan, dear, this is a nice surprise. Are you coming over tonight?"

"I'm sorry, Aunt Flora, I forgot to tell you. I'm on my way to Vermont. To Grace."

"What a splendid idea. Is she picking you up at the airport?"

He could hear the joy in her voice. "Well, that's why I'm calling. I've put myself in a tenuous position. She has no idea I'm coming. What if, once I get to Easton, she rebuffs me?" A soft laugh reached his ears. "Aunt Flora?"

"My dear nephew. I'm sure Grace will be thrilled to see you. Overwhelmed, maybe. But nonetheless, very happy."

"How can you be sure?" He certainly had his doubts.

"The young woman cares for you. Of that I'm sure. But don't get overly pushy or use your negotiating skills. Which is what you usually do when it comes to things out of your comfort zone."

Logan heard the chimes and then the announcement to turn off all electronic devices. "I need to go, but I'll call you when I land."

"You do that, and Logan, have a wonderful time."

As he disconnected, he could hear his aunt chuckling.

He stared out the window. What was so funny? And what did she mean by using his skills? Closing his eyes again, he replayed the scene where he announced to Grace he would set her up with a flat and money. Inwardly he cringed. He had treated that exchange more like a business meeting than a conversation with the woman he adored. But that's who he was, a businessman.

He could feel someone watching him. He turned to the older woman sitting next to him. The corners of her lips twitched upward, her face hardly moving.

"I'm sorry if I disturbed you. I'm a nervous flyer." Her soft gray eyes reminded him of his mother.

"It's no bother." Not one to usually chat with seatmates, he reassured her, "We should have a smooth flight today."

"I certainly hope so." She played with the coffee stirrer in her hand. "Do you fly often?"

"I do. For business."

The wooden stirrer snapped. She looked down. "Oh well."

He leaned in and, in a conspiratorial voice, said, 'I'm sure they have plenty on board."

Her faced relaxed just a bit. "I'm Rachel." She extended her hand.

He clasped her hand with his. "Pleased to meet you, Rachel. I'm Logan." He couldn't help but notice it was like ice. "Do you need a blanket?" He looked up to see if a flight attendant was nearby.

"No, once we take off my nerves will get a bit steadier and I'll be fine." She tucked her hands into her lap, still holding the two parts of the stirrer. "Are you traveling to Boston for business today?"

With a shake of his head, he beamed. "I'm on my way to see the woman I love."

Her face opened up with a larger smile. "That is wonderful. I'm on my way to see my daughter and her husband. They're going to have a baby soon, and I'm coming to stay for a wee bit."

"That sounds nice." Logan's gaze drifted back to the window as the plane punched through the clouds and into smooth flying in the deep, azure-blue sky.

"Tell me about your young lady." Rachel cleared her throat. "If you don't mind, it'll help me take my mind off where we are currently."

Logan hesitated and then figured what the heck, he was certainly spending enough time thinking about her. "Grace is the most amazing woman I've ever met. She is smart, compassionate, tenderhearted but strong, and beautiful." He turned toward Rachel. "And she liked me for me."

"You sound surprised."

"Most women take me at face value. They don't make the effort to look beyond the surface."

"Did you?" Her voice was soft, but her question was a direct hit.

"I guess I didn't either. I just expected the women I dated to be shallow." His thoughts raced. "Maybe some of them weren't like that."

She slowly nodded. "I'm sure you've met a nice girl or two. Before Grace." Her smile grew. "How did you meet?"

"The first time I saw her she was with her sisters and they were getting off the plane in front of me. The moment I looked into her enormous blue eyes, I was hooked. We had just arrived on an early morning flight into Glasgow and her auburn hair was all tousled and curling wildly around her face. I didn't know her name, but it was like *wow*." He remembered that moment vividly.

Rachel's smile warmed her eyes. "And then what happened?"

"We went our separate ways until about six weeks ago. I had just come back from a business trip and I was walking through baggage claim when a woman cried out for help. It was Grace. Someone had lifted her garment bag. I chased the thief and was able to return it to her. It turns out it was her great-grandmother's wedding dress. After that I bumped into her in a market and then at Rosemarkie. That was the first time we spent actually talking. She shared her lunch with me."

Rachel said, "Oh?"

"She had taken a tumble into the stream just as I wandered down the path." He grinned. "She was breathtaking. So unassuming and carefree. She didn't care that her hair was wet or her mascara was smudged." If he closed his eyes, he could see her.

"Is that the moment you fell in love with her?"

He opened his eyes and looked at her. "It was all over for me when she took my hand as I helped her out of the stream. And now I'm on my way to surprise her and find out if she's in love with me."

"You quarreled, didn't you?"

He gazed out the window. Logan didn't want to confess to this stranger he had been an arrogant jerk. "I didn't tell her the truth about my professional life, someone else did before I could get up the nerve." With a derisive laugh he said, "I made her an offer I thought she couldn't refuse, but she did."

"I'm confused. What did you lie to her about?"

"I'm a successful businessman, and I kept it from her because I wanted to be sure she cared about me as a person, not my bank account."

"That's understandable." Rachel put the tray down and set the broken coffee stirrer on it. "Is there something you're not telling me?"

"Well, yeah." He could feel his face grow warm. "I offered to set her up with a place to live and basically support her."

Rachel chuckled and clapped her hands together. "If she's half the girl I think she is, you must have really made her mad."

"Mad enough for her to storm out of my office after telling me I was nuts." His voice dropped low as the airplane engines droned on. "After she got home I sent her a couple of small gifts—a long-stemmed pink rose, some truffles and my sister's favorite book of poems." With a catch in his voice, he said, "My twin sister died almost twenty years ago."

Rachel patted his hand. "That is one of the single most romantic gestures I think I've ever heard."

He pulled his laptop bag out from under the seat. Withdrawing the jeweler's box, he flipped it open. "I had this designed for Grace."

Rachel placed her hand over her heart. "The waterfalls?"

"Yes. To remind her of the first day we spent together. The day I fell in love with her." Logan looked at Rachel. "Do you think she'll like it?'

"Logan, your Grace will love it, and you."

He slipped it back in his bag. Rachel leaned back in the seat. "If you don't mind, I think I'll rest my eyes." She gave him a groggy smile. "Thank you for sharing your love story with me."

Logan said, "I'm not sure if it's a love story yet. But I'm working on it."

He looked out the window. His brain was in overdrive. Talking to Rachel had made him realize he had never gone out of his way before for a woman. Jewelry was easy to purchase. He often had Tracey pick out something small for his current girlfriend. He never knew what she had purchased until the gift had been opened. This time, he selected every stone and worked with the designer to get it perfect.

Would he have ever hopped on a plane and flown three thousand miles as a surprise? There was no guarantee Grace would even be happy to see him. With a slow realization, he knew if she had jumped at the chance to be taken care of, she wouldn't be the woman he cared for. And it wasn't because Grace was the first to rebuff his money, it was because he was hopelessly in love with this woman.

He softly chuckled to himself. After witnessing his friends marry, he knew that when he found the one woman he would love with all his heart, he would do his best to make her happy.

Now it was up to Logan to convince Grace he loved her with all his heart and an ocean was not going to separate them.

CHAPTER 28

Kicking back in sweats, her hair pulled into a messy bun and wrist-deep in mulch, Grace happily dug in her flowers. They were looking woefully neglected from her busy schedule. She was thrilled the day—heck, the week—was in the history books. Kenzie was fine, no ill effects from the deer incident and she was back at work. When she was done there was a bottle of wine chilling in the refrigerator.

She heard a vehicle slow down as it drove past, but she didn't bother to look up, she wasn't expecting company. She brushed her bangs out of her eyes with the back of her hand, took a sip of water and attacked a stubborn dandelion. She tossed it into the wheelbarrow, oblivious to the dirt flying.

"Hello, Grace."

She froze. Those two words and that voice made her heart stop. It sounded almost like Logan. But it couldn't be. Ever so slowly, she cocked her head looked up and into deep green eyes, *his* eyes.

She jumped to her feet, stammering, "Logan?"

His gaze slid from her face to her toes and back again. "You're a sight to behold." His rich brogue was like a loving caress.

She wanted to leap into his arms. Flustered, she pushed her bangs back from her forehead again and smiled. "What are you doing here? Why didn't you tell me you were coming?"

"And miss the opportunity to surprise you?" he teased. He casually glanced around, but Grace knew he was absorbing every detail. It was his way. "Your home is charming and it suits you." His smile grew when he took in the flower gardens. "I can see you have a way with flowers."

She blushed under the intensity of his gaze. "I can't take all the credit. I bought the cottage from Jamie. She did most of the work."

"Modest too." He reached out and touched her cheek. "You've got a little smudge."

Grace could feel the heat flood her face. He closed the distance between them and lowered his mouth to hers. Before they touched, very softly he said, "I've missed you." His lips claimed hers with tenderness and longing.

She sank into his embrace taking a step closer. She slipped her arms under his sports coat and held him close. "Oh Logan," she murmured, his kiss igniting her soul.

She took a step back and glanced at her clothes. Embarrassed, she said, "I must look a mess. Oh no. I've covered your shirt with dirt."

He chuckled. His laugh was low and oh-so sexy. "I have other shirts, but I won't get a second chance to kiss you for the first time on Vermont soil." He pulled her back into his arms. He nuzzled her neck and said, "You are a sight for sore eyes."

She laughed. "I'm a hot mess and don't smell very pretty." She pecked his cheek. "Let me pick up my tools and we can go inside."

He bent over and scooped up her trowel and took the handle on her cart. "Where do you want them?"

Playfully snatching the handle from him, she said, "I've got these. You're already messed up enough." She began to cross the grass and turned to him. "Follow me."

"I like the sound of that..."

Grace felt her heart grow lighter than it had been in weeks. Until she saw Logan standing before her, she hadn't realized just how much she missed him. Her anger had evaporated. She'd dissect everything else later, but for now she just wanted to spend time with him.

"How long are you staying?" she asked.

"I guess that depends on you." His hand brushed hers as they pulled the cart together. "Currently my plans are open ended."

Her mouth dropped. "But don't you have a business to run?"

He nodded and grinned. "I do, and you have to work also. I thought while you're taking care of the medical needs of the community I can open my laptop, call my staff and stay abreast of anything that needs my attention. Otherwise I have a very competent staff who will take care of the day-to-day. Then we can spend every free moment together, if you'd like."

She frowned. "I don't have any vacation time to take while you're here. The family is planning on spending the Christmas holiday in Scotland so I've been working a lot of people's on-call time to bank extra hours for my vacation."

His face lit up. "You're coming back to Scotland?"

She tilted her head and smiled at him. "I am, and it just so happens I was going to invite you to a Boxing Day party.

We're holding a gathering for a few people—Flora and some friends—and I'm hoping you'll be there."

"You couldn't keep me away." He kissed her cheek. "Ah, Grace, it is so wonderful to be walking next to you, talking to you again."

Grace pointed to the patio. "I'm going to put this in the garage, and we can sit out here." She pulled the cart inside, laid the trowel on the bench. She closed the door and taking his hand, she pulled him toward the arbor. "I'm afraid I don't have anything to nosh on, but I do have wine."

"That sounds just perfect. When you get hungry we can run out for a bite to eat."

Grace looked at her outfit. "I can't go anywhere looking like this." Laughing she said, "If I ply you with wine, would you give me time to run through the shower?"

"Absolutely. After all, I did catch you off guard." He quickly hid a hint of a frown. "Am I keeping you from something else?"

"Not at all. My big evening plans consisted of gardening, frozen pizza and wine." She grinned. "I'm happy to share the frozen pizza too."

"As interesting as that sounds, I'd love to take you out so that you can show me some of your charming town." He picked up her hand and turned it over, lightly kissing the delicate skin of her wrist.

Inwardly she melted. "Um. Make yourself at home and I won't be long." She half turned. "Well, ten minutes, maybe?" She snapped her fingers. "Wine first, then shower." She held up a finger. "Be right back."

She ran into the house, poured a large glass of wine and hurried back to Logan. "Is white okay?" she asked.

His smile relaxed her. "Yes, perfect." He took a sip. "Delicious. What kind is it?"

"Something my parents gave to me, Evangeline Wines. It's something new they found."

He took another sip. His eyes met hers over the rim, and then he set the glass on the table and took her hand. "After our last conversation I vowed never to keep anything from you, so full disclosure—I own Evangeline."

Grace's thoughts raced. "It is delicious." She pulled her hand away, with reluctance. "I'm going to get changed. Please relax and enjoy the wine."

"Take your time. I'm going to check email and make sure nothing needs my immediate attention."

She walked into the house. It was times like this she wasn't sure what to do or say. But she had a strong suspicion there were more revelations to come about how broadly his business extended.

Logan reclined in the chair and looked around the tiny backyard. Grace's home was exactly how he pictured it: inviting, comfortable and tidy. He didn't bother to check his cell. Nothing was more important than being in this moment. Grace had his complete attention and he wanted her to feel special. Tonight was the first step in winning her love and asking her to be his wife.

He frowned. How could he convince her moving to Scotland wouldn't be as lonely as she imagined? He'd gladly have a home large enough to accommodate her entire family.

His frown turned into a huge smile. He and Aunt Flora would be part of a big, happy family again.

Now he was really getting ahead of himself. *Slow down, man, you don't want to scare her off.* With a low chuckle, he patted his jacket. He had to remind himself this wasn't business, it was very personal, and he'd better change his tactics or risk blowing the most important deal of his life. *There I go again. This isn't a deal, this is my future.*

He sipped the wine. It *was* good. He picked up the bottle to examine the label. He grinned. Their lives were more entwined than she thought, but he was going to come clean about everything tomorrow. Tonight was for romance.

Logan heard a rustle behind him. He looked up and his mouth went dry. Grace was beautiful. After giving himself permission to drink in every detail, from her painted toes to the graceful turn of her ankle, her casual skirt and blouse and the oh-so kissable mouth, his eyes met hers. Reaching out for her, he stood and kissed the palm of her hand. He could see her shiver and he was fairly certain it wasn't from the late afternoon air.

His voice was low as he said, "You are lovely." He leaned in, his lips grazing her cheeks. She melted into him, her floral perfume igniting his senses. "I have something for you." He reached into his coat and withdrew the small jeweler's box.

Her eyes were bright. "Logan, you didn't need to buy me anything. You being here is the most wonderful gift."

He placed the box in her hand. "Please. Open it."

The lid opened with a *pop*. He could hear her breath catch. "Logan," she said softly. Her fingers trailed over the gems. "It's beautiful. It reminds me of Rosemarkie the first day we really talked." With a quiet laugh, she said, "You helped me out of the stream."

He took the necklace out of the satin-lined box. The twinkling lights made the diamonds and opals sparkle. "I'm glad you were reminded of that day. It was my intention."

He opened the clasp. She turned, and before sliding the

chain around her neck his lips nuzzled the sensitive spot behind her ear. She sighed.

He secured the clasp and adjusted the chain. She turned to face him. The pendant rested in the deep V of her blouse. "It's perfect. Just like I imagined." His voice was husky.

Grace stood on her tiptoes and kissed his mouth. He slid an arm around her waist and held her against his body, reveling in the feel of her lips on his. His heart raced. All he wanted to do was scoop her up in his arms, take her into the house and make love to her. But tonight was all about showing Grace she was loved.

Grace stole a glance at Logan as she drove down the two-lane road towards downtown. "I think Easton will remind you of some villages in Scotland." Her head cocked to one side. "I never really thought about it, but maybe that's why my parents chose to live here."

Without looking at her he said, "It is very charming here. How long have you lived in your home?"

Grace smiled. "I'm in a rent-to-own situation. My sister Jamie sold it to me after she and Caleb moved into their house. So I've been here a few months now."

"I would have guessed you lived there a long time; it suits your style." Grace slowed the car as they approached Main Street.

"Where shall we eat? Do you like Italian?"

"I do. Is there a place here in town?"

She slowed and put on her blinker. "Longer than we've been living here." She pulled into a parking spot. "We can walk. It's just down the street."

Logan did as she suggested, then hurried around the car to open her door.

"You're such a gentleman." She stepped onto the well-worn brick sidewalk.

"Mum made sure I had impeccable manners." He glanced around. "Is Kenzie's gym nearby?"

Grace pointed up the street. "Mac's is her place, and Jamie's office is a couple of streets over. She has her own accounting business."

"Very nice." He took her hand. "Tell me more about Easton."

She glanced at him. "There's not much to tell. We have about seventy-five hundred people in and around town, a couple of grocery and hardware stores. You know, the usual things."

"And you work right here?" Logan asked.

"The medical center is centrally located in the county. It's a regional medical facility. Our patient load is quite diverse."

Slowly he nodded. He seemed to be taking it all in. "Are there any factories in the area?"

She stopped in the middle of the sidewalk. "Logan Campbell, are you thinking about business?"

He shrugged. "Sometimes it's hard to turn off. In my defense, when I look around I see opportunity for growth for the surrounding communities. I'm sure it is harder than in years past to be a farmer, and without new businesses it's difficult to keep young people in the area."

She began walking again. "I guess, but did you come to Vermont to do business or see me?"

He chuckled. "To see you, of course." He playfully squeezed her hand. "Tell me about this restaurant we're going to."

She relaxed and reminded herself to not be so testy. "The Pasta Bowl has been a family favorite for as long as I can remember. We've celebrated major events like birthdays and anniversaries there. They have the best veal marsala, and the tiramisu"—she rolled her eyes—"pure heaven."

She stopped in front of a red door with a jaunty red-and-white awning over the front windows. "Here we are."

Logan held the door for her, and Grace could feel his eyes watching as she sashayed through it.

"Hello, Joey." Grace smiled at an older man standing next to a small wooden podium.

Joey beamed. "Grace, so good to see you again. It's been a while."

"I think since before Kenzie got married." She took his hand.

"Ah!" He laid a hand over his heart, and with a hint of an Italian accent said, "Kenzie was a beautiful bride." He wagged a finger at her and winked. "You know, you're next."

Grace could feel herself blush. Changing the subject, she said, "Joey, do you have a table for two tonight?"

"For you, of course." He picked up two menus and said, "Follow me."

He led the couple to the back of the restaurant. "How's this? The most romantic table in the house." He winked at Logan. "Grace is a very special young woman, you know." He held out a chair for her and Grace sat down, praying this line of conversation would be over quickly.

"Yes, sir. She is one in a million." Logan took his seat and picked up the wine list.

Joey tapped the table. "I'll bring you wine. On the house." He hurried away before Logan could say a word.

He teased, "I think the older gentleman has a wee bit of a crush on you, Ms. MacLellan."

Grace leaned forward in her chair. "He's more like another dad. When my parents are out of the country, my sisters and I come in for dinner. He fusses over us and makes sure we always have leftovers to take home. I think he forgets we're adults, living in our own places and taking care of ourselves."

She leaned back. With a dramatic flair Joey arrived and showed Logan the bottle, poured him a taste and, when Logan smiled, he filled their glasses and then melted away. But before doing so, he said, "I'll bring you a very special dinner."

Logan said, "I see what you're saying." He tossed a look over his shoulder. "I get the feeling I might have his seal of approval."

A bit surprised, Grace said, "I didn't know you needed one."

"I wasn't going to get into this tonight, but Grace, I need to tell you something. And I can promise you with absolute certainty I've never said this to anyone else."

Grace's heart skipped at least one beat. "I'm listening."

He reached across the table and took her hands. She watched him as the candlelight danced, making his eyes glow like the loch.

Caressing her hands, Logan began, "Grace, I never thought I'd find love. It was something for other people. After my mum, dad and sister died, I never wanted to risk that kind of pain again. With the exception of Aunt Flora, I wouldn't allow myself to love."

Her heart ached for him, having so much pain in his life at such a tender age.

"I threw myself into my father's company. It was my way to honor his memory."

She caught sight of Joey approaching their table and he

turned back toward the kitchen. He must have seen the serious expression on Logan's face.

"All that changed the first time I saw you on the plane." Logan's eyes brightened. "Do you remember? You were with your sisters."

With a small smile she said, "I do. It was before Caleb and Jamie got engaged."

"And then when I rescued your wedding dress, I thought for sure that it wasn't meant to be." He said, "It was like I found you and lost you in the span of mere moments."

"I know exactly what you mean. I felt the same way," Grace said. "Gran left me a letter asking me to go to Scotland with the dress and there were instructions on what else I was to do." She drifted back to the farm and putting the dress on and looking in the mirror. "Logan, why did you go to Rosemarkie that day?"

Reluctant to let go of her hands, he moved his chair closer and slipped his arm around her. "It was the strangest thing. It was like I was compelled to go there. I never played hooky from work until that day."

Thoughtfully she nodded. "Did Flora suggest you go out there?"

"No. In fact, I'm not sure I even told her."

"In Gran's letter she told me to go."

He rubbed her shoulder. "The mysterious ways of Scotland were at work on our behalf."

Quietly she asked, "Do you believe in magic?"

He kissed her cheek. "Before meeting you I would have said no. But now I most definitely believe there are a great many things that can't be explained by logic."

"I agree."

He turned her to face him. "Grace, when I'm with you,

I'm the man my mother would be proud of, less driven by business and..."

"Yes?" What more was there for Logan to say?

His eyes held hers captive. "I'm in love with you."

Stunned she drank in the sight of his face and the sound of him saying those words. With a catch in her voice she said, "I've fallen for you too. But nothing can come of it." Tears spilled over her cheeks. "We've been given a brief snip of time to love each other."

She could see him visibly pull back from her. "Are you saying you love me but don't want to be with me?"

She could hear the regret in her voice. "It's not that I don't want to be with you, but that I *can't* be with you. There are too many obstacles in our way."

"Whatever they are, we can overcome them. Haven't you heard love conquers all?"

Grace could see the love in his eyes, and it broke her heart to be the strong one, but she needed for Logan to face the truth. His place was globetrotting and building his empire, and her place was in Easton, with her family.

She laid a hand alongside his face and tenderly kissed his lips. "Can we enjoy this time together for as long as you're here and not think about what might have been?"

"But...Grace," he stuttered. "You can't be serious. You've admitted you love me, and I love you."

"I can't leave Vermont." She hung her head. "My feelings for you have nothing to do with it." She waved Joey over. "We're ready for our salads."

Logan continued to watch her. She said, "Logan, let's plan out the next few days. I am on call this weekend, but as long as we're within cell phone range and I can get to the medical center, I can show you around my hometown."

Logan moved his chair back to the other side of the table. Halfheartedly he said, "That sounds great. Maybe we could invite your family out to dinner. I'd love to see them. Is there someplace in the area that would be extra special?"

"There's the Pillars, it's a great restaurant."

Joey set down the bread basket and salads and hurried away.

"I'll check with them tomorrow and see what night works?" She jabbed a chunk of cucumber. "When are you leaving?"

Logan was intently buttering a piece of bread while Grace waited for an answer. "Logan?"

"I came to the States to win your heart and I'm not leaving until I do." He grinned. "You can be logical and protest all you like. But you said you love me and that is all I need to know." He grew serious. "I know better than most people how fragile life is, and I'm holding onto the dream of a wonderful future."

At a loss for words, Grace toyed with her fork. "You know you are wasting your time."

"It's my time to waste." He picked up the bread basket. "Roll?"

"You're incorrigible." She took one.

He winked. "Thank you!"

Logan thoroughly enjoyed dinner with Grace. Just being with her filled his heart with joy. And now that he knew she was in love with him, there was no stopping him. It would just take some wooing and a reason for Grace to take the step toward a future with him. Meeting her family would give her reassurance that he had no intention of isolating her across the pond. He couldn't wait to meet them. Who knows, maybe Jamie and Kenzie would have some insight into convincing Grace.

He pulled up in front of the bed and breakfast Tracey had booked him into. As much as he didn't want to leave Grace, he also didn't want to overwhelm her with his presence. He had to laugh at himself. Putting her needs in front of his desires? That was something he needed to tell Aunt Flora—for once she'd be proud of how he was handling his romantic affairs. But this wasn't a simple affair, it was his life. His future.

He couldn't sleep. He checked the time back home. His aunt would be at the bakery. He dialed the phone. On the fourth ring he heard, "MacMeekin's."

"Aunt Flora, it's me, Logan."

She chuckled. "You do know I recognize your voice."

"I didn't want to take any chances." Logan smiled into the phone.

"How is Grace? Was she happy to see you?"

Logan stretched out on the bed and leaned against the headboard. This is just what he needed, to talk to his aunt. "Aunt Flora, Grace is in love with me and I told her I love her."

"That's wonderful news. Do I hear a *but* in your voice?"

"There is a little hitch. For some reason she thinks she can't leave Vermont."

Aunt Flora said, "I'm assuming you have an idea of how you can convince her?"

"I'm going to show her that marrying me can give her the freedom to live anywhere she'd like. And if that doesn't work, I don't know what I'll do." Doubts crept into his head. "Maybe I'll buy a house here."

"Logan, Grace is a woman who needs a purpose. You need to give that some thought. If you're asking her to change her life, how will you change yours to blend it with hers?"

"I thought just being together would be enough."

"Spoken like the Logan I've come to know." Aunt Flora's voice held a warning tone. "You need to change the way you think about things. Grace is different, and if you don't come up with an idea you'll lose her. Maybe this time it will be permanent."

"I'm not sure what you mean." Logan could hear what she saying but didn't know what to do about it. "Should I give Grace more of a purpose than just a life with me?"

"Now you're starting to think outside of your narrow brain. What would your mother suggest? She always had the best ideas."

"I'll give it some thought." Logan nodded despite the fact that his aunt couldn't see him. "I'll call you in a few days."

"Goodbye, dear boy, and please tell Grace I said hello."

"I will." Logan disconnected the call and sank into the pillows. While he relaxed, his eyelids grew heavy. He fell asleep wondering what his mom's advice would be.

CHAPTER 29

Grace was drinking coffee in her tidy kitchen when she heard the commotion at the back door. She smiled. Jamie and Kenzie had arrived.

"Grace?" Jamie grinned as she walked into the kitchen. "We got your text, what's going on? Logan is here, in Vermont?"

Kenzie poured two mugs of coffee and handed one to Jamie. "Did you know he was coming?"

"Nope." Grace was smiling from ear to ear. "I was working in the flowers and he appeared. I was covered in dirt and there he was." With a deep sigh she gushed, "He is so handsome and sweet." She pulled the gold chain out from under her T-shirt. "Look at what he gave me."

Kenzie gave a low appreciative whistle. "That's stunning." She took a closer look. "Are those real diamonds and blue opals?"

Jamie leaned in. "The way the light bounces off them, I would say yes."

"Girls, I wouldn't care if they were cubic zirconia. It was

the thought that counts. It reminds me of the day we spent at the waterfalls."

"Is that why he came, to give you the necklace?" Kenzie asked while blowing on her coffee.

Grace plunked on a stool. Her heart fluttered. "He told me he's in love with me."

Jamie's mouth hung open. "And what did you say?"

"I told him I was in love with him too. And then I had to break the bad news that although I have deep feelings for him, I could never leave Easton. This is my home."

Kenzie jumped in. "This will always be home, but you can build a life with Logan too. One doesn't negate the other."

With a flick of her wrist Grace said, "Regardless, he wants to have dinner with the family while he's in town. I was thinking we could go to the Pillars. The castle would remind him of home and the food is always excellent there." She laughed. "You know how much good food is important just in case conversation lags."

Jamie looked at Kenzie and said, "Sounds like fun. Pick any night and we'll be free."

Kenzie said, "Check with Mom to see what they have scheduled. Maybe next weekend."

"You're pretty quick to agree." Grace's eyes narrowed. "You aren't planning on grilling him, are you?"

Jamie exclaimed, "Who, us? Never."

Kenzie shook her head while trying to suppress a grin. "We'll be on our best behavior." She made a cross across her heart. "Promise."

Jamie's grin split her cheeks as she held up her little finger. "I pinky promise."

Grace couldn't help but laugh as her sisters slipped back to their childlike promises. "Now you two need to take off since I'm going to get ready for a day of sightseeing with Logan."

"Oh," Kenzie teased. "You're going to spend the day smooching, gazing longingly into each other's eyes, walking hand in hand and..."

Grace set her mug on the counter and took her sister's coffee mugs away from them too. "All right, you've had your fun, now go." Giving her sisters a playful shove toward the door, she said, "I'll call you later and give you some of the details."

"Just some?" Jamie laughed. "We want you to tell all and spare nothing."

At the door Grace opened it and waited until they stepped outside. Before closing the door, she said, "There will be some details I keep to myself." She blew them each a kiss and with a final wave shut the door.

Laughing, she hurried to change and then she was going to pick up Logan and see what he'd like to do first.

Grace pulled up the long gravel driveway to the B and B and was pleasantly surprised to find Logan lounging on the front steps, waiting for her. She beeped the horn and waved out of the sunroof. His slow, relaxed grin greeted her. Ambling to the car, he leaned in the window.

"Good morning." The deep rumble in his voice echoed in her stomach. "Would you like me to drive?"

"And relieve me of the chance to be your tour guide?" she teased. "Not a chance. Hop in, Mr. Campbell." He came around to the passenger side. "Anything specific you'd like to see?" Grace asked before she put the car in drive.

He looked at her and smiled. "Everything."

She laughed. "Well, there isn't that much to see. After

all, we live in a small town." She put the car in drive and said, "Let's start at Racing Brook Stables. My brother-in-law Robbie's family owns it. Maybe you'd like to ride?"

He buckled up. She handed him a to-go cup of coffee.

"Thank you and you're in charge of our adventure." He looked out the window as the car picked up speed. "It is beautiful here. I can see why you love it."

Slowing alongside the lake she said, "My sisters and I learned to swim in that lake."

Logan's eyes bugged out. "That has to be freezing cold, much like the lochs in Scotland."

She smirked. "You have no idea, but they held swimming lessons in late July and early August, so it was the warmest water possible."

Grace continued to show him points of interest, driving past dairy farms and a large maple sugaring operation. "They have the best maple syrup. Every year after the maple sugar season is over, they hold a huge pancake breakfast for everyone in town."

"That sounds like it's a lot of fun." Logan watched as the huge trees were lined up one after the other. "How old do you think these trees are?"

"Some of them are a couple of hundred years old. They can live four hundred years." She peered through the windshield. "A fun factoid, forty gallons of sap equals one gallon of maple syrup."

"Sounds like a lot of work to me."

She snorted. "This from the man who thrives on hard work."

Logan chuckled. "What can I say? I think what I do isn't as labor intensive as collecting sap, boiling it down, bottling and then distribution."

Grace slowed the car and flicked her blinker on. "We're here."

Horses grazed in the pastures that lined the long gravel drive. She stopped next to a fence. A large black horse hung his head over it. “That would be Pirate. He’s a family favorite.”

“He looks mighty big.” Logan’s voice was strained.

“Logan, do you ride?”

With another look at Pirate, he gulped, “No.”

“Then why did you say you wanted to go riding?” Grace held her amusement in check. Logan wasn’t the first person to be taken aback by the sheer power that Pirate emanated.

Logan looked at Grace with a fierce intensity. “I want to understand and experience everything about this town you love. That includes riding a horse.” He looked at the gelding again. “But is there a less intimidating mount I could ride?”

Grace snickered. “There are several. I’m thinking Snowflake would be just the right horse for you, and we’ll take it nice and easy.” She pointed to a woman standing next to the barn. “There’s Jo, Robbie’s sister. She and George, their dad, manage the place.”

Logan pushed open the door and said, “Let’s get this ride underway.”

Jo hurried over to them. “Hi, Grace.” She eyed Logan. “I’m surprised to see you today.”

Beaming Grace said, “I’d like to introduce you to Logan Campbell, a friend from Scotland.”

“I didn’t know you were expecting company.” Jo smiled and extended her hand. “Welcome.”

“Well, as a matter of fact, I wasn’t expecting him either.” She looped her arm through Logan’s. “He surprised me last night, and today I’m showing him the sites in and around Easton. Our first stop was here.” With a sweeping gesture and a grin, she said,

"So if it's okay, I'd like to saddle up Pirate and Snowflake."

"Snowflake is good to go, but Pirate threw a shoe yesterday and I'm waiting for the farrier, so how about Bandit?"

Logan flashed Jo a look of concern. "Is this Bandit safe?"

Jo laughed softly. "Grace can handle him." She patted his arm. "She has been riding from the moment she could scramble on the back of a Shetland pony."

Logan gave her an admiring look. "Really? I had no idea."

"My sisters and I rode a lot. It's not that big of a deal."

The trio wandered into the barn. Snowflake whinnied softly and Bandit stuck his long deep brown nose over the top of the Dutch door. Grace scratched his nose before patting Snowflake's neck.

"Hey, guys. Ready to stretch your legs?"

She grabbed a lead rope and clicked it on the harness of each horse and opened the stall doors. Jo helped with saddling them up and handed Snowflake's reins to Logan. "Care to lead him out to the paddock?"

Logan tentatively patted her velvety soft nose. "Sure. Grace, are you coming?"

She laughed. "I'm right there with you."

Jo walked alongside Snowflake. Logan said, "I hope you're telling her to be kind to this Scot."

With a quick nod and a fast smile, Jo said, "She'll be a sweetie." They came to a stop and she said, "I'll help you mount and then turn you over to Grace's capable instruction."

Grace waited until Logan was settled, looking slightly uncomfortable but sitting tall in the saddle, before swinging her leg over Bandit.

"Tap your heels very gently on her sides and we'll get going." Grace waited as he did, and Snowflake followed Bandit with a steady, rolling gait. "Be back in a while, Jo."

With a wave she called after them, "Have fun."

The couple made their way down a well-worn path. Logan pulled out his cell phone and took several pictures of Grace.

"Hey, there are better things to capture on your phone than me." She turned her face toward the trail.

"Not in my opinion." He sighed. "So, tell me, is this where your sisters got married?"

Grace held her surprise in check. "It is, but how did you know?"

"Aunt Flora showed me pictures and I made an educated guess." Snowflake picked up her gait to a slow trot. He grabbed the saddle horn and bobbed up and down.

Grace said, "Pull back on the reins."

Logan did, and Snowflake slowed again. "Can we ride up to where they tied the knot?"

She glanced at Logan and redirected Bandit toward the hill. "It's this way." The horses clip-clopped along under the warm sun. Grace could feel Logan watching her. She smoothed her hand down her jacket and said, "Is something wrong?"

"You are very beautiful." He stated it with such simplicity, and the way the words rolled with his brogue had never sounded more endearing to her.

"Thank you." She could feel the heat rise in her cheeks. They came up to the ceremony site, and she pulled Bandit to a halt. Snowflake stamped her feet and waited. Grace slid from the horse's back and Logan followed suit.

She pointed to the edge of the hill. "The arbor was right there for both ceremonies. We had some chairs, and a horse-drawn carriage delivered the bride. The weddings were so romantic."

Logan took her hand. "Can we sit and talk for a bit?"

Grace let him lead her to the edge of the hill overlooking the lush green valley that stretched out for miles. She sank to the ground and patted it. Logan sat down with her and never let go of her hand.

They sat in companionable silence, enjoying nature as birds drifted lazily across the deep blue sky. Grace could sense something was on Logan's mind, and she felt it best to not rush him.

"Grace." He took a deep, calming breath. "When you left Scotland, you were upset with me, and I completely understand why. I want to be totally honest with you about my business and try to explain why I deliberately kept it from you."

Grace tried to pull her hand from his. Her voice was frosty. "Do you really want to go there again?"

"When I told you that I love you, I meant it. I feel we need to be completely honest with each other about everything."

She looked at his face and could see he seemed to be genuine. "Okay, I'm listening."

"It's true I own Tartan Bakery and Aunt Flora is the genius behind the recipes. I took that and used it as a base to expand. I bought a small boutique hotel." He gazed off into the distance. "It was Mum's dream to own a hotel; her specialty was high tea."

Gently she asked, "Each hotel serves high tea?"

He dropped his chin and said, "Yes. We've talked about Evangeline Hotels."

Grace said, "We have."

Proudly he said, "I like taking old manor houses and small castles and restoring them. I'm a huge history buff, as was Mum. It's like a part of her is still with me when I successfully complete a project, but I'm always driven to do one more. If I stop, maybe I won't be able to keep her memory alive."

She held on to his hand. "You must really miss her."

"I do. But I also own a distillery, Tell Spirits. I used the first letters of my family's name, Thomas, Eva, Lisa and Logan. I wanted to honor them and recently I purchased a winery in the states."

"I'm sure they'd be very proud of all you have accomplished."

He looked her in the eyes and said, "I have a few other ideas, but some of that depends on you."

Grace stated, "I'm in the medical field, not the business world."

His face lit up. "I know. Which is perfect! I want to start a foundation for children who don't have access to good medical care and educational opportunities."

"That sounds wonderful…" she began.

Logan held up his hand. "My sister Lisa wanted to be a teacher, so I thought we could call it the Lisa Campbell Foundation for Children."

"We?" Grace could hear his voice was thick with emotion. "That's a wonderful way to honor her, but I'm not sure how I could help. I'm not a doctor."

"That doesn't matter. You have a medical background and you are by far the strongest, most compassionate woman I've ever met. I couldn't think of another person I would trust to help me launch it."

Grace got up from the ground and looked away. "Logan, that is an amazing compliment, but I don't think I can help you. You must know someone else more qualified than me."

Logan stood beside her and slipped his arm around her

waist. "Grace, I've met a lot of people. Most try to figure out a way to profit off me." With a derisive laugh he said, "I'm sure that makes me sounds cynical, but when I met you I knew you were special. As I got to know you, I discovered you were exactly who I had been looking for, not just to head up this foundation, but also to be my partner in all aspects of my life."

At a loss for words, Grace stood ramrod straight, staring at nothing, her heart racing. She longed to be able to say yes, to see what a future with Logan could possibly hold, but she was needed by her family. "Logan…"

"Please don't say no—say you'll think about it. Talk it over with your family before you make a decision." He kissed her cheek. "Think about what we could accomplish with the foundation. Together we would be unstoppable."

She opened her mouth to say no when Logan laid a finger on her lips. "Will you think about it?"

She gave a single nod of her head.

He held her tight. "Thank you, Grace. You won't be sorry. I promise."

CHAPTER 30

After hitting every tourist spot in and around Easton, Grace had made dinner reservations for the family. She was a little nervous having the family and Logan all together. She hadn't told anyone about his foundation idea and she was concerned he might spill the beans tonight. She wondered if there was a way to ask him not to talk about it without hurting his feelings. Well, if she did that, it would just bring more attention to the fact that he was waiting for an answer.

The doorbell rang. She picked up her handbag and scooped her coat up from the sofa.

"Coming!" She glanced at the mirror by the door and was pleased the way her curls were under control for a change. She pulled open the door and there was Logan, with a long-stemmed pink rose in one hand and a small box of Lake truffles in the other.

He seemed to drink in the sight of her and then, leaning in, kissed her lips. "You look radiant." He presented the flower and box to her.

As she accepted them, she said, "And you're spoiling

me." Setting the box on the side table, she laid the flower down too.

"Small tokens of my affection." His eyes smoldered.

She handed her coat to him and he held it while she slipped her arms in the sleeves. She picked up the rose and drank in the scent. "I'm ready."

He took her hand and they strolled to the car. "I'm really looking forward to tonight."

The way his cologne smelled made her knees go weak. "Logan?"

"Hmm." He nuzzled her neck.

"Why haven't you wanted to stay with me here?"

"It's not that I haven't wanted to be with you in every way imaginable, but this way it gives us time to get to know each other." He nuzzled behind her ear. Shivers raced down her spine. He tucked her hair behind her ear. "You've got me under your spell, Grace MacLellan."

She looked into Logan's eyes. "You are the sweetest man I've ever met." She lightly kissed his mouth, lingering a moment longer before saying, "We need to go, we don't want to be late."

He opened the passenger door and tucked her dress inside before closing it. Whistling, he jogged around to the driver's side.

She smiled. "You're really looking forward to tonight, aren't you?"

"I am. Being with family is so important. I never realized how much I missed it until I was getting ready tonight."

"Well, I can guarantee our family is loud, funny, and they'll talk your ears off."

"And what are your parents like?"

She smiled. "Dad is the mighty maple of our family, with deep roots. His branches protect us from any storms we've had to weather." She looked at Logan. "You're going to like him. Mom is the wind that makes his branches sway. Both of them strong in their own way. They complement each other."

"I'm sure I will."

Grace gave Logan directions to the inn. When they pulled in, she recognized all the cars. They were the last to arrive. Butterflies took flight in her stomach. She wondered if Logan was nervous at all.

He stuttered, "Well. Here we are."

Grace poked him. "Hey, you talk in front of large groups in business. This little dinner party shouldn't make you pause at all."

"It's different. I want your family to like me." His eyes searched hers. "It's important."

She laid a hand on his sleeve. "They're going to love you."

~

Grace held Logan's hand as they entered the front entrance. She seemed delighted to discover they had a private room. Jamie and Caleb, along with Kenzie and Robbie, had arrived, and they were beaming.

"Mom, Dad!" Grace exclaimed. "When did you ask for the dining room?"

Mom held up her hands. "It wasn't us. When we got here we were told this is where our party would meet us."

Logan leaned into Grace, inhaling her subtle floral perfume. "I made the change. I didn't want to be rushed in the main dining room." He kissed her cheek and, lingering there, said softly for her ears alone, "I hope you don't mind. I really want to get to know your family."

Flashing him a brilliant smile, she said, "It's a wonderful idea. I wish I had thought of it."

She held tight to his hand. "Logan, I'd like to introduce you to everyone." She pulled him forward. "These are my parents, Olivia and James."

James extended his hand and clasped Logan's in a firm grip. In a deep baritone voice, he said, "Pleased to meet you, Logan." He slipped an arm around his wife's shoulders and said, "Olivia and I are thrilled you wanted to get together tonight."

Logan smiled, and before he could shake her hand, Olivia pulled him into a warm embrace and kissed his cheek. "I've heard a fair bit about you."

Logan quickly looked at Grace and teased, "I hope only the good parts."

Grace's sisters and brothers-in-law pushed back from the table and walked over. He couldn't help but notice both men carried themselves with confidence. He liked them already.

"My sisters, Jamie and Kenzie, and their husbands, Caleb and Robbie."

Logan could see the strong family resemblance between the sisters. He hadn't noticed it that day on the plane. He could see they had James' deep blue eyes and his fair complexion, but their fine bone structure was their mother's. The one unmistakable thing he could feel was their connection to each other. He felt his gut wrench. He hadn't had that in so long he envied all of them.

After shaking Caleb and Robbie's hands and then being hugged by Jamie and Kenzie, he said with sincerity, "It is a pleasure to meet all of you." He gestured to the table. "Shall we sit?"

Logan steered Grace to the two empty chairs and held

one for her before he sat down. *Now this will be a family dinner to remember.* He waved over the server. "Grace, red?"

She looked at the waiter, giving him a polite smile. "Yes, thank you."

Logan said, "I'll have the same."

The waiter finished pouring and slipped away, the plush carpet absorbing any sound except for the soft jazz music playing in the background.

"Isn't this a beautiful place?" Grace said over the top of her glass.

"It is." Logan picked up his glass and said, "I'd like to say a few words."

Seven sets of eyes rested upon him. It was a bit intimidating and nothing like he was used to in a business meeting. He took a sip of his wine, wishing it were something stronger to steady his nerves.

"I'd like to thank you for coming tonight." He gazed at Grace and smiled. "Grace is an amazing woman, and now even after meeting you for just a few minutes, I know why she is the person I have fallen in love with."

Grace's hand flew to her mouth. "Logan," she implored, "What are you doing?"

He took her hand. "Don't worry. I won't embarrass you too much." He loved the way her cheeks flamed pink when he caught her off guard.

"As I was saying, when I saw Grace for the very first time, she was getting off a plane with Jamie and Kenzie. When I saw her for the second time, I rescued her wedding dress, the family wedding dress, and thought I had lost her before I even had the chance to introduce myself. The third time I bumped into her in a market, I was a goner. But it was the fourth time, when I pulled her from the creek at Rosemarkie, that I realized what it felt like to love someone with my entire heart."

Grace wiped the tears that were dampening her cheeks with a napkin. He pulled out a silk handkerchief and handed it to her.

"I've lost most of my family, with the exception of Aunt Flora, so this family dinner tonight is for all of us to get to know each other. I hope at some point, in the future, to become an official member of your family." He held up his glass, relieved he had made his intentions clear. "To family."

Glasses clinked and he sat down. He gazed into Grace's eyes. "Was what I said okay?"

"It was the most romantic thing I've ever heard." She leaned in, tears clinging to her dark eyelashes. "We will find a way to make a long-distance relationship work."

"Love always finds a way, Grace." He tenderly kissed her lips, aware Jamie and Kenzie were watching them.

Conversation and laughter flowed like wine. Throughout dinner Logan relaxed a bit more. He discovered James' brogue grew thicker. He felt like he was beginning to belong. It was more than he could hope for. He couldn't help but smile.

"Logan?" Grace poked his ribs. "You're having a good time?"

"I'm so glad we did this." He clinked his wine glass to hers. "Are you enjoying yourself?"

She beamed as her eyes moved from one family member to the next. "My family means the world to me."

Before he could answer, James stood up. "Logan, would you care to take a short walk to the bar with me?"

"Certainly." He looked at Grace. "I'll be back soon." He squeezed her hand before following James from the room.

James sat on a heavy wooden bar stool in the antique wood-paneled room. The bar was massive and behind it were bottles of fine liqueurs. James held up two fingers and asked for their best Scotch whiskey. "Have a seat."

Logan did as he asked, unsure what was to come next. James took his time and, after taking a small sip of the whiskey, said, "You love my Grace?"

Logan toyed with his glass before looking at James directly. "With all my heart."

"So you *do* plan on marrying her?"

"Yes, sir, I do."

James' brows drew together as he asked, "What about her family? Olivia told me about your brilliant idea of having her give up her life to be with you."

"Sir—"

"The name is James, son."

Logan took a gulp of whiskey. He wasn't prepared to have this conversation, at least not tonight. "James, I was an idiot when I asked Grace to let me take care of her financially. And after giving it a great deal of thought, I've asked her to work with me on a foundation. I'd like to do something for children in my sister's memory. We would have homes here and in Scotland, if that's what Grace wanted."

"And holidays?" James' deep voice seemed to vibrate the very air around them.

"Holidays are for family. The only request I would have is that Aunt Flora be included in all gatherings." He swallowed hard. "She's the only family I have left."

James threw back the last of his whiskey and thumped Logan's back. "Grace is a hard- headed woman. But as long as you promise to treat my little lass with love and respect and never dampen her spirit, you have my blessing."

"Sir—James," Logan stammered. "I promise to do my best every day I draw breath."

"Let's get back to the family." James stood up and tossed a few bills on the bar. He winked at Logan.

~

Grace glanced at the door again. Dad and Logan seemed to have been gone forever. What could they be talking about? "Mom? What is Dad going to say to Logan?"

With a quiet laugh she said, "I can't read your father's mind, but he may just like the fact that he and Logan speak the same language. I'm assuming they're sharing a finger of good Scotch whiskey." She patted Grace's hand. "Don't worry."

The waiter came in the room with a coffeepot. Grace caught his eye. "I'll have a cup, please."

Jamie slid into Logan's chair, and Kenzie stood behind her and said, "Gracie, he is an absolute dream. So handsome and"—with a wave of her hand—"all of this for a family dinner. It is very sweet."

Jamie said, "You've kept him pretty much to yourself these last two weeks. What have you two been doing?" With a wink she said, "I'm sure there's been a bit of romance in the air."

"I've driven more miles than I thought possible. We even went riding and on the top of the hill, where you got married, he asked me to help him run a new foundation in honor of his sister. He told me he wants to help children who need medical and educational support. We can change lives!"

"Really?" Kenzie cried. "That is amazing."

"It was a lot to digest when he first talked to me about

it, but it is an amazing opportunity to help so many more children and families."

"When will you start?" Jamie asked.

With a slow shake of her head Grace said, "I don't think I can. It would mean spending more time in Scotland."

"So?" Kenzie demanded. "It sounds like it will be an opportunity of a lifetime. Think of the impact you can have, far beyond what you're doing today."

Softly Grace said, "I can't leave the family."

Jamie's mouth dropped open. "What do you mean you can't leave us?"

"We've always been the Three Musketeers, and if I'm living an ocean away, how will we do stuff together? How will I be able to be there when you have kids? If you get sick and you need me?"

"Grace," Jamie and Kenzie said at the same time. They each took a hand. Jamie said, "We will always be there for each other, but it's time you put your happiness first."

Kenzie asked, "You do love him, right?"

Grace smiled. "I do."

Jamie rubbed her hand. "He seems like a good man."

Kenzie's head bobbed in agreement. "You deserve the best, and I have a feeling Logan is the best guy for you."

The door to the dining room opened. Logan and Dad came into the room, talking like old friends. Her heart swelled. Maybe Jamie and Kenzie were right. Maybe there was a way to work out a future with Logan.

On the drive back to Grace's cottage, Logan wasn't sure what to say. He had so much to think about, and the biggest question of his life was on the tip of his tongue. When was the right time to ask Grace to be his wife?

"Well, you haven't said—did you enjoy spending time with my family tonight?"

He took her hand and intertwined their fingers. "They're amazing. I feel like I have known them my entire life." He kissed her fingertips. He could feel her shiver. "Are you cold?" He adjusted the heat setting.

"No, I'm fine." She pulled her hand from his and played with the lock of hair that curled right at the base of his neck. "Everyone thinks you're wonderful."

"And you, Grace, what do you think about the last couple of months?" He held his breath. He prayed she would give him the opening he needed.

"I have enjoyed every day we've spent together, each one better than the day before." Her smiled faded. "When do you have to go home, to Scotland? You've already been here much longer than you thought."

"I've discovered I can conduct business wherever I am. In fact, I'm thinking of buying a house right here in Easton."

"Really? Why?"

"You're here," Logan answered simply. For him, Grace was home.

She smiled. "Are you going to rush off tonight?"

"Did you have something in mind?"

Her laugh was low and seductive. "I was thinking a fire in the backyard, some wine and cuddling under a blanket."

A perfect setting. "That sounds too good to pass up." He slowed the car and turned into her driveway.

They strolled to the back door and she said, "I'm going to change into something a bit warmer. I think we might even get a frost tonight."

"I'll get the fire going." He tilted her chin up and claimed her mouth. Then, lightly caressing her bottom lip with his thumb, he said, "I'll meet you out back."

She nodded and headed to her bedroom. Logan watched until she closed the door behind her and wandered into the kitchen, taking two glasses and a bottle of wine with him on the way out the patio door. It didn't take long to have a crackling fire dancing. He pulled the double chaise closer to the warmth and patted the chest pocket of his jacket. A small square box was in the same spot it had been in every day since he arrived.

He looked up as Grace came through the door, her long, curls trailing over her shoulders and down her back. She took her time walking across the patio, as if she was savoring the moment.

Grace wasn't sure why the butterflies in her stomach had decided to take this moment to dance. She was captivated by Logan's raw magnetism. Tonight there had been an important shift for her in many ways. Seeing him with her family, it felt like they were complete, like they had been waiting for Logan Campbell to arrive and claim his spot in their lives.

As she glided across the stones, she felt as if her feet didn't touch the ground. She stepped into the curve of his arms and knew she was home.

After all this time, it clicked. She understood what her sisters had said, how they knew the moment their lives were different.

"I brought our plaid." She pulled him to the chaise and they stretched out. She slipped off her shoes and wiggled her sock-covered feet under the fabric.

"Wine?"

She took the glass he handed to her and leaned back. The stars had filled the sky and Grace felt the rest of the world was a million miles away. She snuggled into his arms. "Logan, are you serious about the foundation?"

"Very." He kissed her forehead. "But I need you by my side."

"I have a few ideas I'd like to run by you."

He chuckled. "Do you think they can wait until tomorrow? I'd like for us to enjoy the evening."

She smiled. "You're right. It would be a shame to waste the rest of the evening talking business. We'll have plenty of time to make our plans."

"Grace?"

She closed her eyes, totally relaxed. "Hmmm?" she murmured.

Logan fumbled with his jacket. "Hang on a minute." He got up and stoked the fire, dropping on another log. He sat on the edge of the chaise and she could feel him looking at her.

She opened her eyes. They grew to the size of saucers. Resting in the palm of his hand was a tiny jeweler's box. He popped it open, and nestled inside was a three-stone engagement ring. The center was a large dark blue sapphire flanked by two exquisite diamonds.

Her hand flew to her mouth. "Logan?"

He dropped to one knee and took her left hand in his. "Grace MacLellan, I know we've known each other for a short time, but you have released my heart from the grief that held me prisoner. We have much to learn about each other, but together we can build a life to share. I don't want us to rush getting married, but will you do me the honor of saying yes and agreeing to be my wife?"

All words escaped her except one. "Yes!"

He took the ring from the box and held it up. "With this ring I promise the best in life is yet to come." He slid it on her finger.

"Logan, I've never seen a ring like this in my life." She held her hand up, the gems dancing in the firelight.

His voice was thick with emotion. "The sapphire is said to come from the Isle of Harris in Scotland, and the diamonds are from my mum's engagement ring. I felt it was only fitting that you have the sapphire; it reminds me of your eyes. And the diamonds keep Mum a part of our new life together."

"When did you—I mean, you planned this before you arrived in Vermont?" She blinked away the happy tears.

"I told you, I've known we were destined for each other from the first moment I saw you on the plane in Glasgow. I couldn't imagine my life without you in it."

With a small laugh in her voice, Grace said, "What if I had said no?"

He kissed her lips. "I knew from the moment I saw you on that plane that you were the one for me and with your Gran and Aunt Flora praying this would happen and a wee bit of magic on our side, it was only a matter of time."

She melted into his arms. "You can never fight the magic of love."

EPILOGUE

The last eighteen months had been a whirlwind of activity, setting up two households, one in Easton and the other in the town of Stirling, Scotland. It had been fun but exhausting. Dad and Mom were thrilled to become involved with the Lisa Campbell Foundation. James' financial expertise along with Mom's educational experience added to Grace's medical training, and Logan's aptitude for raising money helped the foundation launch several tutoring programs. A wellness clinic was scheduled to open after the New Year.

Grace looked out the window from Kenzie's new house at the stables. All their lives had changed so much since the sister-cation trip more than two years ago. Jamie and Kenzie had been right. She found her best life and today was the next step on her amazing journey.

She looked into the cheval mirror. It was her turn to wear the MacLellan family heirloom wedding dress. "Today is the first day of the rest of my life with Logan." She was clear-eyed, no tears in sight.

Jamie and Kenzie came into the room and began fluttering around her, securing the laces on the back of the wedding dress. She was the fifth bride to wear it. Grace smoothed down the front and adjusted the amethyst brooch which secured the plaid to the bodice of the dress with it cascading behind her as her train. Lifting the hem of the dress, she stepped into the pumps Jamie had made for her own wedding, more than two years ago. They were complete with the MacLellan plaid bows. She chose to go without a veil. A crown of blue heather and white roses adorned her upswept hair.

Mom came into the room. "Oh, Grace," she gushed. "Your sisters were stunning in their own way, and now you've taken the gown and created your own distinctive look." Using a lace hankie, she dabbed her eyes. "Gran would be thrilled to see all the Scottish touches you've incorporated.

Grace took a step back and glowed with happiness. "I've got all the traditions covered. The gown is old, my shoes and brooch are borrowed, and for blue I have my Scottish sapphire ring and blue heather in my bouquet and headpiece. And I wanted to make sure our ancestors are with us on this day, so I wear our plaid with honor."

Mom kissed her cheeks and cupped her face in her hands. "I'll see you soon."

Jamie ran a hand over the bump in the middle of her dress. "I'm going to check on the carriage." She kissed Grace's cheek. "See you downstairs."

Grace laid a hand on Kenzie's arm, stopping her from following Jamie, her brow creased. "You'll let me know if Jamie needs me to come home, right?"

"I'll look out for her while you're on your honeymoon, and then when you get back you and Logan will be in Vermont until after the baby is born." She kissed Grace's cheek. "Relax."

"Kenzie? Promise?"

"Gracie, we'll always be the Three Musketeers. I'll give you one last moment alone." She sailed out of the room.

Grace looked at the bride in the mirror. This time she could see her groom standing behind her. It was the image of Logan. "Gran, I did it. I found the love you wanted for me."

A breeze as soft as Gran's touch drifted across her cheek. "I'll make you proud. I promise."

The short ride up the hill at Racing Brook Stables was familiar but different, this time she was the bride going to marry the love of her life. Grace clutched Jamie and Kenzie's hands from the moment she climbed into the carriage until it came to a stop.

Kenzie and then Jamie stepped down. Grace stood and took a deep breath. She was ready to walk down the aisle on Dad's arm.

Dad was very handsome in his traditional Scottish formal dress. He stretched out his hand as Grace stepped from the carriage.

"Lass, you are a vision." He tucked a tendril behind her ear. "Your gran would be very proud of you and your sisters. You all found your futures, just as she wanted."

Grace took her father's arm. "Are you ready to walk your youngest daughter down the aisle?"

"Aye. It's time."

Grace took her first step towards the aisle. She could see Logan waiting for her. She hugged Dad's arm to her and said, "I love you, Dad."

He kissed the top of her head. "Love you more."

She walked down the aisle and looked from right to left at the friends and family who had come to share in this special day with them. Aunt Flora was sitting up front with Tracey, along with George and Jo Burns, Robbie's dad and sister. Joey from the Pasta Bowl sat with Kenzie's right hand at the gym, Cheryl, and her fiancé Artie. Her heart was full of gratitude that these people who had been a part of her life for so long were there to share this special day.

Logan held out his hand to her. His eyes were filled with tears.

Grace's breath caught. "Logan, look."

The couple turned as the June sunset bathed the hilltop in shimmering light. Grace imagined her Great-grandparents, Gran and Grandad, and next to them, Logan's parents and Lisa, were smiling.

She thought she heard Gran's voice say, "Lass, you are a beautiful MacLellan bride."

Logan wiped away the tear from Grace's eye. They faced the minister to recite their vows.

The End

CONNECT WITH LUCINDA

Thank you for reading *The MacLellan Sisters – Blue*.

I hope you enjoyed the story. If you did, please help other readers find this book:

1. This book is lendable. Send it to a friend you think might like it so she can discover me too.
2. Help other people find this book by writing a review.
3. Sign up for my newsletter at http://www.lucindarace.com.
4. Like my Facebook page, https://facebook.com/lucindaraceauthor.
5. Join the Friends who like Lucinda Race group on Facebook.
6. Twitter @lucindarace
7. Instagram @lucindraceauthor

ABOUT THE AUTHOR

Lucinda Race is a lifelong fan of romantic fiction. As a girl, she spent hours reading novels and dreaming of one day becoming a writer. As life twisted and turned, she found herself writing nonfiction articles, but still longed to turn to her true passion, romance. Now living her dream, she spends every free moment clicking computer keys and has published ten books.

Lucinda lives with her husband Rick and two little pups, Jasper and Griffin, in the rolling hills of Western Massachusetts. Her writing is contemporary, fresh, and engaging.

Visit her on:

www.facebook.com/lucindaraceauthor

Twitter @lucindarace

Instagram @lucindaraceauthor

www.lucindarace.com

Lucinda@lucindarace.com

ALSO BY LUCINDA RACE

The MacLellan Sisters (in order)

Old and New – released June 19, 2019

Borrowed – released July 10, 2019

Blue – released July 31, 2019

The Loudon Series (in order)

Between Here and Heaven – released June 2014

Lost and Found – released November 2014

The Journey Home – released July 2015

The Last First Kiss – released November 2015

Ready to Soar – released August 2016

Love in the Looking Glass – released June 2017

Magic in the Rain – released November 2017

Made in the USA
Middletown, DE
02 January 2021